Early praise for
Deep Bitter Roots

Surprises abound in this well-written, delightful, tasty, and fast-paced plot. *Deep Bitter Roots* brings us tantalizing fun in charming settings that ring true in this central Wisconsin small town that includes the Bubble and Bake bakery and wine lounge. The "infestation of the aunts" in this novel creates laugh-out-loud humor. The revelations of many family secrets throughout the community also offer wonderful sparks that deepen the murder mystery. The author seamlessly weaves in interesting facts as Frankie uses her knowledge of journalism, botany, and the grape-growing challenges for Midwest vineyards to bring a perpetrator to justice. *Deep Bitter Roots* is highly recommended for mystery lovers and book clubs.

- **Christine DeSmet,** author of the
  Fudge Shop Mystery Series and *Mischief in Moonstone Series*

Deep Bitter Roots brims with intrigue, old family secrets, and local color. Readers will cheer for Frankie as, while juggling the responsibilities of a baker, vintner, and journalist, she manages to out-sleuth the experts.

- **Kathleen Ernst,** author of the *Chloe Ellefson Mysteries*

Add a deadly curse to a dowager's mysterious death and you get a delectable recipe for Joy Ann Ribar's second mystery of drama and intrigue. In *Deep Bitter Roots*, Frankie Champagne, a baker by day and a bartender by night, again dons her sleuth's cap and plunges into a smart and relentless pursuit of truth destined to delight the fans of Ribar's cozy Midwest series set in charming Deep Lakes, Wisconsin.

- **Patricia Skalka,** author of
 Death By the Bay: A Dave Cubiak Door County Mystery

I fell in love with Frankie, her friends, and her town of Deep Lakes in Joy Ribar's first book *Deep Dark Secrets*. And with her second book, *Deep Bitter Roots*, I am now a devoted fan and you will see me as a regular at Bubble and Bake however, I am content sitting on the sidelines as Frankie investigates another murder and this one hitting her in a way the reader will love and hate at the same time.

-**Cozy Mystery Book Reviews**

Praise for
Deep Dark Secrets

The first book
in the
***Deep Lakes Cozy
Mystery*** series

**Orange Hat
Publishing's
best-selling fiction
book of 2019!**

The winter slumber of Deep Lakes, Wisconsin conceals dark secrets, awakened when the local pastor is found dead in his ice fishing shanty. Baker, vintner Frankie Champagne, owner of Bubble and Bake, is bent on proving her journalism chops and investigates the strange death. What could possibly go wrong as Frankie cuts her teeth on her first reporting gig, bringing to light secrets that were meant to stay in the darkness?

"A great debut by a new mystery author."

- **Christine DeSmet,** author of the *Fudge Shop Mystery* series

"If you love murder mysteries on Hallmark as much as I do, you will love this book!"

- **Doreen V.,** Wisconsin

"A debut that leaves you longing for MORE!"

- **Erika N.,** Wisconsin

"*Deep Dark Secrets* is the first book in the *Deep Lakes Cozy Mystery* series by Joy Ann Ribar, and after reading it, I am moving to Deep Lakes and getting a job working for Frankie."

- Cozy Mystery Book Reviews

"If you like mysteries, read this book. It is a quick and engaging read."

- Kimberly C., Wisconsin

"We're ready for Frankie to tackle another mystery so readers can experience a bit more of Wisconsin local color."

- Thoughts from MillStreet

"What a fun read! I felt like I was a neighbor to Frankie, the main character."

- Jeanne L.

"The setting works very well and has that small-town feel most readers enjoy. The combination of a bakery and a wine-tasting business is original and fun."

- The Cozy Review

"Joy Ann Ribar paints a beautiful picture of a true Wisconsin winter. I would love to visit Bubble and Bake, the bakery/ winery run by Frankie and Carmen, for a lovely baked treat while ignoring the bitter cold that taunts Wisconsin during the winter months."

- Holli

Live La Vida Hygge!

Deep Bitter Roots

Joy Ann Ribar

Joy Ann Ribar

Orange Hat Publishing
www.orangehatpublishing.com - Waukesha, WI

Deep Bitter Roots
Copyrighted © 2020 Joy Ann Ribar
ISBN 978-1-64538-122-8
Library of Congress Control Number: 2020902670
First Edition

Deep Bitter Roots
by Joy Ann Ribar

For information, please contact:

Orange Hat Publishing
www.orangehatpublishing.com
Waukesha, WI

Edited by Kaye Nemec
Proofread by Janelle Bailey
Cover design by Tom Heffron

For Alan Christensen, master wood carver and organic gardener. When I get to heaven, I'll find the quietest flower garden filled with blooms. You'll be there, sitting on a bench, carving a Santa, and we'll catch up. This one's for you, Dad!

The bitter heart comes home
Rooted in bitterness as stone
Stone cannot crush the bitterness
For it has absorbed inside the bone

As Frankie approached the Granite Mansion, a road block of two squad cars awaited. Peering beyond the squads, Frankie saw an ambulance and Alonzo's official sheriff's Jeep. The officer posted at the scene responded to Frankie's probing gaze. "There's been a death at the mansion," she said.

Chapter 1

Happiness is having a large, loving, caring,
close-knit family in another city.
- George Burns

In years to come, Frankie would amusedly label this Spring as the "Aunt-Festation." Not ants as in crawling insects that ruin picnics or scavenge kitchen counters in search of sugary nibbles, but aunts, as in relatives, specifically Frankie's and Carmen's. And while these aunts didn't come with a colony, they were often as difficult to manage as one. The two plucky matrons would give the two Bubble and Bake shop owners plenty of trouble.

Shipped north from Texas by Carmen's mama, Tía Pepita arrived in March, planning to stay with Carmen and Ryan for three months to participate in a clinical trial at the UW Hospital Eye Research Unit in Madison. Pepita suffered from macular degeneration, causing blurred vision and sometimes painful headaches and, because Carmen's mama insisted the doctors in Madison were superior to any in Texas, it was decided she would seek out experimental treatment in Wisconsin. However, Carmen suspected her mother needed a reprieve from her aunt, who had lived on and off with her mother since she relocated to Texas. Tía Pepita was Carmen's grandfather's youngest sister and nobody actually knew how old she was since she wasn't saying, but Carmen imagined she would find out through the medical appointments she would be undertaking with her.

Meanwhile, Tía Pepita, renowned in the Martinez family for her superior cooking skills, was guest starring in the Bubble and Bake kitchen, just to keep her busy and away from trying to micromanage the family sheep farm, owned by Carmen and husband Ryan.

Frankie's Aunt Cecile, CeCe for short, arrived unannounced at Peggy Champagne's just before Easter, loaded down with enough luggage to indicate a long visit. "I just wanted to see Wisconsin one last time before I die," Aunt CeCe told Peggy, a woman of unrattled composure. Frankie's mother lived alone since Frankie's father, Charlie, passed away a few years earlier, but she had recently begun dating a long-time family friend, Dan Fitzpatrick.

Not the stay-at-home type, Peggy had worked full time with Charlie, running their construction firm, "Nothing But the Finest Champagne Builders," until his death. Then she continued while the company was transitioned to the oldest Champagne son, James, and his wife, Shauna. Animal enthusiast Peggy volunteered at Deep Lakes' veterinary clinic, walking dogs and playing with cats, helped at St. Anthony's Catholic church events, and worked Thursdays and Sundays at Frankie's and Carmen's shop.

Bubble and Bake, bakery by morning and wine lounge by evening, combined two of Frankie's passions: sweet eating and wine drinking. Growing up, Frankie learned to bake from her Grandma Sophie, a tiny round Danish woman who patiently taught Frankie the ins and outs of managing dough and shared with her the main ingredient essential to any successful pastry: love. Frankie often heard the melodic voice of Grandma Sophie in her ear when she baked, *"You must put your heart into kneading, rolling and cutting the dough, but be gentle. The bakery knows when your heart isn't in it, and your creations will turn out tough and bitter, my dear one."* Frankie missed her grandmother but felt her warmth and nearness every time she picked up a rolling pin.

From her parents Frankie learned wine appreciation as her parents hosted numerous wine tasting parties, beginning in the late 1970s when they joined a German wine club. At those parties, she learned how to pair foods with different wine varieties, and she memorized the German names for wines of varying sweetness, so she could shop at the liquor store with some sort of pretended expertise. At least she knew a Kabinett from a Spätlese.

Frankie worked an unsatisfying stint at the local newspaper, formerly known as *The Whitman Warbler*, followed by years as a paralegal at a nearby law firm, then leaped off a career cliff six years ago when her house and its contents burned to ashes. Using the insurance money for a fresh start, Frankie bought the old bank building downtown, on the corner of Granite and Meriwether, and turned it into a bakery and wine bar with the help of brothers James, Nick and Will. With Will's backing, she purchased a portion of James' rural property, planted cold climate variety grapes, and began making her own label wine, Bountiful Fruits.

Since March, Frankie and her vineyard manager, Manny Vega, were closely monitoring the vines, awaiting their awakening from a long winter slumber. Spring management was a critical time for Wisconsin grapes. Root stock needed TLC, since vines took a minimum of three years to produce fruit suitable for wine-making. Long before green grass sprouts from the frozen tundra of Wisconsin, pruning must be accomplished to ensure a healthy crop of summer grapes. Frankie, Manny and a couple of hired hands pruned her small vineyard in the cold early March temperatures, taking many breaks to restore frozen fingers back to a nimble state.

Three weeks or so later, pruning completed, Frankie and Manny began equipment maintenance, making sure tillers, spreaders and tractors survived the winter months and were ready to resume their viticulture duties. Fertilizer was calculated and ordered, common or new pests and subsequent pesticides researched, and winter damaged trellises repaired. Frankie hated pesticides and used them only as a last resort, instead applying natural remedies she heard about from other farmers. Fortunately, vineyards tended to suffer least from pest problems compared to most agricultural crops.

With the arrival of the lovely but sometimes fickle April, Frankie and Manny checked the vineyards for the first clusters of buds to appear. Patience was a necessary companion in agriculture because those bud clusters could arrive anytime from mid-April to mid-May, weather pending. In Wisconsin, weather is the most recurring topic of conversation; warm and sunny one day and snowing the next. Residents often joke about seeing all four seasons in the same month, particularly in the spring and fall.

One fortunate consequence of Aunt CeCe's and Tía Pepita's spring visits was the extra time it afforded Frankie to tend the vineyards without neglecting the bakery. This was a boon for Carmen as well, since spring was lambing season at the O'Connor's sheep farm, and all hands on deck were essential for births and feedings at any time of day. Carmen and Ryan, along with teenage twins Carlos and Kyle, managed night-time lambing duties alone, while hired workers assumed most of the daytime duties. Still, the sheep needed to be fed, pens needed to be regularly cleaned, and fences always seemed to need repairing. Carmen's extra assistance at home was gratefully received while the two aunts along with Tess, the culinary intern, and Jovie Luedtke, a hired kitchen helper, tended to most of the spring baking. Frankie and

Carmen were thankful to hire on Jovie after their other intern, Adam, recently left to take a catering position at the famous Concourse Hotel in Madison. The elegant hotel offered to groom Adam for a full-time post after his May graduation.

On this brisk April morning, Frankie arrived at the vineyard with fresh empanadas stuffed with scrambled eggs, chorizo, tomatoes and queso fresco, compliments of Tía Pepita. Living above the bakery/wine lounge had its advantages, Frankie thought, as she paraded through the kitchen around 6:00 a.m., basking in the smell of empanadas and sweet pastries. Tess was humming a different tune this morning, not the traditional Ethiopian song her mother had sung to her as a child, but something that sounded distinctly Latin. Frankie smiled and waved in her direction, not wanting to interrupt.

"Good morning, Frankie," Tess said. "Do you like the song I learned from Tía Pepita?" Tess arched her brows, looking over her shoulder at Tía, who was feeding a piece of empanada to the latest shop kitten, Liberace, a good-natured black and white feline that looked dressed for a formal occasion.

Since Frankie's mother volunteered with the strays at Dr. Sadie Chastain's vet clinic, she brought a cat every few weeks to Bubble and Bake to hang out and hopefully find a forever home with a soft-hearted shop patron. Liberace, named for the famed flamboyant pianist, was reduced to Archie by the aunts. "Better watch out, Tía, you're going to make that kitten so fat nobody will want to adopt him," Frankie teased.

Tía chucked the kitten under the chin, making soft motherly sounds. "Archie is such a good kitty. You are off to your vineyard, no?" Pepita produced a bag containing several wrapped empanadas. "Take these with you for you and your helpers," she said.

Frankie gave her a grateful smile. "Yum. Thank you, they smell like a piece of Heaven." Then she was off in the blue SUV, heading out County K from Deep Lakes to Bountiful Fruits Vineyard on Blackbird Marsh Road.

Manny was already hard at work, mending more broken trellises. Frankie admired this man, a small wiry sun-browned working wizard. Manny could fix anything; he was indispensable to the vineyard, and she was lucky she'd been able to persuade him to come work for her. Manny had spent many years working first for her father, then for James on numerous construction jobs, where the money was good but the wear and tear on the body was inevitable. James recommended Manny to Frankie, so she tried him out for the planting and harvest season after James offered to compensate him for the pay cut he'd have to take. Frankie was indebted to James for it and couldn't imagine how she would be able to keep Manny and pay him what he was worth. The two came to terms, however, and after five seasons, Frankie could finally afford to pay him almost as much as he was worth.

She trotted out to the row where Manny was bending

new wire around a post, somewhere near the end of the Briana grape section. Even without foliage, Frankie had the vineyard's geography memorized, knew where every variety stopped and started, and also knew how the colors of the leaves, the flower clusters, and the glorious grapes differed from one variety to another. Manny had the entire vineyard committed to memory as well. He knew exactly what the vines needed, and she laughingly called him the "grape whisperer." Manny wished Frankie a good morning and took an empanada from the proffered bag.

"Fresh coffee's in the wine shed, boss lady." Manny knew Frankie's morning routine included a couple rounds of java.

The next two hours were spent walking the vineyard, looking for telltale signs of sprouts or swelling buds, making notes for any needed repairs: variety, row number, location number in the row. The two were rounding the final row of the Frontenac plot when they heard tires crunching gravel, announcing a Whitman County brown SUV marked Sheriff's Department. Frankie hoped to see Sheriff and lifelong friend, Alonzo Goodman, exit the vehicle, but instead, the tall imposing frame and unsmiling countenance of Officer Donovan Pflug headed their direction.

Frankie shuddered inwardly; outwardly she sucked in her breath and grimaced. Since Pflug had been on the Whitman County force the past year, he and Frankie'd had a few unpleasant run-ins, the most recent being Frankie's unwanted involvement in a murder investigation. While the investigation took Pflug off on a wild goose chase in Missouri, Frankie uncovered the killer and brought her in to the department to make a confession. Pflug was undoubtedly still smarting from that one.

Now Frankie decided to speak first, "What brings you out this way, Officer Pflug?" She couldn't see his expression hidden behind mirrored sunglasses, but his jaw was set in its usual grim line. Frankie wondered if he had a happy side.

"Here to check on your guest workers, Mrs. Champagne. Make sure all their paperwork is in order." Frankie smarted every time Pflug called her "Mrs." since she wasn't one, a fact she was certain he knew. Despite her desire to keep her temper under wraps, she felt the heat rising from her neck up.

Pflug was known for questioning the migrant workers throughout Whitman County who came north every year, following jobs in agriculture, tourism, and construction. Before Pflug joined the force, the county had only checked on workers if a complaint was filed or if a worker got into legal trouble. Hispanic migrants had been coming to the Deep Lakes area for decades. For as long as Frankie could remember, she had gone to school with Hispanic children in the fall, who went south for the winter months, then returned in the spring. Carmen's father had been one of those migrants until he gained a full-time management position, so the family could stay in Deep Lakes year round. The majority of Frankie's so-called "guest workers" were American citizens, yet they were often lumped together with immigrants who carried work visas.

The county relied on the guest workers and migrants for the seasonal labor to tend and harvest crops. There simply wasn't enough population in the area to fulfill the farmers' needs. Ripe produce doesn't sit pretty in the fields until enough people come along to pick it. In recent years, most of the county youth headed to the city, so migrant workers became essential at hotels and restaurants during the tourist season. A shortage of young, able-bodied workers affected Frankie's brother, too. James relied on the migrants to complete his construction contracts, utilizing their skills, experience and work ethic.

Through James, Frankie was able to find relatives or friends of the construction workers to fill in at the vineyard when it was busiest. Many of the migrants lived on James's property in mobile homes he rented out seasonally. Manny, too, lived just a quarter mile from the vineyard, on a small plot of land with two mobile homes, one of which he rented out to cousins and their cousins, who came to the area for work.

Pflug shifted his head in the direction of Manny. "How many you got living on your property this year? I need to meet them and see their papers. Now would be good." Manny nodded and pointed toward the machine shed where two of his cousins were working on equipment.

Frankie flushed inwardly again. The least Pflug could do was be polite, less demanding, she figured. Frankie wondered if the officer didn't like women or Hispanics or both but then surmised that Donovan Pflug just didn't like anyone. She witnessed the authoritative tone and posture he assumed around both Alonzo, his boss, and Garrett Iverson, the County Coroner, both professionals who were darn good at their jobs. Never mind that Frankie had been dating the handsome coroner on and off for awhile now. She couldn't remember a time she saw Pflug being nice to anyone. Frankie was tempted to trounce after them to get the 411 on the situation.

Restraint took hold of her, however, in the form of her shoulder companions, two fireflies that seemed to intervene when the moment called for it. On her right, a golden one with an angelic pixie face and the voice of Frankie's mother, batted her eyes and hissed in her ear. "Leave it alone, Frankie; the officer's just doing his job."

Frankie looked to her left side for support. The Pirate Firefly, who spoke like Antonio Banderas, shrugged, "It would be safer for you to stay put, I'm afraid, chérie."

Frankie couldn't say how long she'd been living with a split conscience that outfitted itself in fireflies. Maybe since her husband Rick had left her and their two daughters years ago to live in Wyoming with Mary Sue, the rancher. Maybe since her house burned down six years ago, forcing her and the girls to stay with her mother until the investigation was finished and insurance money paid. Maybe since she felt like a divided self, running a bakery, wine bar, vineyard, and moonlighting as a freelance reporter for the *Point Press* newspaper. Maybe. She lost her train of thought, spun around and headed for the wine-making lab, a concrete structure with a cheerful red metal roof and wood-burned sign announcing the name "Bountiful Fruits." This was where the magic happened.

Frankie found Nelson and Zane, the two microbiology interns from UW-Stevens Point, working on the latest wine batch statistics. Nelson was calling out numbers to Zane, who was tapping away on a laptop at his desk. "Oh, hey, Ms. C.," Zane said, looking up for a moment.

Nelson, analysis completed for the time being, was ready to move on to the next vat of fermenting fruits. "Hello, Francine." Nelson, the quirkier of the two interns, always referred to others by their formal first names. He had been working there for nearly a year now, recruiting Zane to join him during second semester a few months ago. Nelson was all business and precise as a Swiss timepiece. He almost always wore khaki, brown, or a variation of the same, kept his hair tidily trimmed in a 1950's cut with a distinct side part, and wore black-framed glasses, the only deviation from brown, except his white lab coat, which was always in pristine condition.

Zane was much looser in his jeans and hoodie, tousled dark hair that stuck up in numerous places as if he'd just gotten out of bed, and often without a lab coat, since he couldn't keep track of it or hadn't done laundry that week. Still, Zane was not loosey-goosey when it came to the wine-making process.

Together, the two interns kept the equipment sparkling and sanitized and kept the interior spotless enough to perform surgery should the need arise. Both took copious notes during each batching of wine, calculating precisely the need for more or less sugar, determining exact yeast temperatures, measuring the specific gravity and keeping a timeline for each batch as it fermented.

Spring marked the beginning of the summer wine variety season, when Frankie specialized in light, sweet fruity varieties that sold well in the wine bar as people planned summer picnics and grilling parties. Five vats of fruits were in the fermentation process right now. Carmen and Frankie located some quality blueberries, cherries and strawberries, turning them into a mash, one fruit, each, in three vats, and a combination of the three in the fourth. Vat number five was reserved for experimenting with new flavors, and it contained apricots that would be combined with a Chardonnay grape juice from the Finger Lakes region in New York. Frankie looked at Nelson, brows raised, anticipating an update on the vats, but Nelson wasn't very perceptive in reading human beings. "So, what's the good word, guys?"

Nelson drew his brows together briefly, then raising his index finger, pronounced, "Auspicious, I believe, is the word you are looking for. As in, the fruit mashes will be qualified and primed tomorrow for stage two of wine making."

Frankie stifled a giggle. "That's great. I'll be here at 8:00 a.m. tomorrow to help you transfer the mash to the tanks."

Bountiful Fruits now had five tanks, so Frankie could batch five varieties at a time. After a few weeks, Frankie would host a bottling party, enlisting the help of ten or so family members, friends, and interns to bottle about 800 bottles of delicious nectar. The use of fresh fruit mash meant fewer bottles per tank but more authentic fruity flavor per bottle. Frankie perused each of the fruit vats, pausing to inhale deeply, savoring the yeasty aroma that many people wouldn't consider appetizing.

She hoped by now Donovan Pflug was off the premises as she left the lab, but his SUV was still parked and running, as was cop protocol. Pflug was marching toward the SUV, the walk of a military man. In fact, his hair was always worn in an army cut, and he was clean-shaven, crisp, and pressed at all times. She wondered if he'd been in service in another life but doubted they would be engaging in that kind of small talk any time soon. She didn't speak to him, waiting for him to say something instead, but he opened the door, stepped inside, and backed out of the parking area, spun around and down the long drive, spitting gravel.

Yep, she couldn't expect him to even give a polite goodbye. Manny was back in the vineyard, mending a trellis as if Pflug had only been a figment of Frankie's imagination.

"Well, Manny? Any problems?" Manny slowly shook his head, offering no words, and in that silence, Frankie guessed Pflug had insulted Manny and his cousins.

Frankie was still thinking about vineyard duties when she pulled into Glen and Meredith Healy's greenhouse on Highway 5, south of town. The Healys accommodated replacement vine stock for Frankie, which was a necessary part of owning a vineyard. Frankie had to replace dying vines annually, determining which ones to order, then have them housed at the Healys, since Frankie had no greenhouse of her own. Luckily, she only needed to replace a few vines a year; this year all five vines were the Frontenac variety, thanks to a woodchuck family who seemed to have an affinity for her only purple grape variety.

It was time to pick the vines up and temper them to the outdoors before planting them in the next couple of weeks. Frontenac grapes yielded depth of flavor and boasted versatility for wine-makers; hence, they were much sought-after by any serious vintner.

Frankie found both Meredith and Glen in the greenhouse, Glen talking to Adele Lundgren, Deep Lakes's mayor, while Meredith was checking on large seed trays of annuals, many of which were just peeking above the cardboard pots' rims. Looking up, Meredith waved Frankie over with one gloved hand.

"Hey, Meredith. I came to collect the Frontenacs you've been graciously babysitting," Frankie smiled broadly.

"Sure, let me just finish up this tray." Meredith carefully sprinkled the tender seedlings, then stuck a marker in the next tray so she knew where to begin again.

The two women headed down the long aisle of endless trays, through an adjoining work area of wide tables, boxes of all sorts to open, and inventory for the flower shop in town, and into the next section of greenhouse where the precious vines were sitting in a cold frame to harden off before the planting stage. Frankie's smile could not be restrained. The vines were healthy, producing tender, waxy yellow-green shoots.

"What would I do without you and Glen? I'm so thankful you're willing to take care of these babies for me, Meredith."

Meredith shrugged off her thanks. "I love it. It gives me another interesting plant to cultivate. Besides, you provide us with the best bakery and bottles of wine, so I think we get the better end of the deal."

The two loaded the vines into a garden wagon and paraded back the way they had come, pausing when Adele called out to Frankie.

"Frankie, do you have a few minutes? You're on my list of people to call about the Deep Lakes Roots Fest. It was meant to be that I bumped into you here."

Adele Lundgren was as astute as she was energetic,

with a sincere devotion to her job as mayor. She'd already served two full terms and was halfway through her third, yet she showed the same contagious enthusiasm from her first year on the job. An expert delegator, Adele was nearly impossible to say no to because a person could rarely get a word in edgewise when conversing with her. Tall and squarely built, Adele raced from topic to topic, losing her conversation partner in the process. Plus, she always managed to be on the move as she spoke, beating her conversation partner to the finish line and leaving that person in the dust, wondering what had just happened. Such was the case now.

"You know the highlight of the festival this year will be re-dedicating Spurgeon Park and unveiling all the new additions: the gazebo, etcetera, etcetera. So, I thought, wouldn't it be perfect to have Emily there - Emily Spurgeon - for the dedication. And you. You're perfect to help write a few words, work with her on a short presentation, you know, something to remind everyone of the history of Deep Lakes. It's 30 years this year - I mean the park, you know. So, Emily agreed to meet you. Here's her phone number - it's unlisted. Try to see her this week."

Frankie was gasping for air, her mind twisting and turning along the pathways of discourse that had just occurred. She had several questions competing for rank and order in her brain but found herself standing alone outside Adele's Cadillac, Adele inside smiling and waving as she drove off.

Frankie stared at the sticky note with Emily Spurgeon's phone number. The daughter of Elmer Spurgeon, owner of Deep Lakes Granite Works and the elegant Granite Mansion the family built around the turn of the century, was a recluse for the past decade or longer. How old would Emily be now, Frankie mused. She had no idea. Oh well, she thought, tucking the paper into her purse and loading up the Frontenac vines. She'd just been given an Adele assignment and dismissed.

How hard could it be, helping Emily Spurgeon write a short speech re-dedicating the park? What had Adele said about a presentation? Frankie had no idea, nor did she have any idea she was walking into a house of tangled secrets, and a deeply rooted past that connected the granite quarry to both happy and disturbing pieces of the town's history, which would soon be unearthed.

Chapter 2

A house built on granite and strong foundations,
not even the onslaught of pouring rain, gushing
torrents and strong winds will be able to pull down.
– Haile Selassie

When you have a lot of solitude,
any living thing becomes a companion.
– Jose Mujica

Frankie parked the SUV in the midsection of the Wellness Center's lot and scooted through the circular doors out of the morning April drizzle. Having not yet transitioned from winter driving gear, she made a mental note that it was time to unearth her umbrellas and stow one in her vehicle. Looking up from the brightly lit lobby that opened up all the way to the second and third floors, Frankie could hear banter of fellow workout warriors and the whirring of blenders, supplying smoothies ordered by the healthy-minded members.

Frankie and Peggy, committed to spending more mother-daughter time together in the new year, decided to do weekly yoga with master instructor Fuji Vang, as flexible as a Slinky but able to demonstrate modifications for the beginner to the expert. As Frankie scanned her membership fob, she was warmly greeted by Taylor, one of the full-time receptionists, whom Frankie could count on for the latest news around the community.

"What's new, Taylor? Any fun weekend plans?" Frankie could count on Taylor to be doing something adventurous or just plain quirky with her boyfriend, Jake.

"Hey, Frankie. Yeah, Jake and I are going to the Grilled Cheese Festival in Dodgeville. In fact, you should compete in it. There will be many versions of grilled cheese. The only rule is that you have to use Wisconsin cheeses." Taylor laughed a little in her recitation, then suddenly lowered her voice and grimaced, "I guess I shouldn't be talking about grilled cheese in a fitness center, huh?"

Frankie just laughed, thinking that only in Wisconsin would there be a celebration centered around the grilled cheese sandwich, albeit a delicious idea for a celebration! Taylor began helping a new member fill out registration forms, so Frankie headed to the yoga room.

Peggy was already in the dimly lit classroom, sitting, legs stretched out in front of her, on a mat, eyes closed. Peggy, whose real name was Marit, a Scandinavian form of Margaret, was still a stunning woman in Frankie's eyes. She was a few inches taller than her daughter with frosty gray hair worn over the shoulders, noticeable icy blue eyes, fair skin that still gleamed with youth, and a lovely figure, despite being a mother of five. Frankie, who barely managed a five-foot-tall stretch, would kill to have her mother's elegant legs.

"Hello, Mother," Frankie said quietly, trying not to disturb the zen in the room.

"Hello, Frankie." Peggy reached out to pat her daughter's shoulder in Peggy's version of a hug. This was how Frankie always remembered receiving affection from her mother- infrequent and distant, fragile - as if Frankie were a glass-blown ornament rather than flesh and bone. Conversely, Charlie Champagne administered huge, protective bear hugs regularly. No wonder she and her father were so close; no wonder losing him left such an empty place within.

Frankie practiced warm, lingering hugs with her own daughters, Sophie and Violet, who carried on the same way, even with their grandmother. Peggy protested at first but soon adjusted as Frankie reminded her, "You're all the grandparents they have; let them love you."

Rick, Frankie's ex, dropped out of the picture when the girls were small, then quickly disappeared to Wyoming to be with Mary Sue, a woman he met long-haul trucking. Frankie received child support for about a year, then Rick apparently left his job and moved elsewhere. Frankie didn't spend time trying to track him down; instead, she made do by working two jobs most of the time.

Rick's parents quickly followed their only son out to Wyoming where, Frankie assumed, the western climate caused people to forget their children and grandchildren. Sophie and Violet received birthday and Christmas gifts for a year or two, then nothing at all. Frankie imagined Rick and his parents were either held captive by a strange religious cult or abducted by aliens; both seemed much more plausible and less painful than self-estrangement from two innocent girls who needed their love. Thank God for Charlie and Peggy, grandparents extraordinaire, and a constant source of support for Frankie. What Peggy lacked in affection, she made up for in loyalty and practical help. In those ways, her love was fierce, making Frankie come to realize that love manifests itself in many forms.

Taking time for an after-yoga smoothie, Frankie and Peggy sat in the modern, brightly-colored plastic chairs and tables in the small café.

"So, Mom, I've been wondering: what's the story on Aunt CeCe? I remember her from when I was a kid, but after I was 10 or so, nothing but birthday cards. And now, she just shows up in Wisconsin for what reason?"

Peggy paused, mid-sip, considering her words before speaking. "It's complicated, Frankie, like so many life circumstances." Peggy explained that Charlie's younger sister wanted to study art, but her mother, Frankie's Grandmother Felicity, would not support that venture. "Your MéMé could be stubborn and difficult, especially when it came to the well-being of her only daughter."

It was hard for Frankie to imagine MéMé behaving this way. Felicity was a fiery red-headed Irish bundle of energy and warmth, who often played games with Frankie and her brothers, romped with them in the snow, and then cooked them hearty meals with luscious desserts before singing them off to sleep. Frankie inherited Felicity's red hair - although Frankie's was a darker cherry version - and her blazing green eyes. Of course, Frankie liked to think she was the best combination of her ancestors but was frequently reminded by both her parents that she could be quick-tempered, reactive, like her MéMé.

Peggy said Aunt CeCe had gone to art school in Milwaukee for almost a year, then abruptly quit, getting married just a couple of months later. The marriage didn't succeed, and Aunt CeCe left Wisconsin, headed out to California, and joined an artists' community. Peggy wasn't certain if Felicity and CeCe ever spoke again. Charlie kept in touch on and off with his sister, but after she moved, Peggy hadn't heard from her and wasn't sure the news of Charlie's death had reached her at the only address Peggy had. But, Aunt CeCe got in touch with Peggy a few months later, expressing her sadness about Charlie and providing vague details about her own life. Aunt CeCe had been living in Orange, California, for years as a caretaker for a woman named Nell, a fellow artist, who apparently died sometime in the past year.

"I think after she lost Nell she was homesick for the only family she had. So, here she is. It doesn't look like she's in a hurry to leave either, so thank you Frankie, for giving her some space in your bakery. She needs a purpose, something to do." Peggy finished, standing up to gather her raincoat and umbrella. Of course her mother, the consummate girl scout, would be prepared for any situation. Frankie's own fleece hoodie would have to accommodate the spring rain for the time being.

Before yoga, Frankie had arrived early at Bountiful Fruits to help Nelson and Zane transfer the vats of fruity fermented liquids to the stainless steel tanks, adding appropriate grape juices from Frankie's suppliers, yeast and other magical ingredients to start the wine processing. Frankie tapped into her phone calendar - a lifeline for all important dates - an approximate date for bottling. She noticed an alert for the day, reminding her to contact Emily Spurgeon to set up an interview. No use putting that off. She looked at the time and decided it wasn't too early to call a recluse, if there was an appropriate time to contact such an individual. The Golden Firefly tsked in Frankie's ear in a scolding manner. It was unfair to mock Emily Spurgeon; after all, Frankie had no idea what prompted her into isolation.

A melodic woman's voice answered the mansion's phone. No, she was not Ms. Spurgeon but rather someone named Alana who worked for her. After a few minutes of waiting on the line for confirmation about the alleged expected meeting, Alana returned, stating this afternoon would be fine, 3:00 p.m., after Ms. Spurgeon's rest time. Frankie puzzled how old Emily Spurgeon would be about now . . . old enough to take daily naps apparently.

Returning to Bubble and Bake, Frankie said quick hellos to Tess, Tía Pepita, and Aunt CeCe, who were finishing up today's cleaning and tomorrow's baking prep, grabbed a cheese empanada, then padded off to the wine lounge to browse the bookshelves for the history of Deep Lakes. Frankie turned to the section about the granite quarry. Better study up somewhat before meeting with Emily Spurgeon, she decided. After all, she wanted to be taken seriously by the quarry heiress. The idea of an heiress in the small town of Deep Lakes made Frankie think of gothic romances - not exactly 21st century stuff, she snickered.

The quarry, situated near the center of downtown Deep Lakes between Highway 5 and Granite Street, had begun as a granite-faced promontory that was being mined by the locals for, among other things, foundations for their houses.

By the mid-1800s, a Chicago-based company purchased the mineral rights to the property, but the quarry operation wasn't born until years later when Milton Spurgeon, Emily's great-grandfather, moved from Chicago to Deep Lakes to operate the quarry with newly designed machinery powerful enough to cut the dense red stone. The combination of Milton's shrewd business style and the highly-rated granite made for a hugely successful business. That is, until both of Milton's sons died, one in World War I, the other from a fall at the quarry site. The latter Spurgeon was Elmer's father, and although Elmer would be heir-apparent to head up the quarry operations, he was just a boy.

The aging Milton sold half the quarry to a hot-shot Pennsylvania bluestone quarry owner, Seamus McCoy, a man looking to broaden his horizons by setting up his three sons with established businesses to run. Clifton McCoy, number three son, moved to Deep Lakes with his socialite wife, Catherine, who hoped to bring culture to the rural Wisconsin town. In 1918, the McCoys built the Granite Mansion, now part of the National Register of Historic Homes.

Meanwhile, Elmer Spurgeon attended business college in Milwaukee, returning afterwards to Deep Lakes to reclaim his inheritance, namely the other half of Deep Lakes Granite Works, preserved in trust by Milton Spurgeon's administrators. Working under the guidance of Clifton, the quarry thrived despite set-backs from a major structural fire to the office and occasional quarry site accidents. Clifton and Elmer employed over 400 men in the quarry's heyday.

Elmer met Clifton's daughter, Cordelia, at a summer company picnic, and began a courtship that turned into marriage a couple years later, forever cementing the two families in the Granite Works Company. Elmer took over the sole operation in 1950 after Clifton died, but he was joined by Cordelia's brother, Edgar, two years later.

As time was flying by, Frankie skipped ahead to the end of the section, where a timeline illustrated the important events in the quarry's history. Here was what she was looking for: the quarry closed in 1984, citing expensive operating costs and logistics of mining in the middle of a city as the reasons. Okay . . . she figured she had enough to go on to speak "quarry" to Emily Spurgeon, who was certainly equipped to fill in more interesting details, she hoped.

An hour later, the SUV was climbing up hilly Whitman Avenue, a wide thoroughfare lined with majestic oaks and maples, the occasional cottonwood giant looming over the curbside. The cottonwoods, with their falling seedlings of fluff that piled up on the avenue in summer, were declared a menace by the city council after years of complaints from the Whitman Avenue residents. However, many of the woody giants were protected due to their advanced age and could not be cut down until they showed signs of dying; now only a few remained.

Frankie laughed as she recalled how many of her schoolmates referenced this part of town as Hog Ridge. Whitman Avenue was the "old money" end of town, if there was such a thing in Deep Lakes as "old money." Mammoth Victorian-style homes flaunted an array of colors, most featuring turrets or gingerbread or both. Foursquare houses were another dominant variety here, but unlike the middle class simple Foursquare manufactured by Sears and Roebuck, these were transformed, breaking tradition with additions to the square shape such as columns, expansive porches, or atriums.

No other structure on Whitman Avenue could compete with the grandeur of the Spurgeon Mansion, however. A Georgian Revival style, unique in its facade of unpolished cobblestone granite chunks, the structure managed to be both breathtaking and homey simultaneously. Its position at the highest point of the street was surely not an accident, nor was its backyard abutting with Lake Joy, making this a city home that felt like a country estate. Frankie admired the well-tended gardens that were just beginning to come to life on this April afternoon.

Maples, beeches, and birches were budding velvety and waxy in their rosy attire, and Frankie spied some willows along the lake as she wound her way along the horseshoe-shaped driveway. She knew the willow buds would be soft in their white fur this time of year, giving them the nickname "pussy willows" and conjuring happy memories of gathering some each year with her father to watch them shed their downy coats, unfurling a delicate pale green leaf, as they sat in a large vase on their dining room table.

The mansion had three entrances, two of which were majestic, covered pediments supported by polished granite columns. Since the house faced the avenue at an angle, it appeared to have two front entry areas. The third entrance was a simple back door, probably used by servants, while the other side of the mansion was occupied in full by a four-season sunroom, featuring a wall of windows, separated into pairs by decorative face-mounted columns. Frankie was uncertain if she qualified as a guest, but imagined it would be more awkward to knock on the back door, so she opted for one of the front entrances, happily hearing the Westminster chime as she pressed the bell.

A lovely young woman in a lavender shift with a white triangular apron opened the door.

"Hello, you must be Ms. Champagne?" Her voice had a pleasant lilt, Frankie noticed, the kind that could lull an ornery child to sleep in no time.

"Yes. I have a three o'clock meeting with Ms. Spurgeon."

The woman nodded, opening the door wide, and offering her hand to Frankie.

"I spoke with you on the phone. I'm Alana West, Ms. Spurgeon's personal assistant."

Personal assistant? Frankie wondered how many hats Alana West was wearing in her job, since she certainly looked more maid or nurse than administrative assistant. Frankie scolded herself for being snobby and old-fashioned, then gasped as she entered an elegant rectangular hallway with marble floor and Persian carpet runner leading to a wide, polished bannister curving its way up three stories, an intricate crystal chandelier dropping halfway down the opening of the foyer.

Alana West led Frankie through a set of patterned maple sliding doors into a room she ventured was the library: floor to ceiling bookcases adorned by art glass windows, a small granite fireplace in the center with a large mahogany desk nearby. Alana offered Frankie a seat in one of the comfortable leather chairs, facing a bay window toward the avenue. On the left side, a set of glass French doors led toward what was probably the sunroom.

"Would you like some tea or coffee while you wait? Ms. Spurgeon is just finishing up with another meeting." Frankie said tea would be wonderful, then regretted her decision as the lengthy list of options was rattled off. She chose an herbal blend recommended by Alana, then sat in silence as the sliding doors were closed.

Frankie recalled Alana saying Emily Spurgeon would be napping before her 3:00 p.m. appointment, so she wondered if this meeting had been scheduled after she called or was a spontaneous one. Just outside the sliding doors, Frankie heard voices, indicating the meeting was likely over. One voice was a woman's, different from Alana's lilting one; this voice sounded older, measured, and formal. The other voice was a man's, but Frankie could hear little of the conversation through those solid doors. Rising to press her ear against the door, it suddenly opened, as Alana carried in a complete tea service, almost losing her balance to avoid running into Frankie, who flushed scarlet.

"I was just going to look for a bathroom," she faltered.

Alana nodded, but Frankie thought she could see through her lame excuse. "Here. Let me show you." Alana set the tray down and led Frankie back into the foyer. There, she could only see the backside of Emily Spurgeon but a full front view of the man whose voice she heard. Dressed in a dark, cheaply made business suit, the man was probably close to six feet tall, his tawny hair on the long side but combed back over his forehead in a modern hipster style. His deep-set eyes were a little uneven, giving him a malicious look, and his bushy mustache was a mistake for sure, Frankie decided. He carried a black briefcase and black umbrella. Frankie wondered how he came to the house, since no other vehicles were in the driveway. Perhaps he walked from downtown; maybe one of the law offices had a new attorney?

Frankie had caught snatches of their conversation when Alana opened the door. How did it go . . . "Well, I'm sure she'll be happy to hear it," was the man talking. "Not certain," that was Emily, followed by a question about when she would be coming. Well, Frankie couldn't put two and two together with so little information. She clearly heard the closing words, though, from the man, who said he'd see her tomorrow morning at eight, followed by the wavering voice of Emily, "Good day to you, Mr. Foster."

Frankie scuttled down the hallway where Alana was waiting by the bathroom door, looking a bit annoyed with Frankie. Frankie lingered long enough to realistically utilize the facilities, then hurried back to the library, where Emily Spurgeon was pouring tea into two lovely porcelain cups. Frankie thought she looked rattled, but then she didn't know what a normal look for Ms. Spurgeon would be. Dressed in a mid-length gray skirt with a flowing sea green blouse over it and simple gray sling-back shoes, Emily Spurgeon looked to be in the realm of 60ish. She wore simple make-up and her salt and pepper dark hair was tied neatly behind her ears in a ponytail. Emily's face was long and a bit fleshy, but she wasn't unattractive, just a little sorrowful-looking. A pair of reading glasses hung on a braided cord around her neck, and she wore an ornate gold wristwatch, something so few people wore these days, since the invention of the cell phone.

Emily was methodically stroking an affectionate Siamese cat, who was purring loudly, encouraging the kitty massage. Frankie smiled in the kitty's direction, prompting Emily to break the ice. "Please meet Pearl, my loyal companion, at least, as long as she gets what she wants!" Emily's eyes twinkled as she continued. "It's a pleasure to meet you, Ms. Champagne. I understand Adele has placed you in charge of my presentation at the Roots Festival rededication of Spurgeon Park. Or should I say, Adele made it impossible for you to say no?" Frankie knew in those moments that she and Emily would get along just fine.

"So, you know Adele, then?" Frankie wondered.

"Yes, we're both in the Whitman County Garden Club," Emily added as she saw the surprise on Frankie's face, "I do get out a little, Ms. Champagne."

"Please, call me Frankie, Ms. Spurgeon."

"And you must call me Emily. Now, tell me what you know about the quarry's history, so we can discuss how the presentation will go."

Frankie was happy she'd taken a little time to review Granite Works' place in Deep Lakes history. Emily added in personal details that the history books didn't include, however.

"Papa always wanted the city to have a park that showed off the beautiful granite outcroppings but thought it would be too dangerous while the quarry was still operating. After Granite Works closed in 1984, he paid a landscaper to bring his design to fruition, including the waterfall. It was finally completed in 1989, you may remember, but then again, you were young."

Frankie wasn't that young, a teenager, for sure, with other things on her mind than the local park. She knew, however, that the waterfall, a grand, white cascade that splashed from the top of the highest precipice, was made possible by piping drilled through the tough granite and a pump system fed by the quarry pond, which flowed into the Blackbird River. She guessed it cost quite a sum of money just for the falls alone.

Emily continued, "I'm so happy Papa was able to speak at its first dedication. He died, you know, in 1991, just two years later. It was good for him to see the park in use by families, for music concerts and picnics." Her voice grew sad and trailed off. She suddenly seemed far away.

Frankie asked about photographs, thinking Emily might feel better reliving memories of her family and the quarry. Frankie offered to create a PowerPoint, featuring some of her favorites.

Emily brightened again. "Oh, yes, that's a splendid idea. We'll need to meet again soon after I pull those photos out. Let's focus on the speech now. I don't want to say too much; nobody likes long speeches, especially at a festival. But, I want to do my father proud, so it has to be a good speech."

Frankie had upgraded from her phone to a tablet for note-taking purposes. Now that she was writing a little more for both the local and regional newspaper, she decided she'd better look the part. She pulled the tablet out of her tote bag, opened its black cover, and began typing ideas the speech should include.

A half hour later, the women were satisfied, deciding the theme of the speech would be about roots - the roots of family, the roots of the community, and how the park intertwined the two. Of course, thank yous and recognition were required. Thanks to many donors and fundraisers, the park had been undergoing renovations the past year to include a new concession building with a mini kitchen and restrooms, a new picnic pavilion next to the concession area, and the showpiece: a new, substantial gazebo that would accommodate larger concerts and other productions. Talk was already underway about "Shakespeare in the Park" and a summer talent show.

"I know I have to thank your brother and his construction company for all the work and materials donated for the gazebo. I can't wait to see it," Emily said.

Indeed, Frankie was proud of James' continued tradition of community service their father had practiced. The gazebo construction had begun last fall, was suspended during the winter, then began again in early March, but the whole enterprise was under wraps, literally, until the unveiling at the festival Memorial weekend.

There was a rap at the sliding door as Alana strolled into the library, clearing her throat.

"Sorry to interrupt, but I'm going to be leaving in a few minutes. Just checking to see if you need anything, Ms. Spurgeon, before I go?"

Ever the curious observer, Frankie noted how Alana spoke with a combination of deference and affection toward Emily. Equally, Emily treated Alana more like a friend or family member than an employee. Alana told Emily that her supper was prepared and keeping warm in the kitchen, reminded her of tomorrow's appointments, and noted that today's mail was on the dining room table. Frankie thought it odd that no mention was made of the 8:00 a.m. meeting with Mr. Foster. Alana must have missed that or maybe didn't hear about it because she had to direct Frankie to a bathroom.

Emily thanked her, wishing her a good night, then added, "Oh, yes, Alana, please add a couple of appointments to my calendar, would you? I need to meet with Ms. Champagne again to finalize my speech and to organize photographs for the presentation."

Alana walked over to the desk, picked up a tablet that was just like Frankie's, and opened it up. "Go ahead. What dates are you looking at?"

Frankie pulled up her calendar as well. The two women agreed to meet again Friday, allowing a couple of days for Emily to browse through her photo albums. A second meeting was set for about a week later, when Frankie promised she would have a preliminary slideshow put together.

"Can you come early Friday, take a little tour of the house and grounds?" Emily wondered. Frankie said she'd love to, mentally noting Emily Spurgeon had not mentioned her 8:00 a.m. meeting tomorrow to Alana.

Chapter 3

Friendship is always a sweet responsibility,
never an opportunity.
- Khalil Gibran

Hold a true friend with both your hands.
- Nigerian Proverb

Finding the need to reconnect with each other and the shop, Frankie and Carmen met in the Bubble and Bake kitchen the next morning to serve customers and get their hands dirty, in the dough, that is. Carmen shared the latest lamb count for the spring season.

"We're up to 192 little wooly babes now with ninety sets of twins," Carmen beamed. "Waiting on a few more ewes. It's going to be a record spring lambing this year."

All of those lambs added up to more wool to sell on the market along with more breeding stock and Frankie shuddered a little, more delicious lamb chops. What could she say, Frankie was a softie when it came to animals, even though she enjoyed a well-prepared lamb chop, too - with a little garlic herb aioli on the side.

"I see that pitiful look, Frankie Champagne. I love

those lambs too, you know, but that's our bread and butter." Having run the O'Connor Farm with Ryan the past fifteen years, Carmen had adjusted to the comings and goings of the livestock.

"I know, Carmie." Frankie gave her dear friend an apologetic look. "I'm coming out soon to see those lambs, and I'm not going to think about where they're going to end up next!"

Carmen tilted her head in Frankie's direction to change topics. "Speaking of coming out for a visit, what's new with you and that handsome M.E.?" Carmen's wide eyes probed Frankie's face.

Garrett Iverson, distinguished yet down to earth medical examiner for Whitman County, had been keeping Frankie company on and off the past few months. The pair got acquainted when Frankie stuck her curious nose into a death investigation during the winter. Frankie and Garrett enjoyed spending time together, going to movies, concerts and plays, but their relationship wasn't exactly what Frankie would call "red hot." Still, she wasn't planning on giving up on it by any means.

"Things are fine," she began, tentatively, wondering what information Carmen expected. Apparently more elaboration was called for, according to the probing eyes and dipping motion of Carmen's head. "We're dating. It's nice. He's been busy the past few weeks taking a course in new forensic practices. He's been in Madison a lot. But, we've been in touch." Frankie sputtered out the information in choppy delivery as Carmen kept waving her hand in a "keep going" fashion. Now, like an expert defense lawyer, she would add her own summation.

"Okay. Well, 'nice' doesn't exactly sound exciting, but give it some time, Frankie. You've been out of the dating game a long time. I'm glad you're going slow, but I'm glad you're out there. Garrett is a good guy." Frankie nodded and smiled enthusiastically, hoping the topic was closed for now.

Frankie was mid-way through her second batch of cookie dough, this one a hazelnut shortbread that she would roll out and cut into acorn shapes, then drizzle with a Nutella icing. Cookie season was another reason Frankie loved spring. Most of autumn and all of winter, Bubble and Bake featured comfort pastries: muffins, cupcakes, tarts, and Frankie's Famous Butterhorns and kringles.

With the arrival of spring, the bakery shifted to lighter fare, a lot more cookies and tarts for picnics and tea parties and less heavy goods, although butterhorns were a staple and still ordered regularly. Both Frankie and Carmen loved to experiment with flavors, adding a variety of herbs, spices, and extracts into basic shortbread dough, sometimes creating an off-putting flop, sometimes a tasty masterpiece.

The kitchen, with its west-facing windows overlooking Sterling Creek in the back, basked in the light of a sunny April morning that promised to be warmer than usual. Frankie slid open a lower cabinet, looking for her tub of cookie cutters, thinking how wonderfully the two aunts had adapted to the organization of the bakery kitchen. Not that it had been easy; Frankie laughed out loud at the thought. Carmen raised her head from the giant mixer she was slicing butter into, arching her brows questioningly.

"I was just thinking about Tía Pepita and Aunt CeCe," Frankie said, "and what a disaster it was at first having them both in here together." Both highly opinionated women thought they knew best how to organize a kitchen, often leaving Carmen, Frankie, Tess, and Jovie in a dither, searching for utensils and ingredients that could turn up anywhere.

Aunt CeCe used the alphabet system instead of organizing by categories, which required a lot of extra thinking on the baker's part, since chocolate chips were in the "C" cupboard, but white chocolate chips were in the "W" cupboard.

Meanwhile, Tía Pepita reorganized items she found using the Spanish alphabet system, meaning sugar was frequently relocated next to the garlic jar! (Sugar in Spanish is azúcar; garlic is ajo.) After a couple weeks of this mayhem, Frankie and Carmen made labels for all the cabinets, something both said was long overdue anyway, and the aunts adjusted with just a few grumbles.

"Yeah, they're both so pig-headed when it comes to cooking and baking, but now it's all good, since they both have their own specialty to make," Carmen laughed.

At first, Frankie and Carmen divided baking duties

among the two aunts, Tess, and Jovie, but disagreements ensued constantly as the aunts fought over what they thought was the best assigned task. After Carmen suggested Tía Pepita start making her family favorite empanadas, she bustled about the bakery like a peacock, pleasing the Deep Lakes customers so much they began ordering empanadas by the dozen.

Frankie was thrilled for Tía but knew she needed to help Aunt CeCe find her own spotlight. A walk down memory lane about MéMé's baking turned the light bulb on for Aunt CeCe, who recalled the colorful, delicate macarons her mother made for every special occasion.

"I brought my recipe book along," CeCe gushed. "I thought you might want some of the family recipes. We just haven't had a chance to look at them yet."

Aunt CeCe's macarons were magical, melt-in-your-mouth fairy bites. She began using a variety of fillings and colors, the customers oohing and aahing over the spring rainbow they created in the bakery case. She, too, was receiving orders for a dozen at a time.

Once each aunt had her sense of place in the bakery, a harmonious rhythm flowed through the kitchen like soft sea waves. Frankie beamed inwardly, thinking of the hygge atmosphere among this gathering of unique women. Tess and Jovie came to love the two older ladies as they sang, laughed, and told stories with the two younger women.

Like a breath of spring air, the Bubble and Bake kitchen was filled with joy and hope, not unlike Deep

Lakes itself, bordered by Lake Joy and Lake Hope to the west. Frankie didn't learn the word *hygge* until after Grandma Sophie passed away but understood its meaning clearly. Difficult to translate simply, *hygge* is a feeling of contentment, manifested by simple pleasures shared with loved ones, like a fire, hot cocoa, singing songs, or roasting marshmallows. After Frankie's divorce, she made it her mission to create happiness for her daughters in little ways each day, and in her bakery/wine lounge, she made it her mission to create a contented space for customers.

The lounge was furnished with oversized cushy floor pillows, Scandinavian lounge chairs and couches, and coffee tables made from old trunks meant for putting your feet up. There were high top and traditional tables and chairs, too, for the non-lounging crowd. A giant bookcase covered one back wall of the lounge, loaded with all kinds of books, games, and puzzles, inviting customers to linger longer.

Beside all the reclaimed wood, Frankie and Carmen hung mason jar lights from the rafters and around the posts and placed flameless candles around tables and nooks where Charlie Champagne's carved birds and nisses (Scandinavian gnomes) could be found socializing.

At 6:30 a.m., the bakery case was filled and wheeled out to the front. Frankie grabbed a coffee mug from the kitchen, while wheeling out the coffee cart with its three airpot dispensers, fresh for the morning rush. Frankie still got a thrill when she flipped on the "open" sign; there was something satisfying in owning this place of passion and sharing it with others, in having others love what she made with her own two hands, in working daily with kindred spirits like Carmen, Tess, and Jovie, who more than shared this passion: they multiplied it.

The shop bell tinkled in an ongoing concert for the next two hours as people were on their way to work or just wanted the cream of the crop in baked goods that morning. Alonzo Goodman was one of those customers, and Frankie was pleased to catch up with her high school friend, Whitman County's two-term sheriff. Alonzo had also been the best man in Rick and Frankie's wedding, and her friendship with the protective sheriff remained resolute after the split. Unfortunately for Rick, his friendship with Lon was a casualty of the divorce.

"Frankie Champagne, I was wondering if you still worked here," Alonzo grinned broadly at his friend. His hair was thinning on top so he kept it short and neat. Frankie hadn't seen Alonzo up close in weeks, and upon inspection, she realized he had dropped a few pounds from the middle-age belly that plagues so many men. Not only was Alonzo looking dapper, but he seemed more cheerful than usual, piquing Frankie's curiosity.

"Wow, Lon, I barely recognize you. Looks like you're getting buff," Frankie bantered back. She hoped maybe the terminal bachelor had a new flame in his life.

Alonzo rolled his eyes dramatically. "I wouldn't call this buff," he said, gesturing toward his midsection.

"The doctor told me to start watching what I eat. Blood pressure's a little high," he ended in a whisper.

"So what brings you to the bakery case, then?" Frankie wanted to know.

Alonzo was picking up goodies for the monthly joint meeting of the sheriff's department staff and county finance committee, getting together to go over the quarterly budget reports. Knowing the meeting was bound to be long and boring, she added an extra supply of cookies to the muffins and empanadas in the order.

Carmen was tending to another customer, so Frankie took the opportunity to ask Alonzo about Donovan Pflug's business at the vineyard.

Alonzo was a little peeved and let out a small sigh. "We've been through this before, Frankie. I can't really do anything unless Pflug gets out of hand. ICE is putting the clamps on local police to keep tabs on guest workers, make sure they have their papers, you know. Pflug is just doing his job."

Frankie instantly felt bad, ruining Lon's cheery mood, taking advantage of their friendship to vent a complaint. She read and saw plenty on the news over the past months about the hot button issue of illegal immigrants crossing the border and how the U.S. Immigration and Customs Enforcement (ICE) was cracking down on illegals all over the country. She supposed she would have to tolerate Donovan Pflug making regular stops at the vineyard during the grape season.

"I'm sorry, Lon. You're right of course. I just wish Pflug could be a little nicer about it. I don't like my workers getting the third degree, especially when both James and I have vetted them. And, I trust Manny. He's not going to risk bringing illegal people here."

Alonzo shrugged. "I know. I don't like this side of police business either, so I'm glad Pflug is doing most of the checking. Better him than me." Changing the subject, he asked, "Any bottling in the near future? I could use a night out."

Same Alonzo; Frankie guessed he was still unattached. She promised to get in touch with him when the new wines were ready to bottle.

"And Frankie? One more thing . . . your aunt . . ."

"Which one? Aunt CeCe?" Frankie asked.

Alonzo shrugged, "The one in the colorful frocks."

Frankie laughed out loud, not just because Aunt CeCe and Tía Pepita both wore colorful dresses, but because Alonzo used the word "frocks," something one might hear on old episodes of *Gunsmoke* or *Little House on the Prairie*.

Alonzo ignored her. "Long gray hair, looks like a flower child from the '60s."

"That would be my Aunt CeCe," Frankie was still giggling.

"Keep an eye on her. I think I saw her bathing in the quarry pond Sunday." Alonzo was suddenly Sergeant Joe Friday in his demeanor, sobering Frankie's own disposition and keeping her from asking him if he was serious. Then the door shut, sounding off the bell, and he was gone.

Carmen was standing behind the counter, mouth agape, holding a bakery bag aloft, staring at the shop door. Frankie assumed she had heard Alonzo's warning about Aunt CeCe, but Carmen cut off her thoughts before she could ask.

"What do you suppose was up with that guy?" Carmen grimaced.

"Alonzo?"

"No, did you see the guy I was waiting on? Cheap suit, briefcase? He booked it out of here without his bakery, when Alonzo looked over at him. Didn't you notice?" Carmen set the bag on the counter, as Frankie grabbed it, flying out the door in time to see the mysterious visitor from the Spurgeon mansion crossing Granite Street.

"Mr. Foster! Mr. Foster!" Frankie called after him, waving the bakery in the air. "Hey, you forgot your bakery!" But Mr. Foster didn't turn around; never stopping his brisk pace, he disappeared down the side street.

Chapter 4

I loved her. I still love her, though I curse her in my sleep,
so nearly one are love and hate, the two most powerful and
devastating emotions that control man, nations, life.
- Edgar Rice Burroughs

The smell of moist earth and lilacs hung in the air
like wisps of the past and hints of the future.
- Margaret Millar

Friday dawned beautiful with abundant sunshine
that promised to expedite both tree and grapevine buds
into leaves and blossoms. Frankie checked on outside
operations at Bountiful Fruits with Manny and inside
wine-making progress with Nelson and Zane. Everything
was running like a well-oiled machine, so she jaunted
down Blackbird Marsh Road, mentally looking for more
tell-tale signs of spring: the emerging green color on the
ground and in the trees, crocuses popping up, migrant
birds returning to northern climes.

This reminded her that the Whitman Bird Club
warbler hike was coming soon, and she wanted to ask
Garrett if he was interested in going with her. Hundreds

of warblers migrate through central Wisconsin on their
way to their northern nesting grounds. They only stayed
a short time in the area, feeding on emerging spring
insects. Warblers come in many varieties, most of them
in various shades of yellows with earth-toned streaks,
caps, throats, or ear patches. Identifying them presented
a veritable treasure hunt as their small, swift bodies
darted among leafy tree branches, never resting long. This
made for a lively and popular birding adventure every
year, the best part being that everyone knew the warblers
previewed the arrival of other returning favorites: orioles,
rose-breasted grosbeaks, bluebirds, hummingbirds and
Frankie's all-time favorite, the striking red-headed
woodpeckers.

Without notice, Frankie was back in the city limits,
heading down the familiar main drag toward her shop.
She pulled into the alleyway between Bubble and Bake
and Deep Lakes Realty, another cream brick building
on Granite Street, and parked on the small cement slab
behind the shop, directly below her first story deck.

Bubble and Bake had the advantage of a corner
location on the main downtown streets, bordering a
small walking trail and green space on Sterling Creek.
The brick building's ground level featured a walk-in
basement entrance where Frankie stored cases of wine,
among other things. Outside stairs led upward to the
wine lounge deck, just large enough for a few patio tables
and comfy outdoor chairs for a sitting area, and a gas

fireplace, inviting evening guests to hang out even when temperatures cooled.

Frankie lived in the second story apartment, a spacious abode with two large bedrooms, a small third bedroom, a living room/dining area facing the creek, and a cute u-kitchen facing the street. Frankie's own deck area was situated directly above the shop's, affording a little more privacy for her personal barbecues or summer hangouts.

Soon, daughter Violet would be home from college in Stevens Point for summer break, a welcome adjustment. Violet was a sophomore, and, thanks to Uncle Will and Aunt Libby, was enjoying a happier year than her freshman year of roommate troubles and homesickness. Frankie's brother, Will, worked in Point as a forester, while his wife, Libby, worked in the Microbiology Lab at the university. They were the family connection the shy Violet needed in her life as she navigated into adulthood.

Frankie walked in the clunky old back door leading to the bakery kitchen, giving it a kick near the bottom where it frequently stuck due to humidity, heat, rain, freezing temperatures, or just plain stubbornness! The loud creak and Frankie's unexpected arrival made Tía Pepita miss a step as she danced around the kitchen in her oven mitts, carrying a fresh hot quiche, her own recipe called the Cha-Cha-Cha Quiche.

"Dios mío, Francisca," Tía scolded, but not seriously. "You could give an old lady a heart attack!" She set the quiche down on a cooling rack and clutched her heart with one oven-mitted hand.

Frankie couldn't keep herself from laughing and was happy to see Tía Pepita smile back. The wine bar sold quiche slices on its limited evening menu and, although Frankie offered her own homemade varieties, she happily added to her menu the spicy Mexican quiche made with chorizo, queso fresco, and pico de gallo. Taking inventory of the kitchen's progress, she was happy to see four more quiches already cooling for evening guests. On the opposite counter, more racks held shortbread cookies, mini muffins and Tess's cardamom nut tarts, a robust African recipe she shared with the bakery.

"Everything looks and smells amazing. I honestly think this place could get along just fine without me and Carmen." Frankie meant that as a compliment, but Tía Pepita interjected.

"Don't get any smart ideas, chica. I'm not staying here forever, you know. Once it gets cold, I'm outta here; it's back to Texas for me!"

Frankie went over and gave Tía a warm hug. "Oh, I know that. I'm just so glad you're here right now. You and Aunt CeCe have brought new life into the kitchen, and your recipes are wonderful. Carmen and I just have to make sure we learn how to make them before you leave."

Frankie grabbed a bakery box and headed out front to raid the pastry case, hoping there weren't any customers to witness it. Tess was out front clearing a couple of tables. Morning rush over, the shop still had two tables of customers: one with two older women chatting away, happily sharing a plate of tarts and mini muffins, and the other, a man sitting alone reading the newspaper, polishing off a large frosted cinnamon bun. Frankie hoped she would find a few leftover cinnamon buns in the case to abscond as she headed to her second meeting with Emily Spurgeon.

"How was the morning, Tess? By the way, good to see you out front." Frankie encouraged Tess, who preferred to work behind the scenes, to make front-of-house appearances, learning to interact with customers, as part of her final preparation for her culinary and hospitality degree from Madison College.

Tess smiled, meeting Frankie's eyes with confidence. "Look for yourself; there's not much left in the bakery case today. So, what can we put together for you to take to that heiress lady?"

There were four cinnamon buns, but Frankie wanted to offer more and to include Emily's staff, namely Alana and the groundskeeper she had not yet met. She wondered if there were more staff as well. She added four mini carrot cake muffins and three lemon poppyseed ones, then decided the iced Door County cherry tarts would round out the variety.

"Just a minute, Frankie," Tess said before disappearing into the kitchen to emerge with four of her freshly baked cardamom nut tarts. "You have to take a few of these, too. Even though they're featured tomorrow. I'm making another pan in a bit." Tess beamed, clearly proud of her contribution to opening up the palates of the Deep Lakes community, none of whom were treated to much, if any, Ethiopian fare.

Bakery box in hand, Frankie left the way she came after retrieving her tablet containing her notes and Emily Spurgeon's speech draft. As she approached the long horseshoe drive of the lofty mansion, she was a little nervous, despite breaking the ice with Emily at their first encounter. Frankie was never comfortable around people she deemed superior to herself, a flaw she recognized but couldn't quite shake. The Golden Firefly took her cue from Frankie's inner uncertainty.

"Stop fidgeting and fluttering and get focused," The Golden One chided. "You're not going to feel high-class if you don't look the part, my dear."

The scolding was only mildly helpful. Thank goodness The Pirate was awake as well, whispering in her other ear, spurring her onward.

"You are smart, Frankie, and beautiful. Hold your head high. You've got this, chérie."

Besides, she brought baked goods. Wasn't that a great way to win over people?

Alana answered the door, taking Frankie's bakery with a professional thank you and asking her if she would like to tour the grounds while Emily was preparing for their meeting. Back out the door she had entered, Alana pointed to a man dressed in denim and flannel, who appeared to be tending one of the many trees on the property.

"That's Mack Perry, Ms. Spurgeon's groundskeeper. He's expecting you. Just walk in the back entrance when you're done. I'll watch for you." Alana closed the front door behind her.

Frankie crossed the greening lawn toward Mack Perry, who seemed to be having a gentle conversation with a tall tree sporting a tapper. A maple no doubt. Mack stood straight when he spied Frankie, allowing her a full appraisal. Something about Mack Perry brought a smile to Frankie's face; his silver hair ended in curls that hung below his shirt collar; his face flushed a healthy pink glow as if the outdoors agreed with him; a smiling mouth peeked out below a silver mustache and above a short, well-kept silver beard. He resembled a cross between a tall leprechaun and a slim Santa. Dodging a wayward branch, he strode forward in green rubber boots, his hand extended in greeting.

"You must be Ms. Champagne. Miss Emily tells me I'm to show you the grounds this morning. Mackenzie Perry at your service." He made a tiny bow as Frankie took his hand and shook it.

"I'm just Frankie, please, Mr. Perry. Nice to meet you. Maple tree?" Frankie gestured toward the budding tree with the tapper partway up its trunk.

"Yes. Bravo, Frankie. And please, call me Mack."

Rather than walking the whole lawn, Mack pointed

out the few maples still being tapped for the sugaring season. Tapping had begun in March, and now that most trees were budding, Mack pulled the taps and began making syrup.

Frankie was interested in the maple sugaring process, telling Mack she would like to see the operation from start to finish next year. "If you're selling the Spurgeon syrup, I'd love to try it," she added sincerely. Mack informed her that sugaring was late this spring due to the relentless winter. But, he hoped to have syrup ready for the Maple Syrup Festival at the Mackenzie Center in Poynette, an event he volunteered at every year.

Frankie impressed Mack with her recognition of the beeches, birches, willows and blue spruce trees. But, she didn't know the ornamental trees and relished learning about the exotic ones adorning the front lawn, including the majestic Chinese chestnut and the shorter American hazelnut, both producing edible nuts in the fall.

Closer to the avenue, Mack pointed out a line of tulip trees that would soon be breathtaking with their large tulip shaped blossoms, later sporting glowing golden autumn foliage. On the southeast side of the mansion, the expansive sunroom was bookended by two smoke trees, which Mack described as a magical show of billowing pink and purple blooms that seemed to float about the tree limbs during the summer.

The sunroom overlooked the formal rose garden, not much to behold in April, but Mack assured Frankie she must visit the garden throughout the summer months as "she changes clothes frequently," in Mack's words. Frankie said she was a little sad Emily's roses would not be featured at the Roots Festival but that her lilacs would be a reasonable substitute. Heading toward the lake side of the property, Mack showed Frankie the lilac thickets, bushes and trees, all loaded with buds; they would no doubt make a spectacular display in the new gazebo at Spurgeon Park.

"I love lilacs, their delicate blossoms, their spring colors, and especially their heavenly smell," Frankie gushed. "They remind me of my grandmother. She had five different types of lilacs, and we could cut them together, so I could bring them home for my mother."

Mack smiled at the reminiscence. "Flowers seem to carry the best memories; maybe that's why I love tending them," he said. "All of these are Miss Emily's favorites. She never could choose just one."

As the pair turned toward Lake Joy, Frankie asked about the camera sticking out of one giant oak trunk.

"Trail camera," Mack explained. "We have three of them posted around the backyard. You'd be surprised what kind of wildlife roams around here, even in town. Miss Emily and I get a kick out of watching the footage. Last week, we saw a red fox and a possum. The animals are starting to forage now that spring's here."

Frankie noticed the personal details Mack added about Emily as he showed her around, and she couldn't help wondering what kind of relationship they had. Was this just loyal affection for his employer, or was there something deeper, at least on Mack's part? She decided to ask a few safe questions.

"Mack, how long have you worked for the Spurgeons?" They had stopped walking and stood inside the pergola overlooking Lake Joy. Frankie noticed all of the ice fishing shanties were off the lake, even though ice remained in the middle; there were too many thin spots, and more open water appeared every day.

"Well, I've known them my whole life. Miss Emily hired me after my father died, so that's going on 29 years. My dad worked in the quarry. Emily and I went to school together for a while."

How did he know so much about flowers and trees? Mack's uncle had a landscape business near Madison. Mack started working for him when he was 12 and continued until he was hired by Emily.

"My uncle was a natural with trees and flowers. He knew what to plant, when and where to plant it, and what to do about pests, blights, and poor soil. He was a great teacher for me. Take that weeping Norway spruce there," Mack pointed to Frankie's left where a tall shaggy evergreen stood, looking much like a dark green "Cousin It." "This is one of Miss Emily's favorite weeping trees, so I was pretty upset when it came down with spider mites. But I saved it using a dish soap solution." Frankie could tell he was proud of his ability, and she noticed many new pink cones sprouting from the Norway, indicating it was thriving.

"I'm going to write that down . . . about using dish soap, I mean. I'm always looking for ways I can take care of pests without using insecticides," she said.

"Oh yes, that works well and might come in handy at your vineyard," Mack noted.

Frankie was taken a little aback. "You know I have a vineyard?"

Mack nodded forthrightly. "I make it my business to know things about anyone who spends time on this property and particularly with Miss Spurgeon."

So, Frankie may have guessed right about Mack having deep feelings for Emily. She probed a little deeper. "Do you know the man that was here the other day? A Mr. Foster? He didn't look familiar to me so I thought he wasn't from here, but then I saw him again yesterday at my shop . . ." Frankie trailed off, hoping Mack would pick up the cue.

"Hmm, that one. Grant Foster is some city slicker from Philadelphia. Wants to reunite Miss Emily with her cousin. I'm keeping my eye on him," Mack indicated, but offered nothing further.

Heading back along the lakefront, Mack pointed out the other many weeping tree varieties on the property, and Frankie admired the weeping Japanese maple for its bonsai-like appearance. Then the tour was finished, and both Mack and Frankie went through the back door, into a large mud room, where Mack took off the green rubber boots, led Frankie through an enormous commercial-style kitchen, down a side hallway, and into the sunroom, where Emily was sitting with Pearl the Siamese cat, several photo albums laid out on the long glass-topped coffee table.

Emily brightened when she looked up; Frankie was certain the reaction was directed more toward Mack than herself. Watching Mack standing with his hands clasped behind his back like a young boy with a crush was endearing to Frankie.

"Tell me, Frankie: did you enjoy the tour of my property?" Emily asked, smiling brightly.

"Mack is a wonderful guide. He gives so much TLC to your trees, shrubs and flowers, Emily. You're lucky to have someone so devoted." Frankie let the last comment hang, watching for a reaction. She was not disappointed, seeing the meaningful look Emily and Mack exchanged.

"Pardon me, ladies," Mack said, "I just want to give Miss Emily the daily outdoors report before I get back to it." Mack shared that all the birdhouses were now cleaned, repaired, and ready for spring arrivals. He gave the robin count of the morning at 17, but he couldn't be sure if he was counting the same robin twice, such were the comings and goings of birds. He added he was on the lookout for other spring migrants, expecting to see more any day now. "The critter camera showed a pair of bluebirds scouting out the house nearest the back driveway." This news produced a little clap from Emily.

Mack resumed his recitation. "I'm happy to tell you the Norway spruce is in the pink - literally; it's sprouting some healthy pink cones, so new growth is happening, and she's on the mend." Frankie thought it was sweet how Mack referred to his trees by gender.

"One more thing: I expect we will finish making syrup next week, especially if these warmer days keep going." Then Mack gave Emily a little bow, eyes twinkling, Emily letting out a little flirtatious giggle. Pearl leaped off Emily's lap to wrap herself around Mack's legs. Clearly, Emily's other devoted companion approved of Mack as well.

At that moment Alana entered the sunroom, carrying a tray with a crystal pitcher, two tall glasses, and a sampling of Bubble and Bake goods. She looked disapprovingly in Mack's direction, making Frankie wonder if her disapproval was his outdoor clothes possibly bringing in some debris, or if it was the man himself. Maybe Alana didn't think Mack belonged on the inside of the mansion.

"Good news, Alana," Emily said warmly. "Mack informs me that the maple syrup will be ready soon. I think French toast and some maple leaf candies are in order."

Emily leaned conspiratorially in Mack's direction as if the two were in cahoots, while Alana produced a withering look at the groundskeeper. Mack disregarded her look or even her presence, walking past Alana as if she were a piece of furniture. He withdrew down the hallway and out the back door, but not before Emily handed him one of the cinnamon buns, wrapped in a napkin.

Alana poured each woman a glass of lemon balm hibiscus iced tea, and explained the healthy levels of vitamin C and cleansing properties from the herb and flower buds. Then she departed as well, leaving Emily to present photos one by one to Frankie, identifying the people and circumstances in each. After aligning the contents of the tray just so, she looked approvingly at the bakery, choosing a cinnamon bun, cutting it precisely into quarters.

"I hope it was okay to bring some goodies from my shop, Emily. I should have asked if anyone here has dietary restrictions first, but I was on the run," Frankie began, but was cut off by a wave of Emily's hand.

"Not to worry, Frankie. I love sweets. Just have to be careful not to eat too many. Mack will be thrilled to enjoy your bakery, and even Alana, I'm sure, will sneak something." Emily added in a confidential whisper, "She's always watching her weight . . . and mine, too." Alana had a fine figure, Frankie thought, but she wasn't surprised to learn that Alana kept tabs on Emily's weight, since she was her personal assistant.

As Emily shared each photo, Frankie took her time entering information into her tablet, checking on names, spellings, dates, and the like. During the hours she spent with Emily, she learned many more personal details about her parents, including that Emily took over hostessing events at both the Granite Works offices and the mansion, since her mother, Cordelia, passed away when Emily was just 12.

An only child, Emily became the mistress of the mansion. Her father relied on Emily as he had relied on her mother, and her childhood abruptly ended. Frankie wondered if Emily had any suitors or even the chance to pursue her own dreams and interests or if her whole world was the quarry company, this house, her father. Frankie found herself feeling sorry for the wealthy heiress, who was, after all, just as human as anyone.

The two went on to review the speech draft for the Roots Festival, making tweaks here and there, until Emily was satisfied it was just right. Frankie promised to print a hard copy of it for her, after Emily disclosed she was not computer capable.

"I leave all my email correspondence to Alana. She reads them to me; I dictate responses to her. I prefer old-fashioned phone calls or face-to-face meetings. It's a much more personal and effective form of communication, if you ask me."

Frankie had to agree, recalling times when her emails or text messages were misconstrued in tone or when she had to request clarification on the meaning of messages from others. Emails were time-saving, no doubt, but not without their downside. Still, Frankie relied on digital communication because she simply had too many irons in the fire.

The meeting about over, Frankie gathered a folder of about a dozen photos from Emily's collection to begin piecing together a slideshow. One photo included the two partners and their families, the Spurgeons and McCoys. Emily was 11 years old, standing tall between her parents. The McCoys were beaming in the photo; Mrs. McCoy looked pregnant - the infamous cousin Mack Perry referred to perhaps? Frankie saw an opportunity and took it.

"Emily, may I ask you something?" Emily nodded, so she continued. "Is your aunt pregnant in this photo?" Emily nodded again. "What happened to your cousin?"

Emily stiffened, slumped a little, then opened another of the photo albums, this one from the 1970s and 1980s. She pulled out a photo of two females; one was certainly a younger Emily looking groovy in wide bell-bottom jeans and flowered peasant top, the other younger girl in plaid culottes and a white smocked shirt, a cute Cocker Spaniel sitting between them on a terrace.

"This is my cousin. It's the last picture of us together, just before she moved away. I was 19; she was seven. Taffy was her dog. She was hit by a truck and killed. It was horrible. I was walking her. She got away." Emily's voice broke as if the accident had just happened yesterday instead of decades ago.

"I'm sure it wasn't your fault. I'm so sorry," Frankie consoled. "What year was this?"

"Let's see. 1978. The quarry closed in 1984 but was already in decline, you see. There were just a few employees left by then. Uncle Edgar wanted to sell his portion and move back to Pennsylvania, where he and Aunt Evelyn still had family. They moved away. Uncle Edgar sold his shares of the company, leaving my father with the fallout. He held on as long as he could, financially, but then he cashed out, too. He was so sad to close the quarry. After they moved, I never saw my uncle, aunt, or cousin again."

Frankie was trying to process this new information, so she wasn't thinking clearly when she blurted out, "But what about Mr. Foster? I mean, isn't he here for your cousin . . ." she faltered now, knowing she'd overstepped.

Emily drew her brows together. "Oh, so Mack's been talking, has he?"

Frankie did not want to get Mack into hot water. "Well, it's just that I saw Mr. Foster here the other day; then I saw him in my bakery, and I wondered if he was new in town. I'm sure Mack didn't mean to be disrespectful." Frankie was uncertain how to proceed.

Emily relaxed a little, but again a sad, distracted worry crossed her face. "Well, the truth is: I'm hoping to reunite with my cousin, and very soon. In fact, I hope she will be standing by my side when I re-dedicate the park to Deep Lakes," she announced.

"So, who is Mr. Foster, then? Your cousin's husband?" Frankie figured she was in this deep, might as well wade in further.

"Well, you certainly have a bit of bulldog journalism in your blood, don't you, Francine?" Emily scolded, as Frankie looked down, embarrassed. "Nevermind, I admire your spunk."

"Mr. Foster is my cousin's representative, here to facilitate our reunion."

This information baffled Frankie. "If your cousin wants to reconnect with you, why didn't she come here herself? Why send a 'representative,' as you called him?"

"Because I located my cousin, or I should say Alana did, using the internet. I asked Mr. Foster to come here to meet with me."

With that, Emily rose, closing out further interrogation on Frankie's part. However, Emily pressed Frankie for another meeting the following week as soon as Frankie had a slideshow drafted. As Emily walked her to the front entrance, Frankie turned to apologize for her probing questions but was stopped by Emily's quiet murmur, "I just hope Delia will agree to the terms."

Driving back to Bubble and Bake, Frankie's mind was in a whirl. *What kind of family negotiates a reconciliation? Is that why a lawyer was involved, if that's what Mr. Foster was? Did Emily's cousin want something from Emily in exchange for reuniting? Clearly, reuniting was important to Emily, maybe because her cousin was all the family she had left.*

Her musings were interrupted by a loud whistle in her ear from The Golden One. "Time out, Francine. A. This is none of your business. B. Stop being so dramatic. C. Not everything is a mystery or a conspiracy. D. Not everyone has an ulterior motive." Frankie shushed both Goldie and her musings for the time being.

Chapter 5

To mourn a mischief that is past and gone,
Is the next way to draw new mischief on.
- William Shakespeare

Frankie had to admit that her heart was aflutter as she anticipated seeing Garrett Iverson this weekend, after three weeks of only scattered phone conversations while Garrett was busy with his forensic practices course in Madison. The weekend was in full swing, and Garrett said he'd be coming to Bubble and Bake Saturday night to see her.

The wine lounge business was picking up now that spring had settled over Deep Lakes, and while Friday nights were generally the busiest, this particular Saturday could actually be called crowded. A bachelorette party had given Frankie a heads-up they would be celebrating at the wine bar, so Frankie and Carmen were both working the evening shift, along with Tess and a seasonal employee, Cherry Parker. The bride and her friends, a chatty, laughing group of nine women, occupied a large corner alcove near the fireplace, ordered two bottles of wine at a time, and snacked on flatbread pizzas, cheese and crackers.

The rest of the lounge's comfy chairs and couches were occupied as well, along with the few high top tables. The only seating room left was at the bar itself. Spring in Wisconsin was reason enough to celebrate, urging people out of hibernation and away from the television. Frankie and Carmen hoped tonight was an auspicious sign for the upcoming summer season.

Around 8:00 p.m., Frankie's brother, James, and his wife, Shauna, showed up for after dinner drinks, quickly heading to a spot perfect for two people near the front window. Frankie waylaid Tess before she could take their order, wanting to talk to James about Donovan Pflug's check-ups on their seasonal workers.

"Hey, good to see you two," Frankie greeted them cheerfully.

Shauna gave Frankie the once-over from head to toe. "Hi, Frankie. You look put together tonight," she offered. Frankie wondered if this was a back-handed compliment: did it mean she usually didn't look put together?

Frankie's relationship with Shauna was an uneasy one; Frankie couldn't quite figure out why that was. Shauna was an attractive beauty with long blonde hair and sky blue eyes. With her more than average height and slim figure, she looked good in everything she wore, while Frankie barely reached five feet and was selective in her clothing choices, as many items didn't hang correctly on her as they'd been designed.

The sisters-in-law sang in St. Anthony's church choir,

where Shauna was frequently featured with solo pieces, while Frankie never had a solo. In fact, Frankie dubbed herself the "blender" as she had a good enough voice to sing with others but nothing as tuneful and sweet as Shauna's voice.

Shauna was an accomplished business partner for James, managing the accounts and clients at the construction company. The two had met in college at the University of Minnesota, both majoring in Business. They went their separate ways but reconnected after Shauna's marriage ended. In fact, James and Shauna had recently celebrated their tenth anniversary.

Frankie suspected moving to Deep Lakes from an exciting city like Minneapolis was unsettling for Shauna, especially since the move included her teenage son, Marcus. But he adapted well to small town life, finished high school, and was now completing a law degree back in Minnesota. Shauna seemed happy here and was good for James, yet she often spoke to Frankie as if she had something to prove. During those times, Frankie's own self-doubts rose within her, and she had to remind herself not to be so analytical.

Painting on a bright professional smile, Frankie tried again. "Did you go somewhere good for dinner?"

James shrugged. "We went to Comé Comé. It's always good, but I hear your place is serving up some awesome homemade Mexican these days," James added with a laugh, causing Frankie to relax. She laughed, too, happily surprised to know the word was out about Tía Pepita's delicious offerings.

"I'd certainly recommend the Cha-Cha-Cha Quiche or some empanadas, but you probably don't have room. So, what can I bring you? I've got some lovely dessert wines on the menu right now."

Frankie returned with a house cherry moscato for Shauna and an area port wine for James, since Frankie didn't produce ports.

"Can I sit with you for a minute? I want to talk to you about something," she began, and was relieved when both nodded and expressed an interest in what she wanted to say.

"Donovan Pflug was at Bountiful Fruits a few days ago, checking up on my seasonal workers, rattling Manny. Has he been out to the construction company, too?" Frankie wanted to know.

It was Shauna who leaned in to answer. "Oh yes, he sure was. I keep all the paperwork on every employee, so I had to show him their documents. There's nothing to worry about. Everyone is legally accounted for, so far that is."

Frankie was glad to hear it but wondered, "How does Pflug act around your office? I mean, is he polite or . . ."

Shauna smirked, producing an abrupt laugh. "Donovan Pflug, polite? I don't think it's in his nature. He's demanding. He looks at me like I'm not smart enough to be in charge of legal documents. It's hard to be respectful when he's around, but I have to be respectful for the sake of the company," Shauna finished, a little flushed. James squeezed her hand, reassuringly. Frankie was happy that she and Shauna had found something in common, even if it was a common adversary of sorts.

Switching subjects, the three chatted about finalizing the Spurgeon Park Gazebo project to prepare for the grand unveiling in May, Frankie offering compliments to both James and Shauna for the volunteer hours expended on behalf of Deep Lakes.

Shauna took the compliment well. "After all, Spurgeon Park is a focal point of downtown. It needs to look like a showpiece for the locals and tourists alike. It's not easy to keep people focused on shopping local and living local with all the other competition out there."

Frankie nodded enthusiastically. "Don't I know it," she said.

James gestured with his head to the bar area where Garrett Iverson was leaning, talking to Carmen. "I think you've got company, Frankie," he said.

Frankie bid the two good night and scampered up to the bar, hoping to surprise Garrett from behind. Instead, Frankie ended up surprised as Garrett turned just as she was about to touch him, threw his arms around Frankie, dipping her in an exaggerated embrace and kissing her deeply, as many customers looked on in variations of shock and approval.

Standing upright a few seconds later, Frankie

smoothed her shirt and apron, never taking her eyes off the handsome face of the man she was falling for.

"You've got some pretty fast moves for someone who's used to dealing with corpses," she said teasingly. "I think you shocked my customers, Mr. Iverson," she giggled.

Garrett looked around the lounge as if noticing for the first time that there were other people there. "A man has to move pretty fast around you, Miss Francine, or he's liable to miss his chance," Garrett said merrily, his eyes blazing with heat from their kiss.

Behind the bar, Carmen was pouring out two glasses of Spring Fever Riesling, a favorite concoction made from Frankie's Edelweiss grapes with vanilla, lemon, and lavender notes. Pushing the glasses toward Frankie and Garrett, she said, "Whoa, it's getting kind of hot in here! Why don't you two go sit somewhere so you can catch up, maybe somewhere more private?" Carmen shooed away Frankie's pretended protest, saying she could manage the next half-hour without her business partner's help.

Frankie and Garrett disappeared into the kitchen, then out to the deck, which wasn't yet open for the season to customers. Although the day had begun sunny and hovering near 70 degrees, afternoon showers brought cooler temperatures and, typical of April nights, temps were now falling into the 40s. Frankie turned on the gas fireplace, grabbed a blanket from the patio storage trunk, and settled next to Garrett on the loveseat for some small talk and serious snuggle time. Neither of them noticed when Carmen set a bottle of wine on the table next to them and quickly tip-toed back inside.

The wine bar closed for the evening, Garrett and Frankie were still in a dreamy place when the back door opened, revealing the brawny frame of Alonzo Goodman. The sheriff immediately cleared his throat loudly after Carmen tipped him off that two lovebirds might be too occupied to notice him otherwise.

Clearing his throat a second time and making a point of walking loudly in his boots, Alonzo called out. "Hey Frankie and Garrett. I need a word with you, Frankie."

The interruption was not part of Frankie's plan at that moment, but she wriggled out of Garrett's arms and sat up straight as a school girl who was caught passing notes. Lon's tone suggested this was a business call, not a friendly chit-chat session. Garrett escaped from the blanket, tucking it in around Frankie's shoulders, tipped a two-finger salute to Alonzo and headed inside.

Alonzo appeared apologetic. "Sorry about this, Frankie. I know you two haven't seen each other in awhile, but it's about the two aunts. I was going to send Shirley to talk to you, but I figured maybe it's better coming from me."

The aunts again! What was it this time? More bathing at the quarry pond, maybe? Frankie realized she hadn't talked to Aunt CeCe about that incident yet, nor had she told Carmen. Well, now she'd have to deal with it. As if in concert with Frankie's mood, dark clouds covered the moonlight, and the air smelled heavy with an imminent storm.

"Why don't we go inside and talk in the kitchen with Carmen?" Frankie began pushing the blanket aside to stand up, as Alonzo averted his eyes.

"Are you decent, Frankie?" he asked.

"What the heck's that supposed to mean, Lon?" Frankie's dander erupted, and she rose her full five feet, standing toe to toe with Alonzo. "Do you honestly think I'd do something sketchy at my place of business, right here in the middle of downtown Deep Lakes?" Frankie couldn't believe Lon's question.

It didn't help that Lon was laughing nonchalantly as he looked down more than a full foot into Frankie's eyes. "That's exactly the answer I expected from you and why we need to talk. Simmer down, Frankie."

Carmen was doing the last closing duties of the night as Tess finished up dishes. Alonzo asked Carmen if the three of them could sit down somewhere private, and Tess decided that was her cue to leave. "I'll put the bar glasses out front and go out the side door," Tess said, adding, "Cherry's already gone. See you Tuesday."

Carmen and Frankie stared dumbfounded, mouths agape, as Alonzo relayed the embarrassing story of Tía Pepita and Aunt CeCe sunbathing on the shop deck that afternoon stark-naked. Lon couldn't believe it himself when the complaint call came to the department around 3:15 p.m. Deciding the best course of action was to send in Officer Shirley Lazaar to deal with the situation, Lon tried to diffuse the gossip around the office instead.

"What in the world was their explanation?" Carmen wondered.

"Did they get ticketed?" Frankie wanted to know, adding, "Who called in the complaint, anyway?" Frankie was mortified for the aunts, her business, and herself. She didn't want her shop to gain any negative publicity; a damaged reputation in a small town could toll the death knell for the business.

Alonzo threw his arms up in the air to quiet the stream of questions. "They said they were enjoying the warmth of the sun, trying to get an even tan . . . I think that's how it went. No tickets issued this time; just a stern warning and reminder of the laws regarding indecent exposure. And Frankie, you know I can't tell you who called it in."

Alonzo was trying not to laugh, but the idea of two older ladies naked on Frankie's shop deck was comical indeed. He couldn't resist jabbing Frankie a little. "Looks like you got more than you bargained for in those two. A little taste of your own medicine, eh Frankie?"

Frankie glowered at Lon, arms crossed under her chest. Carmen, however, pointed one finger at Frankie accusingly. "This has to be your aunt's idea. Why would Tía Pepita need a suntan?"

Hands on both hips, Frankie puffed up like a rooster. "It was your idea for the two of them to spend more time together, keep each other company and all that, Carmen."

She quickly backed down, realizing, whatever the reason, she and Carmen were going to have to sit them down like two little kids and reprimand them.

Carmen agreed. "Better not put it off, Frankie. Let's get them down here tomorrow morning for coffee with a side of piping hot scolding. I'll tell Tía: nine o'clock?"

"Better make it 9:30, Carmen. Church at 8:00 tomorrow. Let's just meet here right after. Meanwhile, we'll practice what we're going to say to them." By now the shock had worn off, and both were smiling and shaking their heads.

"Those two ladies are going to be the death of both of us, Frankie." As an afterthought, Carmen said, "Sorry to ruin your night with Garrett."

"You didn't; he did," Frankie pointed at Alonzo, who decided not to say a word. "Come on, let's finish off this bottle of Spring Fever, you two. I think we earned it."

Alonzo shook his head, indicating he was still on duty for another hour. Walking out the back door, into the rainstorm, he threw back one last witty comment, "Looks like the aunts have a pretty bad case of Spring Fever themselves."

Chapter 6

*The monument of a great man is not of granite
or marble or bronze. It consists of his goodness,
his deeds, his love and his compassion.
- Alfred Armand Montapert*

"Well, that went well!" Carmen and Frankie were sitting on Frankie's couch in her living room above Bubble and Bake, having dismissed the aunts after a heart-to-heart conversation. Punctuated with many emotions, Frankie and Carmen took turns proclaiming their appreciation for the aunts' contributions to the bakery, while explaining the need for proper behavior in public. Both aunts countered with arguments of their own, ranging from people should mind their own business, to being nude is natural - not indecent since people in California do it all the time (according to Aunt CeCe), then eventually to a tearful statement that they should pack up and go back home.

"They are just like children in some ways, Carmen. Fragile. Spirited." Frankie smiled, patting Carmen's leg. "I guess that's why they're so lovable, huh?"

Despite the emotional whirlwind, Carmen and Frankie garnered a promise from the aunts that they would try to behave, at least at the shop. Both stopped pouting when Frankie finished the conversation, pouring accolades upon them for their scrumptious bakery.

"Bottom line: we love having you here and want you to stay," Carmen noted, secretly wondering how long exactly they would remain. Tía Pepita was in a 120-day experimental drug study for her eye condition, meaning she would return to Texas no sooner than late June. Aunt CeCe's visit had no such expiration date; she merely showed up without notice like a surprise spring snowfall. Who knew how long she planned to stay, if she had a plan at all?

"Okay, I'm heading home. The pasture will be a lot less muddy by now so we need to play catch up from yesterday. There's lamb duty, plus the boys are working on a school presentation about sheep production for their Ag Science class. Ryan will be the first to tell you that he's not good at the artistic stuff. So, he'll help with the facts, and I'll help with design," Carmen explained. "I'll be in tomorrow morning to make dough. See you then?"

Frankie started to nod then remembered her plans for Sunday night dinner. "Hey, Garrett and I are going out to dinner with Lon and Jovie. Why don't you and Ryan join us, and we'll make it a triple date?" she asked.

Carmen's open mouth revealed her surprise. "Lon and Jovie, huh? When did that start?"

"As far as I know, it's just starting right now. Anyway, we're leaving at 5:00 for Feil's Supper Club in Randolph.

They're serving a German buffet tonight; it's going to be yummy," Frankie coaxed.

"Ryan and I sure could use a night off. The boys can handle a couple hours of lamb duty, but I'll text you to confirm later. So, who's closing the shop tonight?"

"My mom, Aunt CeCe, and Tess. No worries. Good luck with that sheep presentation. Speaking of presentations, I'm going to work on the quarry slide show for Emily Spurgeon, see how far I get. See you tonight."

Frankie immersed herself in Emily's photos and the history of Deep Lakes Granite Works, reflecting on the impact the quarry had on the community. Like most of America, Deep Lakes was a mini melting pot: quarrymen represented Scotch, Irish, Italian, German, and Polish cultures, working side by side, many joined by their own sons. In later years, Latinos joined the crew of quarrymen, and they produced second generation workers as well. The granite itself, a rich red color with white luminous flecks, was a source of pride for the workers, putting Deep Lakes permanently on the map, as national monuments were produced from the high-quality stone.

The selected photos spanned more than a century of quarry operations. The old black and white pictures showed large teams of horses hauling stone to waiting railcars, boulders being hoisted from the quarry by a thick cable, and eventually, a modern derrick hauling out the rocks. Other photos showed the giant rock crusher, polisher, and saws used to cut the resistant rock.

Frankie marveled at a photo of a man poised over a granite slab, hammer in one hand, chisel in the other, wearing no safety glasses or face covering of any sort. Another photo featured two men hanging in an open metal box suspended over a rock ledge, hanging by a cable. Again, no safety gear of any kind was worn for protection.

The granite may have been valuable, but it was these men in the photos, among hundreds of others, who were the soul of the company. It was their back-breaking labor that brought forth the glorious rocks, their painstaking work that brought the stone to life, their craftsmanship that yielded monuments forever memorializing the lives of others.

Frankie knew the history wasn't all pretty. Workers had died in the quarry over the years, some from equipment malfunctions, some from falling off precipices, some crushed from falling rocks. The work was dangerous to be sure. Looking at the photos, she wondered about the fate of each worker pictured.

She paused to admire a photo showing the corner brick building on Granite and Meriwether, a town landmark that was the original Deep Lakes Bank and now her own, Bubble and Bake. Immediately, Frankie felt a deep connection to the community. Some day, years from now, people would be looking at photos of her shop; she, too, was a part of the Deep Lakes melting pot.

A couple hours later, Frankie, who was bleary-eyed and stiff from sitting, closed the computer, satisfied she had woven together a suitable slide show for the Roots Festival. Now mid-afternoon, she decided to call Emily Spurgeon to see if she could stop by the next morning to show the presentation to her. Then, she needed some sustenance and some movement for her body.

Emily answered the phone herself. "Emily Spurgeon."

Frankie was surprised to hear Emily in person until she told Frankie it was Alana's day off. Of course, Emily would be thrilled to see the slide show tomorrow morning. Nine o'clock would be perfect.

Satisfied, Frankie pried her bottom loose from the chair she'd occupied for hours, mentally reprimanding herself for not getting up every 30 minutes to stretch and move as the experts recommended. Two choices now stood before her: she could take a much-needed walk to wake up her limbs and brain, or she could eat a much-needed meal. The hard-boiled egg and latte she had after church were a distant memory. An insistent growl rose up from Frankie's stomach, putting in a plea for the latter option. Knowing she needed to grocery shop, she figured Bubble and Bake could provide for her quickly and sufficiently. She headed down her steps and into the bright kitchen, finding Tess cutting a Mediterranean flatbread pizza into quarters.

"Yum, Tess. That looks perfect. Any chance you want to make another one of those?" Frankie admired the dark green spinach, rich red sun-dried tomatoes and glossy black olives highlighting the pizza. Frankie's stomach let

out another barking growl. "Never mind. I shouldn't be
eating anything too big since I'm going out for German
buffet later. Besides, you don't need to be waiting on me."
Frankie's mouth began watering as she thought about
dinner, featuring different types of schnitzel, sauerbraten,
red cabbage, and potato pancakes.

Tess laughed easily at Frankie's ways. She wasn't an
authoritative boss, but she eagerly shared her baking and
business knowledge, while praising her workers for their
ideas and dedication. "Sounds like you've been working
without eating again, Boss Lady," Tess clucked, pulling a
plate of apple slices and cheddar cheese from the cooler
and handing it to Frankie. Then she handed her a pizza
quarter, too. "Here, this should keep your stomach happy
until dinner. I didn't expect to see you today. It's supposed
to be your day off. What's keeping you so busy lately,
anyway?"

Frankie told Tess about the Roots Festival and her
part in helping Emily Spurgeon with the re-dedication
of the park and new gazebo. Tess nodded and murmured
as she resumed chopping pizza toppings for the evening
customers. "I hope you don't get all high and mighty,
hanging around that granite heiress. Remember the poor
man and the rich man do not play well together," Tess
teased.

Frankie smiled, relishing Tess's shared proverbs
passed down from her grandparents to her parents, then
to her. "More African words of wisdom?" she asked. "At

least I understand this one. Don't worry about me, Tess. I actually kind of feel sorry for Emily Spurgeon. She seems lonely to me, almost like she's trapped in that mansion. I guess when you have money, you never know whom you can trust." Frankie looked wistful at that thought, trying to fathom the idea of being an heiress.

"Think I'll go out front and mingle with customers for a bit," she grinned. "Oh, and visit with my mother, too." Frankie was feeling gratitude for her business, her co-workers, her friends, her family; she wouldn't trade places with Emily Spurgeon in a million years.

Chapter 7

Knowledge is power only if man knows
what facts not to bother with.
- Robert Staughton Lynd

Frankie's musings from yesterday about her good life were about to return to haunt her. As she approached the Granite Mansion, a road block of two squad cars awaited. Peering beyond the squads, Frankie could see a parked ambulance and Alonzo's official brown Jeep Cherokee.

"Oh no, what in the world . . ." Frankie spoke out loud, pulled her SUV over toward the curb, noticing a few neighborhood residents standing on the sidewalk, speculating. Frankie left the engine running when she exited and marched purposefully up the road where a Whitman County officer was posted, looking officially serious.

"Good morning, Officer Hale," Frankie read the name tag of what appeared to be one of the summer recruits, a formidable woman with wavy cropped hair.

"Good morning, Ma'am," Hale said. "Do you live on this street?"

"No, I was just on my way to see Emily Spurgeon. We have a scheduled meeting at 9:00," Frankie tried to sound authoritative. "I hope she's okay."

Officer Hale responded to Frankie's probing gaze. "There's been a death at the mansion," she said. The recruit held her stance; her poker face gave nothing away. "Sorry, Ma'am. I'm afraid I can't let you pass. The Spurgeon house is off limits."

Frankie refused to be dismissed that easily. Inside, she was reeling, wondering who in the mansion had died. What she needed though, was to muster her manipulative skills to find out what was going on here. "Could I please speak with Alonzo Goodman? I'm a friend of his. I really need to leave something for Emily. She's expecting it. It's very important."

Frankie had to give Hale kudos for being so well-trained. She obviously didn't intend to budge, even though Frankie had pulled her only ace, her connection to the sheriff.

"Ma'am, if you'd like to leave your item with me, I'll see it goes to the mansion."

Frankie was racking her brain for a new approach when she spied Garrett's gray F150 pulling up alongside her and Officer Hale. Garrett rolled down the passenger window, presenting Frankie with a grim face.

"What are you doing here, Frankie?" Garrett asked.

"That's funny; I was just about to ask you the same question," she replied.

"Hop in," Garrett said, then to Hale added, "It's okay. She has business here."

Frankie sprinted to her SUV, turned it off, grabbed her laptop, and climbed into Garrett's truck, making sure to thank Officer Hale for her handling of the situation. Hale just nodded curiously at Frankie, probably wondering if she was going to get in trouble with the sheriff later for letting an unauthorized individual through.

"Well, what's the story? It can't be good, or you wouldn't be here," Frankie said.

"Now wait a minute. You first, Frankie. Why are you here, and how much trouble are you getting me into right now by taking you across a police barrier? Garrett looked serious, although there was one dimple clearly visible, despite his best efforts to conceal it.

"I have an appointment with Emily Spurgeon. I told you I've been helping her with a speech and presentation for the Roots Festival dedication." She paused to hold up her laptop. "We're supposed to review the presentation this morning."

Garrett heaved one long sigh. "I'm sorry, Frankie. That's not going to happen. Emily Spurgeon was found dead this morning in her bed." By now, Garrett had the truck parked behind the mansion. "Tell you what. Just wait here while I go see how things are going." Then, seeing the expectant look on Frankie's face, he added, "I'll see if I can get you inside. But, look, there's nothing you can do here, I think."

Frankie immediately protested. "That's not true. Maybe I can help - with something . . ." Her voice trailed off. What did Frankie think she could help with? She didn't even know why Emily was dead or what would happen next, although she suspected something wasn't quite right. Why were two squad cars posted out front? Why was Alonzo here at all, if not to investigate? Another department vehicle was parked in the driveway, too, meaning a second officer must be inside, probably questioning Alana and Mack. Mack. *Poor Mack. He must be beside himself*, Frankie imagined. A well of sorrow rose within Frankie, and her eyes teared up.

"Hey, Frankie. It's going to be okay." Garrett put his arm around her, drawing her head to his shoulder for a moment. "I guess you and Emily must have hit it off, huh? It's a pretty big shock. Just give me a few minutes." Then Garrett was gone.

Frankie wasn't sure how long she could just sit there; inertia wasn't in her nature. She found her mind wandering a maze of possible scenarios that kept returning to Grant Foster and Emily's cousin Cordelia. Mack said he didn't like that situation, and for some reason, Frankie felt an involuntary feeling to trust Mack's instincts. This conclusion awakened The Golden Firefly, who, up until now, had slept in that morning.

"Don't be ridiculous, Francine," Goldie began. "You don't even know what happened to Emily. Besides, her cousin hasn't even arrived yet. She couldn't have anything to do with this." Frankie waited for Pirate's response, but heard nothing. Frankie had sunk back into the seat and shut her eyes to clear her agitated mind when there was a sharp rap on her side of the truck. Her startled face met the slightly annoyed one belonging to Alonzo. Frankie rolled down the window.

"Hi, Lon. Sorry. I seem to be at the wrong place, wrong time," Frankie said sadly.

Seeing Frankie's face, Alonzo decided to go easy. "Yeah, I'm sorry, too. But, what is it you think you can do? Garrett said you'd like to help. What kind of help, Frankie?"

Frankie said she might have useful information. At the very least, someone should take her statement, since she was supposed to meet with Emily this morning. After all, she told Alonzo, she assumed officers were taking routine statements from Alana and Mack.

"How did you know that?" Alonzo wanted to know, but didn't wait for her answer. "Look, you obviously know the staff and, knowing you, you probably know quite a lot about Emily Spurgeon, so you might as well come in. We'll find a room to put you in. I don't want anyone to see you."

Frankie's curiosity level rose significantly. Why didn't Alonzo want her to be seen? Was Emily's death suspicious? Her mind racing like a madwoman, Frankie's imagination bolted toward a finish line with a murder declaration written across the yellow tape. Shivering from

her dark thoughts, Frankie found herself in the sunroom
- the same sunroom where she and Emily Spurgeon last
met, companionably discussing photographs, planning a
presentation - waiting for an officer to take her statement.
Frankie recalled how happy Emily seemed as she revealed
an upcoming reunion with her cousin. *Life is so unfair
sometimes*, Frankie thought.

It hadn't taken long for Frankie to give her statement,
responding to questions posed by Alonzo himself, while
Donovan Pflug took notes. Frankie suspected Alonzo
was only there for moral support, knowing the history
of discomfort between her and Pflug. For his part, Pflug
appeared to think taking a statement from Frankie was a
huge waste of his time, but with his boss overseeing the
process, he acquiesced.

Frankie made mental notes of all the questions and
answers; she knew she would be analyzing them to death
later on. What could she tell them about Alana? What
had she observed about Alana's relationship with Emily?
What about Mack? Had Emily told Frankie anything
that seemed unusual or worrisome?

Frankie answered as honestly as possible, noting both
Alana and Mack seemed dedicated to serving Emily. She
made a point to suggest there was something off about
Grant Foster, although she couldn't put her finger on
what that was. Pflug scoffed at the insinuation, before
asking her if there was anything else she'd like to add.

"Yes. I should probably tell you that I asked Emily

about Grant Foster because Mack said he didn't trust him. Emily told me herself that she asked Grant Foster to come here to, in her exact words, 'negotiate a reunion with her cousin.'" Pflug sat up straighter, writing down her exact words, giving Alonzo a meaningful look at the same time.

"Thanks, Frankie. I think you've been helpful to us," Alonzo said, telling Pflug he could resume investigating. "I think you should look around the grounds next." Pflug nodded and left.

"Okay, Frankie. Here's the gist of what we know, and I don't want to read about it in the newspaper, at least not yet." Frankie leaned forward attentively, grateful that Lon would share any scraps he could. "Alana West found Emily unresponsive this morning around 8:00 a.m. in her bed. She tried to resuscitate her and called 911 immediately, but it was a no go. First look, probably a heart attack, but we know she was ill, so we need to look into it deeper. Garrett will be doing an autopsy. She's an heiress and a famous one at that, so we need to cover our bases, but I don't think there's anything weird going on here."

That Emily was ill came as a surprise to Frankie, although it seemed like there was medication she was taking during tea? Frankie was trying to recreate the memory, but it was out of reach. Frankie dared to ask Alonzo, "Could I look at her bedroom? You know, I'm pretty observant. Maybe I'll see something, you know, something that doesn't quite fit." Alonzo's jaw begin to twitch.

"You mean you think you'll see something our trained detectives won't see? Just because you solved one case doesn't make you an expert, Frankie." Frankie didn't say anything else, just kept giving Alonzo an imploring stare. "Okay. You can look, but you have to stay out of their way. And you better finish while Pflug is outside looking around. I don't want him to know you're anywhere near that bedroom." Frankie saluted her response, dashing out of the room and up the stairs.

She had never been upstairs before and didn't know what Emily's bedroom was like. Her imagination did not disappoint, as she walked through the door with Alonzo into a spacious room that was a suite. Giant floor to ceiling windows on one side faced the rose garden; another lovely bowed window faced the lake and gatehouse, home to Mack Perry.

The entire room was decked out in purples and greens with wallpaper adorned with violets and silver foil. A plum-colored velvet fainting couch sat in front of the bowed window, a spinet piano beside it. Fine art of all sorts adorned the walls, mounted in ornate antique frames. The four-poster antique mahogany bed spanned one wall, its covers pulled back as if inviting its owner to return to bed, a thought that sobered Frankie back to reality.

At least Emily's body had been removed and, she

assumed, was already loaded into the ambulance headed for Garrett's office.

She surveyed the rest of the furnishings: an oak Grandmother Clock sat in one corner; a burled secretary sporting a swan neck pediment posed majestically in another; a matching burled bookcase holding Emily's personal favorites was next to her bed on one side; a small matching night table on the other. A large door on one end led to an adjoining sitting room filled with more books, a large rolled-top desk, and a pool table. A door on the end nearest the bed led to a private bathroom, replicating the purple and green scheme of Emily's bedroom.

Now that Frankie saw the entire scene, she began to focus with more scrutiny on the small details. She greeted Shirley Lazaar, part-time detective, who retired from a 30-year stint with the Chicago police force, a woman Frankie admired for her no-nonsense approach to her job, a woman not to be trifled with.

Shirley raised a curious eyebrow at Frankie's greeting as she continued to keep a watchful eye on the officer processing the room, whose name fit his rookie status: Officer Green. Alonzo pulled Shirley aside to explain Frankie's presence, causing Shirley to offer an appreciative chuckle in Frankie's honor.

"Green, this is Francine Champagne. She's got an eye for details. Let's see if you were able to find all the necessary information here." Shirley wasn't exactly condescending toward the rookie, but wanted him to know there was a lot to learn in the detective field. Frankie was both amused and pleased Shirley thought she might find something Green had missed. Shirley handed Frankie a pair of gloves, telling her to be careful about what she touched.

Frankie looked at the nightstand, immediately noticing the small jar of honey, a little dribble of the sticky stuff next to it. She frowned. Honey but no other sign of tea - no spoon, no tea cup, no saucer. This didn't quite add up. She made a mental note and continued.

Walking around the room, she was trying to think like Emily. If Emily had felt ill, maybe she went into her bathroom to find something in the medicine cabinet, antacid perhaps, since heart attack symptoms often included heartburn.

In the bathroom, Frankie spied one of Emily's slippers lying between the toilet and vanity, and instantly wondered where the other slipper could be. So, Emily must have been in here after she felt ill and before she died, Frankie surmised, knowing Emily's meticulous tendencies about order. She wouldn't have just left a stray slipper somewhere on purpose.

She pulled back the shower curtain, finding an aromatherapy diffuser sitting in the tub, looking as if it had been recently washed out. There were still drops of water on the outside and in the tub. Another strange thing, Frankie noted.

She could smell what she recognized as balsam,

eucalyptus and tea tree scents when she walked into the bedroom. Frankie was an aficionado of essential oils, diffusing them in the shop during off-hours to create her Danish hygge environment, a combination of sensory delights for her customers. She remembered the library smelled like balsam, as if a Christmas tree had just been cut and brought into the house, and she remembered Emily telling her that all pine scents were her favorites because they reminded Emily of her father.

Frankie's musings were interrupted by a gagging sound nearby. She gingerly began opening doors, finding Pearl the Siamese holed up in the linen closet, hacking up something unpleasant. Not sure what kind of terms she was on with Pearl, Frankie cooed softly to her, reaching out one tentative hand toward Pearl's head. Pearl grunted, gurgled and swallowed, then tucked her head down for Frankie to pat it. Avoiding the kitty spew, Frankie picked up Pearl like a bundle, holding her paws beneath her body, keeping her face forward. Pearl snuggled into the crook of Frankie's arm.

"Look who I found in the bathroom closet," Frankie announced to the surprised faces of the three officers in the bedroom. Pearl wasn't happy to see the strangers and began to curl deeper into Frankie's arms. "I need to find a crate for her or she's going to go hide somewhere else. If I had to guess, there's probably one in the utility room by the back entrance."

Alonzo said he would go look, while Frankie figured

out what to do with the distraught Pearl. Typical cat, Frankie thought: they pretend not to care about their humans but clearly sense when all is not right in their world, turning them into emotional pukers. Thankfully, Alonzo returned quickly with a crate; then Frankie expertly stuffed Pearl into it, deciding a trip to Sadie the vet was in order, just to be sure the cat was okay. Yes, Frankie told the officers, she would do the honors.

First, though, Frankie wanted to finish what she had started. She looked around the bathroom once more, then returned to the bedroom where she tried to locate the missing slipper, finding it behind the drapes near the secretary. She pointed to the slipper, which Officer Green quickly bagged. "The other slipper is in the bathroom between the vanity and toilet. Maybe Emily lost it when she was looking for something to help her feel better," Frankie suggested.

Shirley nodded. "Could be, but there's no way to know that. Maybe that cat dragged the slipper into the bathroom."

Frankie jumped back in. "Cats are not like dogs. They don't drag slippers around. Besides, why is the other slipper over here, by the secretary? Which, by the way, is where the landline is." Frankie pointed to a white provincial French telephone. "Maybe Emily was trying to call for help."

Now Officer Green jumped in. "On that thing? You mean that thing works - like a real phone?" Green looked incredulous. Frankie and Shirley both laughed. Officer Green was part of the cell phone generation, probably never used a landline, except at the office, but nothing that looked like the fancy French phone.

"Hmm, you might be onto something, Francine. Guess we'll be getting Emily Spurgeon's phone records to see if she made any calls last night; that's standard procedure anyway," Shirley said. "Anything else on your mind?"

Frankie mentioned the honey jar and sticky spot on the nightstand. "You see, Miss Spurgeon was OCD when it came to order. If the honey jar is here, where it clearly doesn't belong, she must have had tea or toast or something. But, there are no utensils, no cup, no plate, no napkin. Why would she bother removing those items and not the honey jar?"

At the skeptical expressions on the officers' faces, Frankie recounted how Emily rearranged the tea tray Alana brought in - facing both cup handles in the same direction, lining up the teaspoons, and making a circle pattern out of the pastries. At their first meeting, Frankie remembered Emily constantly adjusting her necklace chain so the pendant was perfectly centered.

"Alright, we'll note that, but I'm not sure it's going to be useful," Shirley relinquished. "Anything else?"

"The diffuser. Emily loved essential oils, and I'm guessing she misted them at bedtime." Officer Green looked confused as a lumberjack at a Mary Kay party.

Frankie gestured one finger at the officers to follow her into the bathroom. Pointing at the bathtub where the diffuser was drying, she said, "That's a diffuser. You add water to it and scented oils. Different oils create different reactions in the human body and psyche. Emily's favorite oils were balsam and other pine scents."

Shirley nodded, a bit impatiently, while Green continued to look bewildered. Frankie cut to the chase. "It doesn't matter if you know how it works. What matters is that the diffuser has been emptied and rinsed out recently. Why?"

"Maybe Emily rinsed it out before she got sick. Maybe that's why she was in the bathroom." Shirley was being practical, pragmatic.

"Maybe," Frankie said, "but then why didn't she put the honey jar away? And why did she leave a sticky puddle on the nightstand? And why was the shower curtain pulled shut, hiding the diffuser?"

Shirley shrugged. "Noted, but I doubt it means anything. You said Emily was OCD, so maybe an open shower curtain would drive her crazy. And maybe she felt too ill to finish cleaning up the honey spill."

Frankie felt a bit defeated and decided now was a good time to take Pearl to the vet clinic. She cheered up a little when Shirley told her to keep them posted about anything else she might remember later.

As Frankie drove to the vet clinic, Pearl announced her displeasure with throaty growls coming from the back seat. She either still felt ill or just didn't want to be confined in her kitty crate. Frankie tried to console Pearl with soft reassurances, but the growls continued. Luckily, the vet clinic was only a few minutes away.

Sadie Chastain, veterinarian extraordinaire, was posed at the reception desk tapping on the computer keyboard. She offered Frankie a warm smile, peering curiously at the kitty crate.

"Is something wrong with Liberace?" Sadie asked. Frankie marveled at the vet's memory of her patients' names.

Frankie shook her head, looking woeful. "I'm afraid I have sad news, Sadie. This is Emily Spurgeon's cat, Pearl. Emily was found dead this morning in her bedroom. I found Pearl hiding in the bathroom, vomiting."

As an afterthought, Frankie added, "Wow, I'm probably not supposed to tell you that - about Emily, I mean." Frankie was obviously more rattled than she realized.

Sadie's expression went from shocked to inquisitive as she wondered how Frankie discovered the cat at the Spurgeon mansion. Frankie read her face, and quickly added, "I've been working with Emily on a presentation for the Roots Festival. We were supposed to meet this morning. I just can't believe she's gone."

Sadie shook off her shock to deal with the cat at hand. "Let's take Pearl back to the exam room and see what's going on. She's probably just upset from the change of routine and maybe . . ." Sadie's sentence trailed off as she opened the crate and lifted out the unhappy cat. "Wait, this is not Pearl!" she exclaimed.

Frankie's mouth formed a perfect "o." "What do you mean? Emily introduced Pearl to me at our first meeting and again at the second meeting. This is the same cat."

"All I can tell you is that I've been treating Pearl for several years. The Pearl I know is a Blue Point Siamese. This cat is a Chocolate Point Siamese. Excuse me a moment; I'm going to grab Pearl's chart." Sadie returned and showed Frankie the photo of the original Pearl from the chart. Frankie immediately noticed the differences in their faces, including the colored markings.

"I last treated Pearl One eight months ago. Emily brought her in for her yearly exam. She was healthy then, eight years old. I have never seen this Pearl before."

Frankie didn't know what to make of the information. She felt certain Emily would have told her about the first Pearl, considering how affectionate she was with her feline, especially if she lost the first Pearl recently. But, then again, Emily seemed emotionally fragile about certain subjects, including her family and her cousin's dog that was killed by a car. Sadie broke into Frankie's thoughts.

"I'll draw some blood and examine this Pearl, take her photo and make a new chart. I'll call you when she's ready to be picked up, if that's okay. The blood test results should be in this afternoon. I'll see if I can get some sputum from her, too." Sadie was in full professional mode now.

Frankie wasn't sure if she should return to the mansion or Bubble and Bake. Her mind was swirling with too many ideas. She wondered how Mack and Alana were handling Emily's death. She wondered if Emily's cousin would come to Deep Lakes. She wondered if Grant Foster was still in town and if he played a part in Emily's death. She wondered about Pearl. She wondered what time it was as her stomach grumbled for lack of food. Yes, it was noon on the dot. What a morning it had been. Frankie swung the SUV into the back alley behind Bubble and Bake, parked, and went through the back door of the shop.

The kitchen was empty except for a snoozing Liberace, who barely looked up at Frankie as she padded to the cooler to find some lunch. Since today was a dough making day for tomorrow's customers, Frankie found batches of dough in the cooler that would be proofed early tomorrow morning or maybe even tonight if someone planned to return to the shop.

Frankie found a tub of mixed greens for a salad, some baby carrots and mini peppers, and her favorite dressing: lemon citrus vinaigrette. She tossed everything in a bowl and added a lemon pepper tuna pouch, giving up a small portion of tuna to Liberace's dish. The little tuxedo cat slept soundly as Frankie chomped her salad, pondering her next move. Frankie decided she needed her tablet to take notes about the morning. Hopefully, writing down the details would ease her muddled mind.

The notes came out in a long stream, which made Frankie feel a little better until she checked the time. Only 45 minutes had passed since she came to the shop. Who knows how long it would be before Sadie called her to pick up Pearl. She needed to do something.

Frankie found relief for a troubled mind in baking or wandering her vineyard, so when in Rome, she thought. She began pulling ingredients from the cupboards to make shortbread dough, using the microwave judiciously to soften the butter just a little without destroying its integrity. Working with cold or cool butter produced the best results. For this batch of cookies, Frankie added lemon and orange zest, a little orange juice and chopped Macadamia nuts. After cutting the dough into diamond shapes, she would later ice them with a pineapple glaze, and if they tasted good enough to sell, she would christen them "Tropical Gems."

When Frankie's mind was thrown off-balance, she often created the tastiest concoctions. Today was no exception. Questions about Emily trailed into the cookie batter, trickled into the rolled out dough, and sliced into the individual cut-outs, where they would bake into something more solid. At least, that's what Frankie imagined.

Her cell phone sang out as she removed the last pan from the oven, breathing in the warm tropical aroma. It was Dr. Sadie.

"Hi Frankie. You can pick up Pearl, but before you do,

you might want to call someone to collect Pearl's spew. I'd like to send it in to the State Lab to be analyzed. She may have ingested some poison. It's not conclusive since I only retrieved a small sample, but she ingested something that her feline system didn't like. I gave her a general antidote just in case and a tranquilizer to calm her down. By the way, this cat is only about a year old."

Frankie was momentarily immobile ruminating on the word "poison." Is it possible Emily was poisoned? If so, how and by whom? She sprung into action now, feeling the need to get into the mansion and do some snooping. She began formulating a plan to talk to Alana and Mack without creating suspicion about her questions.

But first, she rang Shirley Lazaar's cell number. "Shirley, this is Frankie Champagne. Are you still at the mansion?" Shirley affirmed she was. "Good, because the vet would like a sample of Pearl's vomit." Shirley couldn't remember who Pearl was. "The cat. I'll be there shortly." Frankie hung up before Shirley could tell her that the vomit had already been cleaned up.

Chapter 8

*In vino Veritas. In Aqua satietas. In . . . What is
the Latin for Tea? What! Is there no Latin word
for Tea? Upon my soul, if I had known that
I would have let the vulgar stuff alone.*
- Hilaire Belloc, "On Tea," 1908

Tea is drunk to forget the din of the world.
- T'ien Yiheng

The rookie officer was no longer blocking the
driveway at the Granite Mansion when Frankie returned,
but yellow police tape was strung around the property's
perimeter. Frankie parked on the street, slid the kitty crate
under the tape, then ducked under it herself to proceed
up the paved drive. Alonzo's jeep was gone, and only
one squad car remained, parked near the back entrance.
Frankie rapped on the door and didn't wait for a response
before entering. After all, she had Pearl, a legitimate
reason for being on the premises.

Frankie heard footsteps coming into the kitchen and
was prepared to see Mack Perry, whose muddy garden
boots were planted by the back door. Instead, Alana

appeared, still in uniform, her face a puffy tear-stained mess. She glowered at Frankie and the kitty crate, both hands on her hips.

"Who told you to take Pearl, anyway? That's my job." Alana looked loaded for bear. "And what are you doing here in the first place? Who invited you? You can't just barge in here without permission."

Frankie took a step backwards. She hadn't been prepared for such an onslaught, but then she reminded herself that Alana was likely in shock. She looked sympathetically at the young woman, who was still clearly infuriated, and set down the kitty crate, opening it up to reveal the sedated Siamese.

"I'm so sorry for your loss. It must have been terrible to find Emily this morning. And I imagine you've been run through the mill answering questions." Frankie offered to make some tea for Alana, who was staring gingerly into the kitty crate, as if Pearl might dive out at any moment. "Pearl's been sedated. Dr. Sadie said it should help her recover faster."

Alana's reply was sharp. "Recover? From what exactly?"

Frankie hesitated, choosing her words carefully. After all, Alana could be a suspect, couldn't she? The Golden Firefly pricked her ears at Frankie's thoughts. "Suspect? Don't jump to conclusions, Francine." Frankie still proceeded with caution.

"Well, Pearl threw up. I found her. She was trying to hide. Clearly, all the clamor of the police upset her routine. That's a cat for you." Frankie was trying to sound jovial despite the circumstances. "Why don't you leave Pearl here in the crate where she can sleep it off, or does she have a favorite spot where you can put her?"

Alana appeared calmer with a mundane task in front of her. "Yes. That cat loves the sunroom. I'll just take the carrier in there and put it by the windows."

Again, Frankie offered to make tea and bring it to the sunroom, adding, "Are you hungry, Alana? When's the last time you ate something? I can make you something, a sandwich maybe?" Alana nodded dimly, resigning herself to Frankie's presence for the moment.

Frankie saw a chance to snoop around the kitchen, although she didn't know what she was looking for. She opened a couple of cupboards before finding an assortment of loose teas in labeled canisters. She selected a soothing chamomile bergamot blend and searched for spoons and a tea ball. Another cupboard contained a variety of dishes, including tea cups and saucers. Frankie pulled out two sets and began looking around for sandwich fixings while water was heating on the stove in the teakettle.

The bread in the old-fashioned bread box looked good, so she pulled out two slices, slathering them with chunky almond butter and raspberry jam she found in the fridge. She was surprised to find the fridge mostly empty, except for some lettuce, carrots, condiments, butter, eggs and a bunch of green grapes. She assumed she would find leftovers of Emily's Sunday night dinner, but there were none. Frankie tried not to place too much stock in this. Maybe Monday was Alana's grocery shopping day.

As the tea steeped, Frankie started opening more cupboards and drawers. Under the sink, Frankie found the same sanitizer wash she used at the bakery and the winery for sterilizing equipment and sanitizing pans, dishes, and wine bottles. She was surprised to find a commercial sanitizer in a residential house, especially since Emily did not entertain guests. Still, Frankie supposed the use of sanitizer matched up with Emily's obsessive tendencies. Frankie stepped into the pantry and was startled to hear Shirley Lazaar's voice in the kitchen.

"Finding anything important?" she asked, louder than necessary. "I'm looking for Ms. West."

"You'll find her in the sunroom. I offered to bring her something to eat. She looks awful," Frankie said. "Did you get a sample of the cat's mess?"

Shirley shook her head. "Sorry, no. Ms. West cleaned it up before you called. She asked if it was okay. I didn't think anything of it. She even used a heavy duty sanitizer." Shirley gave Frankie a curious look. "So, what did the vet say, anyway?"

Frankie told Shirley it was possible the cat had gotten into some poison, but that Sadie didn't seem overly concerned. "Sadie says cats get into things they shouldn't eat all the time. Anyway, she administered some general antidote, just in case, and gave her a tranquilizer to sleep off her shock."

Shirley nodded, thoughtfully. "Well, maybe Ms. West knows something about the cat we don't know." Frankie wondered the same thing: *Did Alana know anything about the disappearance of Pearl One and the arrival of Pearl Two?* Frankie didn't share the tale of two Pearls with Shirley, deciding it was irrelevant.

Shirley continued, "I have to tie up some loose ends with her before I head out. By the way, you were right about the honey jar on the nightstand. Emily has tea every night in her room. Ms. West cleaned it up after she called 911. And, before you ask, Francine, there will be an autopsy. Just in case," she added meaningfully.

"How long before I can get the results of the autopsy?" Frankie asked automatically, thinking she must have a typical journalist's nature.

Shirley anticipated Frankie's response and grinned broadly. "Call in a couple days, and we'll have more information for you."

Frankie was adding pieces to her mind puzzle. *So, Alana had cleaned up the teacup and saucer and the cat puke. What else had Alana cleaned up? What about the oil diffuser? Didn't Alana know a person shouldn't disturb a crime scene? Or maybe she cleaned up to hide something?*

The Golden One hissed in Frankie's ear, urging her back to her right mind. "Crime scene? You have no reason to think this is a crime scene. Stop jumping to conclusions, Francine," Goldie scolded, as The Pirate chimed in.

"You have to keep your wits about you, Caramio.

Stick to the facts, one step at a time," The Pirate pitched his calming influence upon Frankie.

Frankie shook herself back to the present, remembering Alana was waiting in the sunroom. She quickly finished a tray, adding the sandwich and some grapes for Emily's assistant. The sunroom was brightly lit and warm with the flooding afternoon sunlight. Pearl was still asleep, and Alana was staring at Shirley Lazaar, who was just leaving as Frankie came through the French doors.

"Here you go. I couldn't find much, so I hope you like almond butter and jam." Alana nodded numbly, picked up one-half of the sandwich and took a small bite while Frankie poured out the tea.

"I couldn't find any honey, so I hope sugar is okay," Frankie baited Alana, pretending not to know the honey jar was upstairs in Emily's bedroom.

"Oh, I might have left the honey upstairs in Ms. Spurgeon's room," Alana said absently, choking out the last words.

Frankie instantly felt sympathy for Alana and reproached herself for suspecting her. "I imagine Emily was like family to you. Do you have any family around that you can talk to while you're going through this?" Frankie was trying to be helpful, knowing she would go to Carmen or her brother, Will, any time she was hurting. From the bitter look on Alana's face, she doubted the woman had close ties to her family.

"I don't have any family around here, and even if I did, they wouldn't be any help to me," Alana stared at Frankie with a hurtful expression.

"I'm sorry to hear that. I guess I'm fortunate to have family around me that I can count on." Frankie wasn't sure why she decided to share this information when it clearly wouldn't help Alana feel any better. From somewhere inside herself, Frankie felt compelled to say it.

Alana tossed Frankie a scathing look over her teacup. "Well, aren't you the lucky one! My father died when I was little, leaving my mother to work two crappy jobs just to try to make ends meet for me and my sister." Alana was choking back tears with the memory, her words coming out in a biting tone.

"That must have been so difficult for all of you. Where are your mother and sister now?" Frankie asked, automatically.

"My mother eventually met a man who could take care of her - of all of us. He was a plumbing contractor and made good money. But, my step-father didn't want the family package. Eventually, he cut my sister and me out of the picture and moved away with my mother. We haven't been in touch since." Alana stood up on the last words, ending the conversation. "If you don't mind, I need to get some things ready for Ms. Spurgeon's cousin, who will be arriving any day."

Frankie looked surprised to hear this, assuming the cousin, who had been absent from Emily's life for years, would not bother coming for the funeral. Unless - maybe the cousin was checking on a possible inheritance? Another wave of emotional questions shot through Frankie's mind: What would happen to Mack Perry? He was skilled but aging; there were only so many jobs around for which he would qualify. Did Alana have a degree in anything? Would it be difficult for her to find employment? Would Granite Mansion be sold, or would Emily's cousin move in?

Frankie wondered if she should stay until Shirley Lazaar left or until Pearl was awake but thought that neither idea made sense. Alana was here and could tend Pearl, and Frankie had no good excuse to be here. Going back through the kitchen to the back door, she glanced around the room and left.

The afternoon sun was replaced by gray clouds, suggesting April showers were on the way. Frankie scanned the grounds, looking for what - she didn't know, then caught sight of Mack Perry near the lakefront walkway. Getting closer, she saw Mack peering sadly at the weeping Norway pine, softly touching its new tender shoots.

"Hello, Mack," Frankie spoke quietly. "I'm so sorry about Miss Emily. If there's anything I can do to help, please let me know."

Mack nodded, just once, lips trembling. "Thank you, Francine. She was my whole world, you know. Emily. This house. These grounds. The lake. Even the quarry. This is all I have to my name." Frankie felt obliged to place one hand on Mack's shoulder.

"I'll come over another time and we can talk, Mack. I want to ask you a few questions, but I think you've answered enough questions for today."

"I'd answer a thousand more if it would bring her back," Mack choked. Frankie patted his shoulder one more time before saying goodbye.

*   *   *

Although late in the day, Frankie had baking on her mind, or rather, baking therapy. She slumped into the back door of her kitchen, finding both Tía Pepita and Carmen busy with dough. She could smell the fryer at work, likely cooking empanadas, and she made a mental note to turn on the diffusers full throttle after everyone left, perhaps using peppermint and rosemary oils combined to cleanse the air. Carmen was icing a batch of yeast donuts, taking turns with piping bags of maple, chocolate, and almond for tomorrow's offerings. She looked up at Frankie, startled to see her friend looking tired and drawn.

"What's wrong, Frankie? Didn't it go well at the Spurgeon house?"

Frankie looked dumbly at Carmen. "You mean, you haven't heard? I thought it would be all over town by now. Emily Spurgeon died sometime before 8:00 this morning."

Carmen dropped the piping bag to hug her stressed friend. "No, I haven't heard. I'm surprised none of our customers said anything. What happened to her?"

Frankie told Carmen and Tía what she knew for certain, which wasn't much, now that she narrated it. She ended with the strange story of Pearl the cat.

Carmen, who was piping again, asked. "Well, what do the police think? You were there a long time, so you must have some idea. Besides, I know the wheels are spinning up there; you must have a theory of some sort." Carmen pointed to her own head, but her meaning was clear.

Frankie spoke as if divulging a secret. "I don't think she died of natural causes, but we'll see. The police said she was ill, which I didn't know, but what kind of illness?" Frankie's thoughts were disconnected for now. "Anyway, someone has something to gain from her death. I need to find out about her will."

Carmen stopped piping to look squarely at her friend. "Oh boy, here we go again. How are you going to find that out?"

Tía Pepita jumped into the conversation. "Oh, there are dozens of ways to find someone's will. You live in a small town. I guarantee there are lots of people who know what's in that will."

Frankie had to smile at Tía Pepita, if for no other reason than in response to Carmen's glare at her aunt. "You're right, Tía. I just need to find the law firm that drew up the will, the witnesses who signed it and . . ."

she trailed off as a light bulb shined boldly in her brain. "Emily Spurgeon was reclusive, but she belonged to the Garden Club, and I just bet someone in that club signed her will. I'll start with our mayor."

Frankie relished the idea of discovering information, and she felt better for the first time that day. Maybe she could be helpful to the police.

"Or maybe there's nothing to help with; did you consider that?" The Golden One chided Frankie and was simultaneously joined by Carmen.

"Take it easy, Frankie. Wait until the autopsy comes back before you start digging into this. Can you promise me that much?" Carmen asked.

Frankie backed down. "You're right. I need to wait, and besides: I don't want there to be foul play. Emily's death is just so sudden and, to me, she didn't seem sick. She didn't show any signs I can think of that she was suffering. She was excited about reuniting with her cousin and about rededicating the park."

Frankie thrived on action, so she planned to call Adele Lundgren after dinner. Meanwhile, she dove into bakery work, pulling out the icing for the Tropical Gems shortbread cookies she'd baked earlier. Making diagonal stripes with the pineapple icing, she offered one to both Carmen and Tía, who exclaimed affirmatively. She iced the other batch of cookies, Crantastics, an excellent shortbread made with craisins and white chocolate, with white chocolate icing in concentric circles around the disks.

Frankie always marveled at the workings of her kitchen, loving the hands that prepared the dough, loving the cozy warmth emanating from the ovens, loving the confluence of smells that somehow created harmony. Maybe it was Frankie's sense of Danish hygge, which Frankie tried to practice most days. Maybe it was the company Frankie chose to keep - surrounding herself with positive, bona fide, kind-hearted people - people who kept Frankie's inner compass pointing to True North.

Chapter 9

Death pays all debts.
- William Shakespeare

Sometimes legends make reality,
and become more useful than the facts.
- Salman Rushdie

After a hastily thrown-together supper, Frankie sat at her kitchen breakfast bar, staring out the back window facing Sterling Creek, watching the mid-April showers. She opened her tablet of notes from the folder she named "Quarry Heiress Mystery," then punched in Mayor Adele's home number on her cell.

"Lundgren residence," Adele's brisk voice answered on the first ring. Frankie had scripted her end of the conversation and proceeded as planned.

"Hi, Adele. Frankie Champagne. Sorry to call you at home, but it's been quite the day with poor Emily's death," she began. "I spent a few hours there today." The information piqued Adele's curiosity.

"Oh my, Frankie. Were you there to meet Emily about the Roots Festival?"

"Exactly that," Frankie continued. "But, the police were there when I arrived, and she was already gone. I tried to help by providing information since I spent a lot of time with her recently."

Adele's voice wavered a bit. "I just cannot believe she's dead. Do you know how it happened? What kind of information did you give the police?" Adele quickly reverted back to her normal modus operandus, stringing out more than one topic of conversation, like a fisherman with several baited poles in the water.

Frankie told Adele what she knew, which was next to nothing, other than there would be an autopsy and maybe an investigation if the autopsy revealed anything unusual. She left out her expedition of Emily's bedroom suite and the possible poisoned kitty. She also refrained from giving out any details about Alana West and Mack Perry. Tonight, Frankie was fishing in other waters.

"Adele, do you know anything about Emily's will?" She wanted to leave the question as open-ended as possible.

Adele paused to think. Perhaps the question threw her off-kilter a bit. "You mean, who's getting her estate, don't you? Frankie, do you think someone meant her harm?"

"Not that I know of, but I'm guessing she has a substantial fortune. Her home is a virtual museum. She doesn't have a husband or children, so I'm wondering who will inherit." It was a question.

"We-ell," Adele began slowly, which Frankie found odd behavior for the mayor. "I know she planned to leave her home and some of the antiquities to the historical society. As a member of the Society Board, I can even say Granite Mansion will be the new location of the Deep Lakes Historical Society."

Frankie wasn't surprised to hear that Adele had inside information, but she was surprised about the substantial bequest to the historical society. Frankie knew Emily was fond of the community, yet it was difficult to fathom such wealth. "Did you see the will, Adele? Were you a witness?"

"Oh, no, I couldn't be a witness with the city receiving an endowment and the Society receiving property. That would be a conflict where someone could contest the will. But, I have a copy of the will at my office, come to think of it." Frankie could see Adele trailing the conversation in another direction, so she quickly cut her off.

"You said the city is receiving an endowment?" Frankie asked.

"Of course, for upkeep of Spurgeon Park, but I wonder what else was in the will. I filed it long ago, and it didn't seem terribly important at the time . . ." Adele trailed off. Frankie knew her call had precipitated plenty of speculation on Adele's part. She needed to switch topics.

"The real reason I called is to ask you what to do about Emily's speech and presentation at the festival. Do you have any thoughts as to who could speak on behalf of the family? Or, do you plan to take that over - you know, as mayor."

The distress came back into Adele's voice as she contemplated those words. "Well, I just don't know, Frankie. I'm going to have to think about that. If only Emily had family or even a close friend . . ." Frankie pounced like a waiting cat.

"Well, there is her cousin, I suppose." Frankie drew out her words, allowing them to sink in.

"Cousin?" Adele, not a life-long resident of town, was clearly clueless about a cousin.

"Yes, Cordelia McCoy. I understand Emily has been in contact with her recently and that she may be coming to Deep Lakes. Probably for the funeral now instead of a reunion, sadly." Frankie was hoping the astute Adele would pounce on the opportunity for a family member to make the festival presentation, which was certain to draw a curious crowd to the park.

"Frankie, why don't you look into that? Go meet her as soon as you have a chance. Show her the presentation, etc. Tell her that she is just the right person to rededicate the park. After all this time, wouldn't it be a shock for the town to see the other half of the Granite Quarry family?" Adele was gushing to the point where she must have momentarily forgotten about Emily's death. Frankie's sober comments dialed down Adele's enthusiasm.

"I'll try to connect with Cordelia McCoy, but it won't be the same as having Emily Spurgeon, a true pillar of the community. She was an interesting person to know, even if only briefly," Frankie finished.

"Yes, you're right, Frankie. I forgot myself for a moment. I was fond of Emily, and she died too soon, if you ask me. Well, keep me posted, please. There's much to do before the festival."

Frankie tapped a few notes about Emily's will on the tablet, chastising herself for not asking Adele if she knew that Emily was ill. Furthermore, she might have asked Adele if she could stop by her office tomorrow to look at the will, but Frankie knew she didn't have a legitimate reason to ask. Besides, despite Adele's flighty nature, she was professional in her mayoral duties, and Frankie respected that. Furthermore, Frankie had another source she could draw on to view Emily's will, and she planned to tap that source tomorrow morning, bakery box in tow.

*　*　*

Frankie paused to admire spring's progression as she drove down Meriwether Street, lined with budding crab apples and pagoda dogwoods, which would promenade their rose-red and creamy white blossoms in May. She loved the season, marking the return of many of her favorite birds that had migrated as far as South America while Deep Lakes lay frozen in ice and snow. Every day of the short spring season was a new discovery: bulb plants popped from the ground, grass turned from brown to green overnight, daylight extended into night's territory, the late dark of evening brought forth a chorus from tiny frogs known as Spring Peepers, and more.

Frankie came back from her reverie, turned right onto Kilbourn, passed the Sheriff's Department, and swung into the next parking lot adjacent to the Whitman County Courthouse building, one of Frankie's favorite buildings in the city. At least a century old, the three-story building was a neo-classical design of limestone and deep red granite. The jewel in the crown, though, was the ornate metal-clad dome at the building's center, boasting four clocks facing the four cardinal directions. The courthouse was a stark contrast to the recently built sheriff's department, a limestone and concrete structure with flat features. Maybe the proximity of the two buildings made people appreciate the courthouse's beauty more, Frankie surmised.

Opting to take the marble stairs rather than the elevator, Frankie climbed to the third floor where the Clerk of Court's office was located. She paused at the top of the final flight to catch her breath, mentally calculating when her last workout had taken place. She'd been so occupied with readying the vineyard and running Bubble and Bake, she hadn't spent much time at the fitness center. The Golden Firefly quickly offered to add a workout routine to Frankie's agenda.

Breathing normally, Frankie proceeded down the hallway, toting an offering of her new Tropical Gems cookies, Crantastics and chocolate glazed yeast donuts.

She stepped through the Clerk of Court's office to find Verna Krause at the reception desk, scowling at her computer. Verna was a fixture in the office, having been Deputy Clerk for forty-plus years. Now in her 70s, it didn't appear she planned to retire anytime soon, much to the chagrin of the Whitman County Board.

County jobs were a hot commodity in the area; they offered the highest wages and prized benefits. Verna was hired at a time when nepotism prevailed and nobody bothered to protest. Back then, Verna's uncle was the county judge, and he hired both Verna and her sister, Thelma, as his two Deputy Clerks. Thelma, just a year Verna's senior, was still working in the file room. Frankie bet neither of the two women had much for computer skills, but there they were, still employed in jobs they probably were no longer qualified to fill.

Verna raised her gray salon-curled head at Frankie, a residual scowl still present. Peering over gold-framed glasses, she greeted Frankie. "What can I do for you today?"

Frankie almost asked if she could assist her in any technological way, but decided that could open up a proverbial hornet's nest. Instead she asked to see Virginia Busby, the Clerk of Court. Verna gestured to an inner office with one gnarled, somewhat shaky finger. Frankie thanked her, telling her to be sure to have some bakery when she took a break. Verna stared blankly at Frankie, blinked a few times, and then the bakery box registered, and she nodded absently. Frankie wondered if she should check Verna for a pulse; this thought brought a poke in the ribs from Goldie. But Frankie just smiled.

Virginia's office was the last bastion before the sacred chambers of the two Whitman County judges, and Virginia was a formidable guard. Nobody would describe her as fat, yet she was as large as a Green Bay Packer linebacker and probably could hit just as hard. She dressed in form-fitting clothing that accentuated her broad frame, as if to remind people to take care when approaching her. Her large hairstyle was fresh from the 1980s, frizzed out and poofy on top, fused in place with Aqua-Net; the color was indescribable. It was probably supposed to be some kind of blonde, but it was a burnt yellow at best.

That this woman, the polar opposite of Frankie's mother, was a long-time friend of Peggy's, was difficult for Frankie to fathom. Both women had been county 4-H leaders when Frankie was in elementary school. Virginia was a young mother, while Peggy was more than a decade older, but she took the inexperienced and hesitant Virginia under her wing, molding her into a confident leader.

Virginia looked up from her paperwork and smiled broadly at Frankie with bright coral lips. "Hey, Frankie," she boomed. "What brings y'all up here?" For some Wisconsinites, "y'all" had migrated into the vernacular.

Frankie set the bakery on Virginia's desk, careful not to cover any papers. "I had other business but wanted to ask you a question," she said in a quiet voice, suggesting confidentiality.

"Liar!" The Golden One clapped loudly in Frankie's ear like a gunshot. "You don't have any other business," she said accusingly. Frankie actually flushed with guilt; Goldie was right, and Frankie despised lying. Virginia looked concerned and told her to sit down.

"You okay there, Frankie? Do ya need a glassa water or somethin'?" Frankie recovered and shook her head no. Virginia persisted. "Ain't you a little young for hot flashes?"

Well, Frankie thought, this is starting off just great. As if on cue, Judge Bryant's door opened, and he walked into Virginia's office, recognizing Frankie on the spot.

"Well, if it isn't little Frankie Champagne," he said. Dicky Bryant had been a partner at the Dickens Law Office in its origin, when Ward Dickens' father owned it. After he passed the practice on to Ward, Bryant worked part-time as a consulting attorney, until he was elected judge.

Frankie worked at the law firm as a paralegal until she opened Bubble and Bake. She didn't much like Dicky Bryant, whose ego could barely fit into the room if someone else was present. In Dicky's prime, many male bosses demeaned their female employees or, in some cases, did even worse things. He always referred to Frankie as "little," something she didn't appreciate. Still, he was a judge, and Frankie was inclined to be polite.

"How are you doing these days, Judge?" she asked, hoping their conversation would be a quick one.

"Can't complain. What brings you here? Not in any legal muck, I hope," he said, chuckling to himself, as if legal trouble was a laughing matter. He didn't wait for an answer, informing Virginia he was going to lunch and would be back at one to go over the Spurgeon files with her. Frankie brushed aside the judge's snub, having honed in on the topic at hand.

"Are you handling the Spurgeon estate? I was sorry to hear about Emily. I've been working with her on a presentation for the Roots Festival." To her surprise, Dicky sat down in the chair beside Frankie.

"The Quarry Curse strikes again!" Dicky said matter-of-factly.

"I'm sorry. What?" Frankie looked at Dicky, dumb-founded.

"Now don't tell me you haven't heard about the curse," Dicky said. "Everyone in Deep Lakes knows about it. Of course, you might be too young . . ."

Frankie didn't feel like enduring a demeaning speech by Dicky, so she pasted on her business face and took the direct approach. "Would you kindly enlighten me about this so-called curse."

The judge settled his ample frame more deeply into the chair, like a kindly granddad preparing for storytime. Clearly, he enjoyed enlightening the ignorant, Frankie thought. She looked over at Virginia to gauge her interest, not surprised to see the rapt attention she offered to her boss. Knowing Virginia, she probably hoped to glean some new nuggets of gossip she could share right from the horse's mouth. Frankie inwardly grimaced, wondering if Whitman County residents knew much about the woman they continuously re-elected to handle confidential information.

Dicky rubbed his palms together, revving up his storytelling engine. "Well, let me see if I can remember all the tragic events surrounding the quarry. Early on, the quarry used wooden derricks with guy wires to move the granite, but the derricks caught fire one night - maybe struck by lightning, maybe not. The quarry had to suspend operation until they could rebuild. When the timber came in on the train, the quarry supervisor got his leg caught between rail cars - doctor couldn't save the leg." The judge paused to let this sink in a minute, but Frankie didn't seem impressed, just expectant.

"Then there's the Ides of March disaster of 1925. Two workers got crushed by the stone crusher; nobody knows how they landed under the machine. The same day, a worker fell off a high rock face, broke his neck. Another man drowned by the quarry dam. That night, the quarry office burned to the ground, along with a storage shed."

"Well, working conditions weren't too safe in those days, and saving buildings from a fire was almost impossible then, too," Frankie responded, not ready to believe in a curse.

Dicky just grinned like a Cheshire cat. "Oh, there's plenty more. Five years later on March 15th - same date as in 1925 - the boarding house built for the quarry workers burned down, killed 42 people, almost everybody. The next day, two workers died: one got caught in the water wheel, and the other one died trying to save him. An explosion that afternoon took out another three workers and injured a few more. Every few years there were more accidents, always around the Ides of March. How do you explain that?"

Frankie admitted to herself the list of tragedies was formidable. But, she still didn't believe in curses. "Did the accidents stop happening when the quarry adopted safer standards, used steel cranes, and built brick buildings?"

There was the judge with that grin again. "Well, you'd think so wouldn't you? I'm sure McCoy and Spurgeon thought so, too. But, there were just other kinds of problems. A lot of men got quarry sickness; that's what they called it in the '60s and '70s. Silicosis is a fatal lung disease caused by breathing in granite dust. It mostly happened to the pavers, the workers who cut and shaped the giant slabs into headstones and monuments. I saw it first-hand, but that was before you worked at Dickens. Our firm represented those families ..."

Frankie gulped as she saw Dicky Bryant getting misty-eyed with a faraway look. He rose from the chair then, no longer in the mood to talk about curses or conjure quarry ghosts. Frankie couldn't speak, suddenly overwhelmed by sadness.

"Of course, the Spurgeon and McCoy families had

their own misfortunes, I suppose," Dicky said, then abruptly dismissed the topic. "I'm going to lunch now," he said. "See you in an hour, Virginia. Good day, Frankie."

Virginia broke the silent gloom that had descended. "I've never heard him tell it that way before. Well, I for one, believe in the curse. Judge didn't finish the story, but there's proof."

Frankie was all ears to hear it.

"You know, the quarry lands were owned by the Ho-Chunk. They had a village on the property, fished the Blackbird River, hunted the area. They buried their dead on that land. The original buyers cheated the remaining Ho-Chunk into practically giving the property away. The state came in and annexed it into the county, giving the tribe a pittance of its value. The dates of those tragedies line up with the Blood Moon; that's the Ho-Chunk, getting their revenge."

Frankie shivered, feeling like she was on a fourth grade campout, telling scary stories in the dark. She didn't believe for a minute the Ho-Chunk had anything to do with the quarry accidents, but it certainly added to the colorful history of the place.

She was a little surprised that Emily hadn't told her about any of the tragic events or illnesses and began to feel a little miffed about the whitewashed history in Emily's photos and notes. Was it plausible the heiress didn't know the history? Frankie shook herself back to the present to broach Virginia with the reason for her visit.

"Well, that's a lot of history to digest, Virginia. And it's connected to the reason I'm here. You see, I've been working on a presentation with Emily Spurgeon for the Roots Festival. She was supposed to be rededicating the park to Deep Lakes and now, well, I don't know. I came here to look at her will. It's public record, correct?" Frankie spoke with formality.

Virginia was taken aback for a moment. "Well, sure. The will's been filed. Just a minute. It's on the judge's desk." She returned quickly, walking past her own desk to shut the inner office door so the sharp eyes and ears of Verna and Thelma wouldn't pry. Virginia gripped the file with long manicured black nails - every other nail studded with a red jewel - making Frankie think momentarily that she was in a horror flick. Virginia snapped the folder open to a rather long document, Emily's will.

"If you like, you can take a picture of it with your phone. I'd rather not go out front to make copies, if ya know what I mean." She leaned toward Frankie conspiratorially.

Frankie found it amusing that Virginia, a woman of loose lips, did not trust Verna and Thelma. Gosh, this whole office might be corrupted, she thought. Frankie pulled out her phone, switched on the camera, and snapped each page.

"Anything in particular that stands out to you, Virginia?" she asked, assuming Virginia had already passed judgment on Emily's last wishes.

"You could say that. I mean, I'm glad to see the city and county benefitting from the Spurgeon fortune. But, look at this, here on page three," she pointed to three specific paragraphs.

The first left the gatehouse on the mansion property to Mack Perry, including a monthly stipend from a trust fund. Frankie wasn't surprised. Mack had been living in the gatehouse for years, and given their personal affection for each other, she imagined Emily would take care of him.

The second paragraph indicated a transfer of some profitable stock shares to Alana West. The third bequeathed most of Emily's jewelry to Alana West minus a few heirloom pieces that would go to the Historical Society. Frankie arched an eyebrow and met Virginia's deadpan expression.

"Well, I guess Emily and Alana West were close? She must have trusted Alana. Or something..." Frankie trailed off, unable to come up with a satisfactory reason for such a substantial inheritance.

Virginia smirked. "I don't know Alana West, and I didn't know Emily Spurgeon, but I don't trust common folk when it comes to the opportunity for big money. I just wonder why Emily left nothing to her own flesh and blood."

Frankie jumped on that comment. "You know she has a cousin!"

Virginia nodded. "You bet I do. She called our office yesterday afternoon, before Emily's body was even cold.

Asked about the will. She's the only surviving next of kin, so I faxed her a copy of the will right off. She called back to say the court would be hearing from her attorney - soon. I'd bet my last dime Cousin Cordelia will be contesting this will. Talk about a mess!"

"Thanks for your time and the information, Virginia. Looks like you're going to be busy working out this estate. I wish you good luck. Hope you like the bakery."

The excursion to the Clerk's office provided more than Frankie had bargained for. One thing was certain: Frankie had a lot of work ahead of her. Natural death or not, there were a number of people with ample motive to end Emily's life, and the fight over her assets was just beginning. Other than reading over the will, there was nothing to do for a couple of days but stew while she waited for the autopsy report.

Chapter 10

I like hashtags because they look like waffles #
- Unknown

Frankie paused long enough in the Bubble and Bake kitchen to bid a late good morning to Tía Pepita, Aunt CeCe, and Tess, who informed her she had missed Carmen by just a few minutes.

"She'd like an update from you, Frankie. So give her a call when you can," Tess looked up from the dough she was rolling out for cinnamon pecan tarts, giggling at Liberace, who was perched in the back windowsill on high alert, his tail puffed out like a bushy squirrel as he watched chickadees eating seeds off the outside ledge.

Frankie nodded at Tess, gave Liberace's tail a friendly stroke, then decided she should check in to see if her baking assistants needed help today. "After all, this is *your* business, Francine, remember?" The Golden Firefly rebuked her sharply, and Frankie turned around to peruse the kitchen.

"How's it going here today?" she asked.

The three women assured Frankie that all was under control. Tía Pepita was making caramel custard-filled empanadas, having finished date and cheese versions for tomorrow. Aunt CeCe's macarons were drying on sheet pans, displayed in lovely spring colors and awaiting creamy fillings. Tess was working on tarts and pointed to Carmen's finished yeast donuts frosted with strawberry, vanilla, and dark chocolate icings.

"You all are indispensable!" Frankie gushed sincerely. "What a nice variety of offerings for tomorrow! It looks like you don't need me, so I'm going upstairs to look at a will." Frankie arched her brows mysteriously, reached for a leftover donut, then decided against it. She bounded up the back stairs to her apartment, where she pounced on a banana sitting on the counter.

Opening her tablet, she located the photos of Emily's will and began reading, pen and notebook by her side. Frankie found that writing down notes by hand was her best method for committing important information to memory.

She wasn't surprised to see money left to Deep Lakes for the preservation and upkeep of Spurgeon Park, nor the Emily Spurgeon Trust Fund on behalf of the Whitman County Historical Society, promising them the mansion for the Society's location, along with a list of household art, antiques and jewelry that would stay in the mansion for display.

The first item making Frankie pause with curiosity was a pledge of ongoing payments from the Spurgeon-St. Jude Trust Fund on behalf of a facility in Texas known as "The Ranch." Frankie made a note to look into the facility, wondering how Emily was connected to it.

Item number four left a lump sum from the sale of specific stocks to The American Kidney Fund. Frankie knew Emily's mother, Cordelia, died from pregnancy complications brought on by her kidney disease, at the young age of 40. She had not carried the baby to full term, so the infant died with her. She marveled that, even after decades of medical advancements, kidney disease was still prevalent and largely incurable. That fact brought a sudden chill down Frankie's arms. *Alonzo and Shirley said Emily had been ill for some time - could she have suffered from the same disease that ended her mother's life?* She jotted her thoughts on the notepad.

Next, she read Items five and six, the two notations Virginia mentioned at the courthouse: (5) Mack Perry inherits the gatehouse residence on the Whitman Avenue property until his death, and (6) Emily Spurgeon Trust Fund of 2016, created from the sale of stocks, on behalf of Alana (Brophy) West, who will receive a monthly stipend of $4,000 until her death or age 65, whichever comes first. The year 2016 caught Frankie's attention, being quite recent.

Items seven, eight, and nine were all charitable contributions, which would be accomplished from the sale of specified stocks and bonds. Frankie wasn't surprised to see The Wisconsin Humane Society, The Wisconsin Chapter of the Nature Conservancy and The

Natural Resources Foundation of Wisconsin listed there. Finally, Item 10 was a $25,000 bequest to her beloved Garden Club.

Frankie skipped over some of the legal jargon, having seen the boilerplate language of wills numerous times when she worked as a paralegal. She skipped to the preparer, pleased to see the law firm of Dickens and Probst listed, since she might be able to jar loose some details from her former bosses.

Scanning the list of witnesses, she was surprised to find, not the typical two signatures, but five witnesses to Emily's last wishes. The will was dated January 27, 2016. There was that year again. It made Frankie wonder if this will replaced a previously filed will.

She opened her office computer, locating the screen where she used a sticky notes app to create a bulletin board. Frankie lived by notes and lists, so she had boards dedicated to various shop events. Now, however, she began with a blank board, entitled "Emily Spurgeon's Death: Suspects."

Although the autopsy was pending, Frankie had a feeling and decided to go with it. She began making a web of possible names, including Grant Foster, Cordelia McCoy, Alana West and yes, even Mack Perry. All of them had something to gain from Emily's death, after all. After she listed facts and possible motives under each name, she made a Post-it note labeled "Questions." Under it, she wrote a note to ask about Emily's illness, another to ask how long Alana West had worked for Emily, and another about wills created before 2016. She added: *What is The Ranch in Texas? Why are there five witnesses on the will?* She wrote down the witnesses' names, just in case they knew some worthwhile tidbits.

When she closed her computer and tablet, Frankie found she had lost track of time. No wonder she felt stiff and tired - she'd been sitting on the breakfast bar stool for hours. A single banana did not a meal make, a fact for which her stomach reminded her loudly. She wondered if Garrett might be free to grab some dinner, and she picked up her phone to call him just as it began singing her catchy ringtone. It was Garrett.

"Hey, Garrett. You must be a mind reader because I was just about to call you," Frankie's voice sounded upbeat, conveying her pleasure at hearing Garrett's voice.

"Oh, really, Miss Francine?" Garrett sounded upbeat, too. "It's been a long day. I thought just maybe I could catch you before dinner. How's bar food sound to you?"

Frankie replied with relish. "Sounds like just what the doctor ordered, or should I say what the ME ordered?" She giggled. "Meet you at The Mud Puppy in half an hour?"

"You're on. See you there, Sunshine." Garrett clicked off.

Frankie ran to her bedroom to assess her appearance. What could she pull off in less than 30 minutes, she wondered. She splashed some water on her face, along with a rejuvenating cleanser, then spritzed some texture spray into her straight, fine locks, poofing her bangs and crown with her fingers.

Good enough, she decided, opening her closet door to pull on a fresh, casual shirt in place of her Bountiful Fruits tee. She liked her dark blue jeans as is but opted to swap out her tennies for navy blue loafers. A lover of jewelry, Frankie chose a pair of interlocking hoop earrings that cascaded almost to her neckline. Now, she looked like she was dressed for a date, albeit an informal bar dinner. Best of all, she could enjoy some catch-up time with Garrett, who may be too busy after Emily's autopsy report is finalized.

Frankie and Garrett were engrossed in conversation over bacon cheddar-cheeseburgers and a shared basket of beer fries at the rustic Mud Puppy, a couple of blocks from Bubble and Bake on Meriwether. Country music sang out from the jukebox as owner Kerby Hahn busied himself filling beer glasses and mixing the official state cocktail, the Old Fashioned, made with brandy and served sour or sweet per the customers' wishes.

For a Tuesday night, the place was bustling, with more than ten patrons seated at the polished oaken bar and more than half of the dozen or so tables filled. Although the three pool tables were presently unoccupied, in an hour league teams would fill the bar for an 8-ball competition - a popular winter pastime in Deep Lakes that dribbled into spring. Kerby's sister, Steffie, was already dancing around the dining room, looking like a busy bee in black jeans and bright yellow tee, and Frankie wondered if another waitress would be coming in to help her out.

Garrett and Frankie clinked beer glasses, toasting the arrival of spring, locking eyes in an electrifying connection that wasn't lost on either of them. Frankie felt her cheeks grow warm as Garrett's foot made contact with her shin, making Garrett smile from ear to ear.

Frankie was planning to dig into Emily Spurgeon's death, but that topic now relocated itself to some file folder in the back of Frankie's brain, urged on by both The Golden One and The Pirate. Instead, conversation traveled from the progress of Frankie's grapevines to current wine varieties, Garrett's recent courses in updated techniques in evidence examination, and news on their children.

Garrett's daughter Amanda, a veterinarian graduate, was about to embark on her first year of residency at Cornell University in New York. Frankie's daughter Violet, conversely, would be moving home for the summer in just a few weeks. Violet planned to work at the wine lab with Nelson and Zane, learning the science of viticulture, to Frankie's great joy.

The Mud Puppy's noise level had grown several decibels since the pool teams were set up, drinking, joking and knocking balls around the tables, so Garrett suggested they might scoot outside for a nighttime walk in the spring air.

"Where's your car?" Frankie asked, not minding Garrett's arm around her shoulders, keeping her warm in the cool evening temperature.

"I parked at Spurgeon Park, hoping my instincts were right that you walked here and wouldn't mind a quiet walk in the moonlight," he answered softly near Frankie's ear, creating a little tingle.

"It's a beautiful night. My first evening walk of the season," she smiled and moved in closer beside Garrett.

Arriving at Spurgeon Park, the two took in the progress of the construction and landscaping, well underway. The old pavilion had been removed, weed barrier and grass seed taking its place. The new pavilion was concealed by barriers and tarps, surrounded by construction equipment. On the other side of the equipment, the new concrete block and log building that was the concession stand, kitchen and new restrooms stood proudly. Both agreed that all would be ready by Memorial weekend for the Roots Festival.

Thoughts of the festival brought a frown to Frankie's face as she tried to imagine someone else delivering the speech and presentation meant for Emily. Garrett read her thoughts and stood to face her, clasping both of her hands in his.

"I'm sorry about Emily. I know you and the committee will come up with someone who will do her justice at the festival." Frankie squeezed his hands, feeling a little encouraged.

"And, by the way, Frankie, " Garrett added, "I sent my initial findings on Emily up to the Wausau Crime Lab for further analysis. I hope to hear from them by the end of the week, but you never know. It depends on how busy they are and if other cases have precedence." Frankie raised her brows, inquiringly. She hadn't brought up the subject, practicing unusual restraint, she thought.

"Call me a mind reader," Garrett laughed. "I know you care about the autopsy, and I know how that curious mind of yours works - on overdrive." When she pulled her hands away, Garrett pulled her in for a kiss. "That's one of the things I like most about you, that spirited intellect of yours." Frankie pressed against Garrett, looked up at the full moon for a moment, then melted into Garrett's waiting mouth for an ardent kiss.

*   *   *

Frankie was unable to sleep, perhaps from over-indulging in bar fare, "Or maybe overindulging in Garrett Iverson," The Golden One chirped, flitting around Frankie's brain, a sly smirk on her haloed face.

"Hmm, maybe," Frankie answered aloud, not at all bothered by the accusation. Padding out to the kitchen, she opened up the computer, sat down at the breakfast bar and began an internet search for The Ranch in Texas. Of course, the search yielded more than two million results, including a radio station, a church, and a number of restaurants, for starters. Frankie knew she needed more specific information than she had, so she scrapped the search and looked up Grant Foster instead, which yielded exactly nothing in Philadelphia. After noting this on her board, she searched for Cordelia McCoy instead.

Here, she struck gold. If the internet had located *her* Cordelia McCoy, the first entry was an address, leading to a street photo of a small townhouse on the northeast side of Philadelphia. Frankie browsed the neighborhood, found out it was ranked fairly high in crime and quite low in desirability as a place to live. On the upside, rents were cheap. Frankie concluded that Cordelia wasn't living a wealthy lifestyle, a probability she noted on her Post-it board.

Going back to her initial search, she clicked on Cordelia's social media accounts, finding numerous posts and photos, going back several years. The amount of information to digest was overwhelming, and Frankie knew she could easily become lost in the maze of this woman's personal history.

Again, she reminded herself how painstaking investigative work could be and truly appreciated police detectives and big-time journalists who did this work on the daily. Shaking herself back to the matter at hand, she decided to look at the past few months of Cordelia's chronicles to see if she could piece together a truthful picture of her present life.

Several photos of Cordelia dressed in formal wear,

showed her cozied up to the social elite of Philadelphia at various charitable events. Her posts had the same things in common: praise for the celebrity who hosted the event, excitement at being part of such a noble cause, and gratitude to someone named Toby Sparks.

Frankie made a quick list of events and hosts from the past year, double underlining Toby Sparks. She was disappointed, however, when she searched Sparks, finding no photos and no hard information, except that he was named in several hashtags on social media. What did that mean? Frankie wasn't fluent in social media, despite the shop having a website and media page for events and announcements. Violet and Sophie managed most of the pages, posting the pictures and articles Frankie provided. Frankie had to admit it: she just wasn't terribly interested in that part of her business.

Yawning repeatedly, Frankie closed the laptop, padded back to bed, and decided to pay a morning visit to Nelson and Zane, her resident tech experts, at the winery. Hopefully, they could shed some light on hashtags and Toby Sparks.

Chapter 11

A lot of life is dealing with your curse, dealing with the
cards you were given that aren't so nice. Does it make
you into a monster, or can you temper it in some way,
or accept it and go in some other direction?
– Wes Craven

When Carmen swung in the back door of Bubble and
Bake Wednesday morning, Frankie was already whipping
up a fourth flavor of shortbread cookie dough. Several
pounds of butter lined up in quarter pound sticks on the
counter, like Lincoln Logs, caused Carmen to quip, "Oh,
oh, it's kringle construction season!"

Before Carmen shifted gears to begin scolding
Frankie for not calling her yesterday, Frankie took the
lead with a genuine apology to her dear friend.

"I'm sorry for not calling you yesterday, Carmie. Time
just got away from me, but I have lots to tell you." Carmen
donned an apron and started preparing the familiar yeast
donut dough, something she could do in her sleep since it
was a staple shop item. Carmen could work on the more
imaginative baking after Frankie updated her.

Frankie shared her list of suspicious persons who would

benefit from Emily Spurgeon's death, along with tidbits of information she knew about each one. She listed the beneficiaries from the will, including the mysterious Ranch in Texas, and she noted the 2016 trust fund for Alana. She described the social media posts and pictures of Cordelia McCoy, too, and the mysterious Toby Sparks, conveying her plan to talk to her techies at the vineyard this morning.

"So, I'm guessing you got next to no sleep last night, huh Frankie? I know that brain of yours - all those questions swirling around your noggin, bumping into each other!" Carmen laughed and pointed a baking spatula directly at her friend. "Did some early morning baking shake anything into place?"

Frankie had to admit that it didn't. "Not this morning anyway. I have more questions than answers, plus a voice inside my head telling me to slow down and wait for the autopsy. But . . ."

"Go on." Carmen stuck a tub of dough by a sunny window, and covered it with a towel.

"I have a feeling about this. I know Emily was ill, but the timing of her death doesn't seem right. She was excited about seeing her cousin, excited about the festival presentation. When people have something to look forward to - well - their illness usually takes a hiatus."

"I hate to say this, Frankie, but I trust your instincts most of the time and you should, too. Just don't dive in too deep until you see the autopsy report. Okay?" Carmen was the practical and cautious one of the two.

Frankie nodded. During their exchange, she'd been measuring large quantities of flour, counting out yeast portions and zesting lemons and oranges. Now the back door opened to reveal Tess, Jovie, and Tía Pepita in one convergence of chit-chat. Frankie was pleased to have them there all at once, for today she planned to share the secrets of kringle preparation, exactly as she was taught by her Grandma Sophie Petersen decades ago.

Frankie needed all hands on deck to prepare the 200-plus kringles for their booth at the Roots Festival. Since the shop had opened more than five years ago, Frankie prided herself in making the kringles herself, pouring all of Sophie's love into each formed pastry. Now, however, she knew it was time to share the process with her trusted bakers. She just couldn't keep up with kringle demand alone any longer.

"Good morning, Tess, Jovie, Tía. Are you ready to begin?" Frankie smiled and bounced a little on her toes. She was truly thrilled to share this important piece of her heritage and her childhood. All three nodded enthusiastically. Tess and Jovie would learn the delicate process of rolling layers of butter over layers of thin translucent pastry, folding them over and over again to form the buttery crust. Tía promised to watch the process but admitted her eyesight would be a hindrance, so for now she would dedicate her efforts to learning all the varieties of fillings Frankie offered.

Frankie demonstrated rolling the butter layer, then

watched Tess and Jovie do the same. Each rolled several butter layers, placed them in the cooler, then imitated Frankie's directions in pastry rolling, placing the pastry dough in the cooler, too. Tomorrow, they would complete the second stage of kringles, rolling the butter layers into the dough layers. Making kringles required three days of patience to ensure the appropriate temperature before the buttery dough met the filling.

Frankie asked Tess and Jovie to roll out, cut, and bake the four kinds of shortbread dough she'd made earlier, as she prepared to head out to the vineyard. The two made a plan to divide and conquer the four batches, and then Tess asked, "Did you uncover anything interesting in the will you looked at? You were sort of mysterious when you came in yesterday."

Frankie let out a whew. "A few curiosities, for certain. But the mystery might just be the Quarry Curse!"

Frankie meant that to be a lighthearted bit of blather, so she was surprised to see the reactions it evoked. Carmen and Tía Pepita exclaimed "Dios mío" and made the sign of the cross simultaneously. Tess ducked for cover as if lightning might strike any moment, her cheerful head wrap the only thing Frankie could see of her from the other side of the counter. Even Liberace let loose a low meow-yowl, tucked his tail and bolted out the kitchen door, just as Aunt CeCe was coming in, pushing the bakery case from the day's sales. Jovie wore an expression of mild curiosity mixed with amusement; she seemed to view curses the way Frankie did.

"What in the Devil is going on in here anyway?" Aunt CeCe asked, looking at the frozen faces around the kitchen. "Something seems to have terrified Archie; he jumped out the door like he was being chased by a ghost!" Aunt CeCe's words did nothing to lighten the mood of her co-bakers. Before Frankie could explain, Tía Pepita found her voice.

"It's that quarry woman's death, CeCe. The curse, the Quarry Curse." Tía sounded spooked. Aunt CeCe continued to look dumbfounded.

Frankie shared the list of tragic events she could recount from Judge Dicky Bryant's tale of the granite quarry's history, adding his suspicion about Emily's untimely death. "But, it's all just local lore, an interesting legend," Frankie put in, cheerfully.

But Tía Pepita waved away Frankie's dismissal. "Curses like chickens come home to roost. Maybe that woman is paying for the sins of her family." Tía was matter-of-fact. "All those poor workers who lost their lives is a big shame on her family."

Hearing Tía speak so passionately, Frankie wondered if the woman knew any of the victims first-hand. Frankie attempted to minimize the tragedies somewhat. "Yes, there were so many workers in every industry who were injured or killed back then because safety practices were not in place. It must have been a terrible time."

Tía was having none of it, however. "And whose fault was it? Do you think the owners would risk their own safety? Nope, poor people don't matter."

Frankie nodded her understanding, continuing. "Well, at least things improved. I mean safety standards, wages, benefits - those things." But Tía jumped right back in.

"Oh, yeah? Then how come all those people got sick? That was in the '80s, not old times!" Tía was quite riled, and Frankie was certain this was personal for her.

"Weren't the Spurgeons and McCoys generous to the families with sick loved ones? It seems I heard they took care of their medical bills and such," Frankie noted.

Tía Pepita sent sharp dagger eyes in Frankie's direction. "Un uh, no way. Tell that to the Gomez family. You remember your parents talking about their bad luck, Carmen."

Carmen raised questioning brows at her aunt. Tía Pepita held up two fingers in a grand gesture. "Dos hombres," she said, making a sign of the cross from forehead to abdomen. "The Gomezes lost two men to that quarry!"

Tía recounted the first tragic tale of José, the patriarch of the Gomez family. The man kept working despite a diagnosis of quarry sickness, only to be killed by an explosion at the quarry in 1982, she was certain.

"Three niños Señora Gomez was left to fend for," Tía crossed her fingers and raised them up toward the ceiling, her eyes floating upward as well. She picked up the account with Jose's son, who went to work in the quarry at 15 to help keep the family afloat, but he died too, falling from the crane platform where he was working on a rock face. He died just months after his father, leaving Rona Gomez with two daughters and no prospects.

Carmen nodded, remembering. "Yes, I remember my parents talking about it, but it happened when I was a kid. I think they said the quarry owners paid for the Gomezes' house though."

Tía Pepita spat on the floor, leaving Frankie to wonder if this was a common occurrence, and maybe she'd better mop more than once a day. "Those rich people - what do they care if Rona Gomez had to work two full-time jobs just to keep food in her niños' bellies, huh?"

Tía's face showed disgust for the Spurgeons and maybe all the wealthy people in the world. She was gearing up for a stormy lecture, evidenced by her huffs and rapid packing of cooled empanadas in storage containers. Frankie and Carmen gave each other a knowing look and steadied themselves for the onslaught.

"Of course, nobody understands loss as much as me," Tía sighed heavily, the weight of grief fresh on her face. Married three times, she had buried all three husbands; bearing the mark of a sorrowing widow, she always wore or carried something black since the passing of number three.

Tía Pepita's first husband, Emilio, went missing in Vietnam and was never recovered. By 1980, he was officially declared dead and the family held a funeral service that seemed futile as it offered no real closure to any of Emilio's loved ones.

Finally, Tía moved on, marrying Luis, the man Carmen would call her Tío. They moved from Wisconsin to El Paso, Texas, where they ran a small grocery store. By the 1990s, their neighborhood was overrun with barrio gangs. Tía begged Luis to sell the store and leave, but buyers were not lining up to purchase businesses in their neighborhood, so they stayed.

One day, the grocery was robbed at gunpoint by a young teen whom Luis recognized. Tía explained that the boy had grown up in their barrio, came shopping with his abuela and mama, gone to their church.

"My Luis couldn't see the teen with the gun, just the boy he knew." Tía grew tearful at the re-telling. "He tried to reason with the boy, but he couldn't. My Luis died right on the floor of his own store." She choked on the last words, bringing Carmen around the counter to embrace her aunt. But there was more to tell.

Tía married a third time in 2000. "Clive was a handsome German-American man and rich, too. He was also younger than me," she finished in a whisper that conveyed scandalous behavior; marrying outside her culture and a younger man no less was surely shocking for someone her age. By now, a weary Tía was losing the threads of her story. She insisted Clive was a fishing captain who was killed by a sea monster right on the deck of his boat in the Gulf of Mexico.

"So, you see ladies, I know what it is to have grief. Now you know why I believe in curses." On those words, Tía headed to the bathroom, Aunt CeCe following close behind. Frankie knew her aunt was burdened with sorrows of her own, but somehow she managed them, or worse, buried them below her flower-child exterior.

Carmen hastily relayed the truth about husband three. Clive was nothing but a blowfish, as she called him, meaning he liked to brag, but he wasn't rich at all, nor was he younger than Tía; he just said he was. Clive was a captain on a tourist excursion boat that ran three cruises daily around San Padre Island. One morning, hungover, he slipped on the boat deck, fell into the water, and drowned. Tía's story was a much better ending, they all decided.

Frankie didn't want to leave the shop in an atmosphere of evil curses and sorrowful tales, so she turned on the radio, opened a can of tuna, and enticed Liberace back to the kitchen.

As it was nearing lunch time, she tossed a few flatbreads on a baking sheet, added sauce from the cooler, a few veggies, and a mountain of mixed cheeses. She placed them under the broiler, then retrieved two bottles of wine from the lounge - Dark Deeds and Singin' the Blues - apropos for the occasion, she figured. Despite the associated names, the black cherry Lambrusco and blueberry Riesling were two of Frankie's favorite multi-purpose wines, appropriate for most occasions.

When Tía and CeCe returned to the kitchen, the others had gathered around pizza squares and were pouring wine. Tía gasped and looked at the clock. "Should we be drinking wine before noon?"

Frankie nodded her head. "I suppose we can have wine in our shop anytime we wish, right Carmen?"

Carmen giggled her affirmation, brushing up alongside Frankie to whisper, "Way to restore the hygge in here." The ladies toasted to sunny spring days.

It was time for Frankie to head out to Bountiful Fruits to pick the brains of Nelson and Zane. She asked Aunt CeCe how the sales were that morning and looked over the leftovers in the bakery case.

"The universe was smiling on the bakery today. Everyone seemed happy, and some bought extra goodies, too!" That was Aunt CeCe, always channeling the positive vibes of the universe. Frankie suspected she had some sort of magical qualities, as bakery sales were always up on days she ran the retail side. Of course, her cheerful clothing contributed to the shop atmosphere, too. Today she wore a white gauzy peasant top loaded with bouquets of daisies.

"If you're looking for something to take out to the men at the vineyard, I set aside this blueberry-cream cheese coffee cake. I think they'll find it spell-binding." Frankie knitted her brows quizzically. How did Aunt CeCe know she was going to the vineyard?

"Thank you, Auntie," Frankie said, planting a kiss on her cheek. "This looks scrumptious. I think I'll bag up some meaty empanadas, too, Tía, since it's lunch time, if that's okay with you."

Tía Pepita spread her arms wide, as if presenting a display of jewels. She looked happy again. "Of course! There's plenty. Take all you want."

* * *

On Frankie's drive out to Bountiful, she managed two phone calls. The first came from Abe Arnold, editor of *The Whitman Watch*, the local newspaper where Frankie submitted articles about grape cultivation, wine making, and shop events. She and Abe had become rivals after Frankie scooped his paper on the story of a local pastor's death during the winter. Frankie did irregular part-time reporting for *Point Press*, a daily in Stevens Point that ran Frankie's exclusive story about the pastor's death.

"Frankie Champagne. It's Abe Arnold. Rumor has it you were at the Granite Mansion during the police investigation of the Spurgeon woman's death. True?" Abe began.

Frankie proceeded with caution as she could hear the hunger in his voice to garner any inside information he could. "Yes, I had a meeting with Ms. Spurgeon that morning, so I gave a routine statement. No big deal." Frankie was being dismissive on purpose. "Why do you ask?"

"Just preparing to get the autopsy report. I want to

cross all the t's and dot the i's, so to speak. Did you hear or see anything strange?"

Frankie was holding her cards close. No way was she going to reveal anything to Abe Arnold - not yet, anyway. "Not really. When do you expect the autopsy report?" Frankie wondered if Abe knew something she didn't. She doubted that he did since Garrett promised to let her know as soon as the report was in.

"Report should be any time now. Nothing definite, though." Abe ventured further now. "Hey, Frankie, do you think we could work together on this one - I mean, if it amounts to anything. You know, share information - divide and conquer?" Frankie said she'd think about it and signed off.

Not a minute later, her editor, Magda, was calling from *Point Press*. "Frankie. Magda here. Just checking in with you. Ann from Obits flagged Deep Lakes this morning. Seems like a well-known heiress died. She was only 60, so I wondered what you knew about it."

Frankie filled Magda in but not completely. "I'm staying on top of it, in case there's more to it than natural causes, Magda. I'm waiting on the autopsy report, which is coming any day."

"This could be a big story, Frankie. I'm counting on you to come through. If there's anything odd at all about that report, I expect you'll be working it." Magda was loud, emphatic, and multi-tasking, as usual. Frankie could hear her handing something to someone and responding to a question. Frankie assured Magda she would stay in touch. "Okay, good. Gotta run," Magda's phone clicked.

By the time the call ended, Frankie was parked on the cement slab in front of the winery building. Before going in, she walked through the vineyard, assessing the clusters of budding grape blossoms, pausing to check the moisture of the soil. She waved at Manny, who was outside the equipment shed eating lunch with two workers.

"Everything looks good here," Frankie called down the hillside. Manny gave her two thumbs up. "Have you seen anymore of Officer Pflug?" Manny shook his head, then scrambled up the sloping grass to meet Frankie.

"Pflug came by last week to remind me to call him when more workers arrive. I told him it would be a long time before we needed more people. I'll let him know, though; I don't want any trouble for you, or me, or them," Manny confided. Frankie knew she could trust her vineyard manager.

Stepping inside the winery lab, Frankie was greeted by a stack of empty energy drink cans and fancy coffee bottles. She looked over at Zane first, who might have slept at the lab, noting his disheveled appearance was beyond the norm for him. "Are you feeling okay, Zane?" Frankie asked.

"Never better, Frankie, now that I've re-energized!" Zane, sporting more than a five o'clock shadow and wearing Star Trek lounge pants, pointed to the tower of empty cans.

Even Nelson, who always wore khaki pants and a polo or button-down shirt, was dressed in sweat pants under his lab coat. "What gives, Nelson?" Frankie wanted to know.

"Excuse me, gives what?" Nelson asked, peering at her above his black-framed glasses. Frankie often had to remind herself that Nelson operated in the literal world, often oblivious to informal exchanges. She was reminded of the "Who's on First" schtick and switched gears immediately.

"What I mean to say is, what's going on around here? I've never seen you two dress this way, and what's with all the empty caffeinated drinks?"

Nelson looked squarely at Frankie. "As I explained in my email to you this morning, Ms. Champagne, Zane and I were running behind schedule due to studying for exams. Neither one of us has slept much, hence the stack of energy beverages before you." He made a grand gesture toward the tower. Frankie laughed inwardly, but she hadn't checked email today so was unaware.

"Of course, Nelson. Not a problem. I hope your exams go well. I brought you some brain food," she added, producing the coffee cake, empanadas and paper plates, "in exchange for a technology favor."

The two techies were thrilled, only now realizing how hungry they were for something other than caffeine. They both grabbed plates, piling on empanadas and cutting large chunks of cake.

"Shoot, Boss. What do you need from us?" Zane asked.

Frankie slid a spare chair into Zane's computer space, then opened a tab with Cordelia McCoy's social media posts. "This woman right here," she pointed to a tall, willowy blonde, "her pictures seem to be with important or famous people, and her posts always mention Toby Sparks. I've seen other posts with that name as well, but I can't find out anything about him. Can you help?" Frankie moved over, letting Zane go to work, as Nelson, on her other side, did the same.

It was fun watching the two hammering away at the keyboards, focused determination on their faces, like they were in a competitive challenge. Zane was the first to sit back, grin crookedly in Frankie's direction, and pronounce success.

"Here you go, found him. His name is Toby Freyberg. He just uses Sparks for his business."

"Which is what exactly?" Frankie asked Zane.

"He's a connector. He knows people - rich, famous people. And for a fee, he will connect the unconnected with the rich and famous." Zane was pleased with himself.

Frankie's jaw dropped. "You mean, people will pay someone so they can rub elbows with the rich?" Zane and Nelson both nodded.

"You see, Ms. Champagne, in this day and age of social media, people want to be seen with celebrities. Many believe it increases their value, you know." Frankie still couldn't convince Nelson to call her by her first name.

"So, Cordelia paid Toby Sparks to connect her to these people? I wonder why." Frankie's mind was trying to piece potential reasons together.

But now it was Nelson's turn for show and tell. While Zane was sharing his information on Toby Sparks, Nelson was searching for intel on Cordelia and found some fascinating dirt.

"Take a look at this. Cordelia McCoy used to live in Santa Clara County, California, in The Highlands in the 1990s and 2000s. Back then, she was Cordelia Ainsley, married to banker Julian Ainsley of Lehman Brothers. He lost his fortune in the Great Recession of 2008."

Nelson showed Frankie a photo of their luxury home in The Highlands, which was lost in bankruptcy in December 2008. Shortly afterwards, the couple divorced. Cordelia reclaimed her maiden name, returned to Philadelphia in 2009, and moved into a townhouse on the seamy side of the city.

Zane took over the conversation, showing his latest results from searching for photos of Cordelia in the 2000s. Frankie immediately noticed the contrast from the latest photos. She wasn't as thin and appeared much more glamorous. Falling on hard times changed a person dramatically, Frankie supposed. She herself knew how stress wreaked havoc on her body when she divorced.

"I wonder what Cordelia's been doing the past ten

years. How is she earning a living? And how can she afford a personal representative?" Frankie was firing questions into the air.

"Personal representative?" Nelson asked.

Frankie shook herself back to reality to answer Nelson. "Grant Foster. He's been in Deep Lakes on and off. I saw him at Emily Spurgeon's house after they'd had a meeting. He's supposed to be Cordelia's representative - so an attorney of some kind?" Frankie admitted she couldn't locate him in her internet searches.

"I'm guessing Cordelia has spent the last ten years trying to rebuild her reputation, looking to get into the good graces of the moneyed, maybe hoping to land a wealthy husband or situation." Zane speculated.

"Hmmm," Frankie chimed in, "a real Eliza Doolittle of sorts."

Both men stared blankly at Frankie, clearly not up to par in their knowledge of musicals. Frankie tried again. "You know, a pig in a fur coat." Zane hazarded a guess to her reference this time.

"You mean she can dress up and look rich, but she's still just a pretender."

"Exactly." Frankie smiled.

Nelson offered his lesson on the current vernacular. "We would call Cordelia a *poser*, Miss Champagne." Frankie had heard the word but didn't use it.

"So what you're saying, is maybe Cordelia is not the real McCoy." Frankie laughed at her own joke. So did

Zane, who apparently knew the expression, but Nelson looked skeptical.

"Well, we wouldn't know that without DNA testing," he offered. Frankie giggled inwardly but was careful not to poke fun at Nelson. She respected him too much and knew he could be sensitive about his lack of understanding jokes and sarcasm.

"Zane and I will look into this Grant Foster and see what we can find out for you. We'll keep you posted." Frankie thanked them both, offering them a salute before heading back to town. She had a dinner date with her mother and Aunt CeCe and didn't dare show up late.

Chapter 12

Snake's poison is life to the snake;
it is in relation to man that it means death.
– Rumi

Frankie rose early, despite the half-light of a drizzly April morning. Stretching as she traipsed to the kitchen, she rinsed out yesterday's coffee mug and fired up the brewer, replaying pieces of last night's after-dinner conversation with her mother.

They made small talk about Garrett, the growing season, and wine varieties currently being batched. Then Peggy shared upcoming plans with Dan Fitzpatrick, an old family friend and widower whom Peggy began dating a couple months earlier.

"Dan and I are hosting a pontoon party in June, probably on a Sunday, later in the day, so you can come after the shop closes," Peggy invited. "Of course, bring Garrett, too."

Frankie said that sounded fun. "Let me know when you pick a date, so I can get someone to close that day."

Frankie pulled out her laptop, at the same time asking her mother for her opinion. "I've been poking around the internet, looking for information on Cordelia McCoy and Grant Foster," Frankie admitted, waiting for her mother to voice disapproval at her nosiness. But Peggy surprised her by smiling wryly, and scooted her chair in closer so she could view the photos Frankie pointed out. Frankie had two open tabs, one with photos from the early 2000s, the other with more recent photos. She shared the information Nelson and Zane uncovered that afternoon.

Peggy, with eyes like a hawk, perused each page of images, adjusting her reading glasses from time to time to scrutinize them more closely. Finally, she spoke.

"Well, I could have told you Cordelia McCoy had fallen into hard times without having to do any further searching," she pronounced. Frankie's expression urged her mother to tell more. "She looks positively bleak in these recent photos. She's lost the youthful color in her face. It's clear she's no longer having her hair professionally managed, nor her nails."

Frankie scrunched her brows together, squinting to see what her mother saw. Peggy pointed out two images that showed Cordelia's hands, noting a chipped nail in one and worn polish on another. In the recent pictures, Cordelia wore the same hairstyle, nothing salon worthy. Frankie was amazed by her mother's meticulous attention to detail, something Frankie had not inherited when it came to her own physical appearance.

Peggy continued. "Look at her evening gowns in

these recent photos. They were in fashion 10 to 20 years ago. Clearly, she isn't able to afford an updated wardrobe." Peggy pressed one finger on a black and white gown with a giant back bow and another Bohemian floral gown with diagonal ruffles to demonstrate. "Nobody wears these styles anymore. And look at this one . . ." It was Cordelia in a strapless fuschia Grecian gown with a front slit that traveled above the knee. "Fuschia is not an *in-color*, and nowadays slits go all the way above the thigh. Shamefully."

Similar to a lawyer making a closing argument, Peggy showed her daughter an image from 2006 of a smiling Cordelia and her banker husband presenting a large check to a children's hospital. Cordelia was wearing a tasteful one-shoulder black gown adorned with a glittery broach and sequins. Peggy clicked on the next tab and jabbed her finger at a photo from 2016. Yes, Cordelia was wearing the same black gown. "And I'm sure if you took some time, you would find more of these recycled gown pictures," Peggy ended crisply. Frankie wasn't sure if her mother was acting the snob or if she was simply showing off her power of observation.

"Wow, Mom, you are amazing. I wish I had your gift for style." Frankie meant that sincerely. As the only girl in the family, she wondered if she was a disappointment to her fashion-conscious mother. But, Peggy was having none of Frankie's self doubt.

"You, my dear, are meticulous in other ways. Your baking, for example. Your palate is one to be envied.

And your wines, too. And more recently, you seem to be cultivating an intuitive side that's razor-sharp."

It was rare to receive such praise from her mother, and Frankie spontaneously reached over to hug her tightly. To her pleasant surprise, Peggy didn't stiffen like a board but squeezed her daughter briefly. Maybe Aunt CeCe, who was so open and warm, was rubbing off a little on Peggy.

Standing in her own kitchen, Frankie smiled at the warm memory. She concluded the evening was a winner all the way around. There was no more time for reflection as she needed to get downstairs to the shop kitchen and tend to the kringle dough in the cooler. She hoped everyone else was coming in early today because she was determined to pay a visit to the Granite Mansion before the autopsy report arrived. And, she decided not to call ahead, hoping to catch Cordelia McCoy off-guard, and maybe the others, as well. Donning her comfy yet chic steel blue casual pull-ons and a Bubble and Bake tee, she raced down the steps, ready to begin the day.

The next three hours proceeded like clockwork. Carmen, Tía Pepita, Jovie, and Tess all joined Frankie in preparing fillings for the kringles. Fillings could easily be cooked in advance, then frozen for later use.

At the Roots Festival, kringles would be sold in quarters, featuring the most popular flavors: almond, pecan, raspberry, cherry and blueberry. Frankie offered more flavors at the holidays, but since the shop would sell out at their festival booth, she needed to pare down the varieties.

After the fillings cooled, she removed yesterday's dough from the cooler and showed Jovie and Tess how to fill them, watching each as they practiced shaping the buttery pastry into a large oval, spreading the filling down the center and folding the dough over the top. Several kringles were baking when Aunt CeCe pushed the bakery case back into the kitchen at 9:30 a.m, nearly bare from another successful day of sales.

Frankie excused herself after tucking some tarts and cookies into a bakery box, leaving the others to prep for tomorrow. Just before heading out the back door, she remembered today was Thursday. The wine lounge would be open and quiches needed to be readied as well as tomorrow's bakery. "Hey, I'm coming back later to prep the quiches for tonight," Frankie told her crew.

"Not to worry, Francine," Tess chirped. "We have enough hands. We will probably finish okay." Tess was an angel. Jovie nodded enthusiastically, as Carmen shooed Frankie out the door, reminding Frankie that Thursday was supposed to be her day off, in case she'd forgotten.

"You know, it's hard to stay away when I've got such great friends to work with here," Frankie cooed, meaning every word of it. She seldom took a full day off from the shop. Such was the life of owning a small business.

A few minutes later, Frankie knocked on the front entrance at the Spurgeon house, and was surprised when the door was opened by none other than Cordelia McCoy in the flesh. At least, what little flesh she had. If a pencil had a head and face, Frankie imagined it would look like the waif in front of her. Cordelia's face was almost a perfect triangle with visible freckles, despite her attempt at concealing them with too much bronzer. The rest of her face was occupied by wide eyes that glinted like graphite points. Her long hair was the color and texture of straw, and she was smoking a strange-looking brown cigarette that smelled like a holiday ham. Frankie had succeeded in catching Cordelia off-guard to be sure.

"Yes?" Cordelia looked directly at Frankie, blinking a couple of times in an exaggerated fashion. Frankie expected the woman would at least be able to conjure a polite greeting. She was taken aback by her abrasive demeanor.

"Hello," Frankie faltered. "My name is Francine Champagne. I've been working with your cousin Emily on a presentation for our community festival." She paused to allow this to sink in but went on hastily. "I'm so sorry for your loss, Ms. McCoy and I'm sorry to bother you. I was hoping we could discuss how to proceed with the presentation." Frankie decided to be business-like and direct.

Cordelia continued to blink as if Frankie were a speck in her eye she could rub away. "I have no idea what you're talking about. Just a minute." She turned around and called over her shoulder, "Helena! Helena! Come here. I need you to deal with this."

Frankie wondered who Helena was, but soon found out as Alana appeared at the door, dressed in uniform, looking displeased, but trying to hide it.

"Oh, hello, Ms. Champagne. What are you doing here?" Alana asked, brusquely. Meanwhile, Cordelia disappeared into the house.

Frankie confessed that she hoped to meet Cordelia and speak with her about the presentation and funeral plans. Frankie said she would help with anything regarding the funeral. Alana seemed surprised at this but invited Frankie to come inside.

Speaking softly in the foyer, Alana said Cordelia had arrived two days ago and everything seemed up in the air. "We're not sure when the funeral will take place yet, but I suppose plans should be made. I don't even know how long I will be working here. I have no idea what Ms. McCoy's plans are." Alana's thoughts seemed scattered, and she looked frazzled.

Cordelia's voice spoke loudly from one of the first floor rooms. "Elena, did you get rid of her? I need you. Come here." Alana rolled her eyes, looking weary.

"Has it been like this since she arrived?" Frankie inquired, secretively, inviting Alana's confidence. Alana nodded, held up a finger for Frankie to wait, then proceeded down the hall to see what the new mistress of the mansion wanted.

When Alana returned, she ushered Frankie into the familiar library and shut the double doors. Frankie noticed the library still smelled the same; the heady pine scents had not been replaced by the smoky ham smell. She guessed Cordelia didn't spend time in the library.

"Let me get Ms. McCoy some breakfast, and I'll convince her to join you here afterwards. Just give me 10 or 15 minutes, okay?"

Frankie nodded her agreement, and offered the bakery box to Alana for Cordelia and anyone else there. Alana took the box skeptically. "Thanks. I'll offer this to her, but I promise you that she won't touch this stuff."

Frankie wondered what Alana would say to convince this woman to meet her when she clearly wanted nothing to do with Frankie. Meanwhile, Frankie would not pass the time idly. She had some snooping to do and was in the perfect room to do it.

She spied a laptop computer sitting atop the large mahogany desk, a stack of papers sitting next to it, and a book about Midwest trees nearby. Moving the mouse, she was happy to see the computer didn't have a screen lock, so she could see the open pages.

The first screen was a website of herbal remedies in alphabetical order, opened to the home page. She didn't see anything unusual about it, knowing how Emily loved to use herbs; her kitchen was full of herbal teas, and she used herbal oils as well.

She moved on to the second tab, which was an overview of the types of kidney dialysis, methods and side effects of each. "Hmm. Was it possible Emily had the same kidney disease her mother had died from?" Frankie repeated the idea again in a whisper. "Dialysis! Just how sick was Emily?"

Suddenly, papers on the desk scattered as Pearl launched onto the desktop, causing Frankie to jump out of her skin. "Yikes, Pearl! You scared me out of my wits, cat!" Frankie said out loud. In response, the Siamese brushed her whole body against Frankie's left arm and shoulder, purring encouragingly. Frankie relaxed, stroked Pearl for a bit, then quickly began gathering the fallen papers, placing them back neatly, although in what order, who could tell.

Frankie's racing heart had calmed a bit, and she resumed. Pearl was perched right next to the mouse, and Frankie had to nudge her a little to regain her own snooping position. She clicked her phone camera for a shot of the kidney screen, then opened the final tab, revealing the Wisconsin Law Library site on the Trusts and Wills webpage. That was curious, but of course, she knew Cordelia planned to contest Emily's will, so maybe she was reading up on Wisconsin laws to get the lowdown. She clicked a picture of that page, too.

Hearing approaching footsteps, she quickly skittered back to the leather sofa, picked up the book on the coffee table about American rose gardens, and tried to relax. Alana walked in to inform Frankie that Ms. McCoy would meet her in a few minutes after she freshened up.

"Can I bring you something to drink? Tea or coffee? I doubt Ms. McCoy will ask you." Frankie noticed Alana did little to conceal her disdain for the woman. Of course, Cordelia couldn't even call her by the correct name, so why should Alana hide her feelings?

Frankie said she'd love some tea and that Alana could choose, then added, "How are you holding up? So many changes around here must not be easy for you."

Alana's posture slumped a little, showing her melancholy. "Well, it's not at all the same. The worst part is looking for a new job. I don't know if Ms. McCoy plans to stay here, or even if she does, whether or not she wants me to stay."

Alana sniffled a little, then straightened when she saw Pearl perched on the desktop. Frankie's heart skipped a beat, as Alana marched toward the cat to shoo her off. Frankie prayed the computer screen wouldn't be in view or that it had gone back to sleep mode. It didn't help that The Golden One was singing loudly in her ear, "Well, well, well, you might be in a little pickle, Missy."

As luck would have it, Pearl jumped from the desk before Alana got there, hissing sassily as she ran under one of the wing chairs by the window. The mood had been broken, and Alana was off to retrieve the tea. Frankie whispered a silent *thank you* to the kitty.

Frankie considered returning to the desk, despite warning whistles from both Goldie and Pirate. "I'm just going to peek at the top paper," she told herself. It turned out to be medical notes from a recent doctor visit, dated a week before Emily's death. The paper just below it was a prescription. Before reading any of it, Frankie snapped pictures of both, deciding to view them later. She desperately wanted to dig through that stack, guessing it was about two inches high, but the risk was too great, so she returned to the sofa and the rose garden book.

Cordelia showed up before the tea, her hair in a bun. She changed from loungewear to a pink sheath, which accented her bony frame, a strand of creamy pearls around her neck, and pearl studs in her ears. Frankie noticed her cream shoes were scuffed and worn, however. Maybe Frankie had a little of her mother's observation skills after all.

"Hello, Ms. Champagne. You must excuse my earlier mood. Things are quite undone around here at the moment. So, you're a baker?" Cordelia asked, a note of condescension in her tone. "Can you make gluten free products? I'm dying here in this little area where a person just can't find what they need."

Frankie planted a fake smile and attempted to sweeten her own tone. "I don't bake gluten free products as a rule. There isn't much call for that around here, but I assure you that I can. If you have something particular in mind, please let me know."

Alana brought in tea just then for Frankie, with a large espresso drink for Cordelia, who pounced on it immediately. "Did you use soy milk, Anita? And two sugars?" Alana nodded twice, asked if anything was needed, then backed her way out of the library.

Frankie figured her time was being measured in seconds, so she got straight to the point, asking Cordelia if she would be interested in representing the family for the re-dedication of Spurgeon Park, indicating she was still working through the quarry photos.

"Oh, I honestly don't know if I'll be here for the festival. It just depends, you know. And, I'm not a Spurgeon; that's not *my family*."

Frankie interjected here. "Well, they are your closest family. I mean, your Aunt Cordelia was your father's sister." Frankie wanted to show Cordelia a thing or two. "Your parents and you are featured in the presentation, too." Cordelia made a face as if she'd sucked a lemon.

"We-ell, that may be true, but . . . look, why don't you finish going through the photos you need for the presentation, then I'll take a look at it. Yes?" Frankie knew she was being dismissed but was inwardly pleased at the access she would have to the mansion for the time being.

"Certainly. Thank you, Ms. McCoy. Please let me know the details for Emily's funeral. I'd like to help any way I can."

"Yes, of course. I'll have Elena call you. I can't say right now when the funeral will take place. Again, it all depends." Cordelia was being vague again and seemed distracted. Of course, Frankie knew the reason for all of it. Everything depended upon the autopsy and the legality of the will. She didn't intend to press Cordelia for answers -

not yet, anyway. Today was all about establishing a cordial rapport, just in case.

An hour later, back at Bubble and Bake, Garrett called to tell Frankie the autopsy report was in. He sounded strangely formal, and Frankie was trying to guess why.

"The department reviewed the report this morning and are now prepared to brief the press on its findings." He sounded like he was reading an official statement.

"Okay, so what are the findings?" Frankie asked, rather business-like, but clearly unsure of her approach.

Garrett sighed, drawing a strained breath. "I can't disclose that over the phone. The department has set aside a 2:00 p.m. slot for you to review the report and ask questions. Alonzo will be there."

Awareness dawned on Frankie then. Garrett was being official because he was instructed to be, and that instruction came from Sheriff Alonzo Goodman directly. So, she was being treated like just another member of the press, then. The insight provoked a sharp poke from The Golden One. "Come now, Francine, isn't that what you wanted - to be treated like a professional? You can't have your cake and eat it, too, dear." Goldie was right, of course; Frankie did want professional recognition.

"Yes, Garrett. I will be there at 2:00 p.m. sharp. Your office?"

"No, we will be in the sheriff's department conference room." Now Frankie wondered how many reporters would be there at the same time. As if reading her thoughts, Garrett added, "This is a specific time slot for you alone. Other reporters will be briefed later. Come prepared because you only have 30 minutes before the press conference."

Frankie said she'd be ready and thanked Garrett for the call. She wondered if she was getting special treatment because she was dating Garrett or because she was Alonzo's friend. Indignation rose within her at the thought of being treated differently, as her sense of fairness took over. Now it was The Pirate who stepped in to quash her feelings. "You caught a lucky break. Gratitude is the sign of a noble soul, querida."

Having ducked out to the shop office for the call, Frankie returned to the kitchen, still staring at her phone screen, lost in thought. Carmen looked up from the pie plates she was filling with quiche mixture, concerned. "Do you want to talk about it, Frankie?"

Frankie set the phone down and began methodically moving baked quiches to the cooler. "Hm. That was Garrett. Autopsy report is in. I'm supposed to view it at 2:00 this afternoon."

"That's good, right? What you've been waiting for?" Frankie nodded at her friend. "Then what gives?"

"Oh, it's Alonzo. He wants this to be professional, formal, you know? Like I'm a stranger or something." Frankie sounded perturbed.

Carmen began moving quiches to the ovens. "Well, you wanted to be the hot-shot reporter. Now that's how you're being treated. I mean, what did you expect, Frankie?"

Frankie huffed a little, having just heard the same thing from her two-sided conscience and now her closest friend. "I don't know what I expected. It just feels weird. Makes me wonder if Alonzo and I will ever be the same, you know?"

"Give it time, Frankie. Your relationship is changing, evolving. That doesn't mean it's a bad thing. I think you should be excited about sinking your teeth into this report. You know, you need to get your head in the right place."

Carmen was one hundred percent correct about that. "But now I'm not sure what to wear," Frankie said, a bit huffily, as Carmen burst into laughter.

"I'm sorry. What were you planning to wear before the sheriff decided to treat you like a member of the press?" She tried to stifle another giggle then decided to be more helpful since Frankie shot her a dirty look. "Well, you can't wear jeans. That's too informal. And a Bubble and Bake shirt is out of the question," she was perusing Frankie's current outfit. "A dress makes it look like you're trying too hard. Change into some church slacks and a casual top. You can't look like you're going on a date, either, so maybe a polo or button shirt." Carmen rested her case, and Frankie went upstairs to change.

She returned in black slacks and a red long-sleeve v-neck top with a placket of crossed gray laces down the front, looking somewhat nautical. Carmen nodded her approval, and Frankie headed out the back door, tablet and notebook in hand, just in case the wifi in the concrete block sheriff's building wasn't functioning on all cylinders today.

As Frankie expected, Garrett and Alonzo were waiting in the conference room when Shirley Lazaar ushered her through the door then closed it and took a seat to join them. Frankie supposed she was happy Donovan Pflug wouldn't be present. He always had a way of making her nervous or angry, or both.

Alonzo nodded his hello to Frankie then slid a copy of the report across the table toward her. Garrett, Shirley, and Alonzo each had their own copies for reference.

The first note indicated the cause of death: renal failure. Frankie tried to control her facial expressions but felt more certain than ever that Emily had the same kidney disease that had taken her mother's life.

She continued reading, logging away the initial information. Two narratives followed, one on the external exam, the other on the internal. Frankie assessed the narrative as a normal detailed recording of the process, so she moved on to the lab data.

Of note, the urine contained the chemical Polyethylene glycol 3350, which didn't mean anything to Frankie except that the report indicated high levels of the compound. She knew she would need to ask where such a chemical came from.

Moving on, the liver panel showed small amounts of Tanacetum vulgare, but the narrative noted this was "unremarkable." Still, Frankie intended to find out what the Latin term meant, as it seemed familiar to her somehow.

A high amount of Methyl salicylate was found in the digestive system. *So, Emily died from something she ate?* Frankie mused. She returned to the internal exam to find that only a small amount of undigested food was removed from the stomach.

The final opinion was inconclusive yet suspicious, stating multiple potential causes of death, including the chemicals mentioned in the urine and digestive analyses, combined with the decedent's advanced renal disease. The time of death was between 2100 and 2300 hours.

Reading the report a second and third time, Frankie looked up at Alonzo, who was watching her with a sort of amused expression, making her feel prickly. Her gaze turned to Garrett, who just looked tired but also ready to answer Frankie's questions. Ignoring Alonzo entirely, she turned her body away from him and directed her questions to Garrett.

She began with the fancy chemical names, learning that Polyethylene glycol 3350 was most commonly found in over-the-counter laxative, while Methyl salicylate was found in Wintergreen oil, most commonly in topical pain relievers, like BenGay or Icy Hot. Frankie's red flags were popping up everywhere now.

"So, somehow she ate Icy Hot or something like it?" she asked. Garrett shrugged.

"Well, that doesn't seem likely. With the strong aroma

and flavor, it seems likely Emily would have noticed that in her food and not eaten it," Garrett suggested. Shirley Lazaar nodded to confirm.

Frankie tried to conjure up the bedroom scene where she was allowed inside for observation. The only scent she recalled was the evergreen fragrance common in Emily's house, as it was her favorite. She jotted on her tablet: *Could the evergreen scent have been masking the Wintergreen oil?* "Well, what about in her tea?" Frankie asked.

Shirley and Garrett both nodded approvingly at Frankie's inquiry. "Maybe. We're going to have to go through the mansion again," Shirley admitted.

Frankie resumed. "Okay. Next question: Emily had a chronic kidney disease?" All three officers nodded. "What kind of treatment was she receiving for it? Dialysis?"

Shirley Lazaar took the lead. "Not dialysis, although she was getting ready for it. She had the equipment at her house in an adjoining room. But, we talked to her doctor, and he indicated she was on an experimental medication to help build red blood cells, another to assist with eliminating potassium and another to control blood pressure. Of course, the laxative rid her system of these medications."

Frankie jumped on the information. "So, why would she even take a laxative? That was so risky, considering her condition." Trying to keep pace with Shirley's monologue, Frankie frantically tapped the medication details onto the tablet, followed by her own question about the laxative.

Frankie quickly diverted her question path before

the precious 30 minutes was up. "Where did you find the body?" She hated calling Emily "the body" but knew that now was not the time to be emotional.

Again Shirley answered she was found in her bed.

"What condition was the bed in? I mean, were there fluids on her sheets?" Frankie swallowed hard to stay technical, detached.

"Yes. Plenty of fluids. Including on her pajama bottoms," Shirley answered.

"And on her pajama top?" Frankie asked.

"No fluids or residues on the top, no," Shirley stated.

"Had she called anyone that evening?" Frankie wanted to know.

Alonzo broke in. "Yes, there was one call, around 8:00 p.m. to her treating physician. Before you ask, he didn't answer. Dr. Barnard was at the Performing Arts Center in Appleton with his wife." Frankie wondered if Alonzo disclosed the doctor's name intentionally; there was no way he would make a professional slip-up.

"Did he call her back afterwards? Oh, did she leave a message?" Frankie asked.

Garrett grinned, as Frankie was digging. Alonzo said no message was left and the doctor called back the next morning at 7:00 a.m., but of course she was already deceased.

Alonzo rose from his chair, looking at the clock. "We have to wrap this up, Frankie. You're welcome to head downstairs to the main lobby for the press conference.

Maybe someone else will ask a good question, and you can pick up some additional information." Frankie wondered if Lon was making fun of her, but again, that was not his style.

Garrett ushered her down the back stairs, which allowed her to enter the lobby without anyone seeing she had come via the second floor. Clearly, Alonzo didn't want anyone to know Frankie had had a private viewing of the report before others.

She spotted Abe Arnold from *The Watch* immediately, as he stood several inches above most people. There were only a few other reporters there from the area, most armed with recorders to catch exact words. There were no TV cameras, but there were photographers.

Frankie chastised herself for not bringing her good camera and settled for using her cell phone to take a photo of Alonzo before using the same cell phone to record the conference. She felt like a rookie once again. At least she would scoop the TV stations, who wouldn't pick up the story until tomorrow at the earliest.

Alonzo read an official statement from the autopsy report to the press but answered nearly every question with, "I cannot comment right now due to the ongoing investigation." At least Frankie knew the department was going to treat Emily's death as a possible homicide until the investigation was completed. And that information gave Frankie a license to delve into her own fact-finding mission.

Chapter 13

Ambition is a gilded misery, a secret poison, a hidden plague, the engineer of deceit, the mother of hypocrisy, the parent of envy, the original of vices, the moth of holiness, the blinder of hearts, turning medicines into maladies, and remedies into diseases.
– Thomas Brooks

After calling Magda, Frankie wrote a brief article, sticking to the information Alonzo released at the official press conference, and emailed it to *Point Press*. In her phone conversation, she told Magda she would be looking into potential suspects and talking with folks who knew Emily. Magda approved, hoping the *Press* would be the first to report new findings.

"But, be careful Frankie. Don't take any unnecessary risks. And, be sure to keep me informed." Magda was relentless and ambitious. She didn't intend to be a regional editor forever. Frankie could read around Magda's words; she was expected to take *necessary* risks and to figure out which risks were necessary to get the scoop.

Frankie searched the internet for Tanacetum vulgare, which had shown up in trace amounts in Emily's liver panel. She nodded in recollection as the search yielded the common name, Tansy, a perennial plant found almost everywhere in their area.

Tansy was often used in the garden to control insects, but she soon discovered that the oil could be lethal if taken internally. Additionally, one article warned users not to confuse this Tansy with Blue Tansy oil, commonly used in diffusers for its calming properties and as an antihistamine. Blue Tansy is not toxic. Frankie's fingers drummed the countertop. *How did tansy oil come to be in Emily's liver?* The only two people who came to mind with access to Tansy oil were Mack Perry and Alana West. She didn't like to think that either of them could have knowingly given the oil to Emily.

She wasted no time calling Shirley Lazaar. "Hi, Shirley. This is Frankie Champagne. I was looking up Tanacetum vulgare - you know from the autopsy - and I wondered if the department collected any of the loose teas Emily Spurgeon had in her kitchen cupboard?"

Shirley confirmed that samples of the teas were collected just that afternoon, following the autopsy findings. Frankie admired Shirley's thoroughness. Having been an officer for years in the Chicago PD, Shirley - Frankie suspected - had seen it all and knew to cover all the bases. Shirley added, "There's a lot of different herbs in those teas, though, and it could take a long time to test every one of them."

"May I suggest you start by talking to Alan

Christensen? He's the local herb expert around here. If you take the teas to him, I bet he can narrow down which ones to have tested. Just a thought," Frankie wanted to be helpful. Besides, there could be more in those teas than Tansy oil. Emily had high levels of Wintergreen oil in her system, and she drank tea every day.

"Hm. It's a bit unconventional, but I'll run it past the boss. Thanks. By the way, word on the street is that the funeral will be Monday." Shirley clicked off.

Frankie had missed morning yoga with her mother, so the two decided to meet for the five o'clock class with Quiver Royce. Unlike Fuji, their normal Yogi, Quiver was less forgiving when it came to modifications for the less flexible. She often said things like, "Your body is yearning to open like a butterfly." And, "Don't let your brain get in the way of your serpent energy."

Frankie wanted to understand Quiver's silky comments, but she felt like she missed the Yoga train. However, an hour later, anointed with wild orange, basil and bergamot oils, Frankie was feeling focused and renewed.

"Mom, do you happen to know a Dr. Barnard?" Frankie queried, on the off chance the versatile Peggy Champagne might know him.

Peggy raised both eyebrows, questioningly. "Do you mean Fitz Barnard? He's the president of the Historical Society. Are you feeling okay, honey?" Leave it to a mother to automatically think the worst.

"Yes, I'm fine, Mother. I'm not sure if that's the Dr. Barnard I'm asking about, but maybe. What kind of doctor is he?" Frankie wanted to know.

"Well, he's a local of sorts. He practices in Madison but lives in Whitman County. He's young, so he's building his resume, if you get my meaning. I think that's why he became involved in the historical society. He's trying to gain some notoriety."

Peggy prided herself on her ability to accurately assess others. "Would you like to meet him? Come to our meeting tonight and see for yourself. It starts at seven. Open to the public." That said, Peggy excused herself so she could go home and change for the meeting, which would be held at the historic Sterling Creek Grist Mill, now a Bed and Breakfast, on Sunset Avenue.

An hour later, Frankie, back in her press conference outfit, stepped into the lovely dark red and fieldstone mill and was welcomed by owners Sam and Nicole Beachem. The couple purchased the mill a couple of years ago, relocated from a suburb of Chicago, and were looking forward to their second full tourist season in business. Frankie was acquainted with them from Chamber of Commerce meetings and their patronage at the wine lounge, but she had not been in the renovated Grist Mill until now.

Nicole took Frankie and a few others on the tour, revealing five bedroom/bath combinations decorated rustically in a 1950's farmhouse style. Frankie admired

Nicole's taste in decor, and enjoyed the sample baked goods she offered at the meeting from the B and B's menu.

Frankie took a seat near the back of the meeting area, hoping to avoid any probing eyes, while she observed the Society President in action. It was obvious to Frankie that Dr. Barnard had ambitious plans for the Society, including preserving the former Hensen Mercantile building on Granite Street and the former Johnson Livery and Blacksmith shop on Kilbourn.

Both buildings were vacant and needed extensive structural repairs. While many members supported the doctor's ideas, the Society had limited resources to support them. Dr. Barnard shrugged off their worries and criticism, saying the upcoming fundraisers, especially the art auction, were sure to be profitable.

After the business of the night was completed, Peggy veered her daughter in the direction of Dr. Barnard, who was conversing with one of Frankie's least favorite citizens, real estate developer Bram Callahan. Bram seemed to have his fingers in every money-making pie in the county, and while that was certainly no crime in Frankie's mind, she didn't like his lofty, self-important attitude. Peggy edged over toward Bram, cutting him off physically by placing herself between the two men, as she procured two drinks from the refreshment table. Frankie smiled inwardly at her mother's tactical maneuvers.

"Fitz, I'd like to introduce you to my daughter, Francine. She's new to the historical society," Peggy said, giving Frankie a nudge toward the doctor. Frankie was surprised at how young the man was, guessing he could not be long out of medical school. She thought she might be able to use his age to gain the upper hand.

"Hello, Ms. Champagne. Nice to meet you. I enjoy your mother's historical knowledge on so many subjects. She's better than Wikipedia." Frankie hoped Dr. Barnard didn't rely on Wikipedia for his professional research. She filed away the comment for the time being, hoping to cut right to the chase. But, the doctor continued, "So, you're interested in becoming a member of the society? We are always looking for new members, and we can use your help with the upcoming fundraisers." The last thing Frankie wanted to do was add a commitment to her already full plate, so she bluntly switched topics.

"Dr. Barnard, I was acquainted with Emily Spurgeon. In fact, we were becoming friends. I feel terrible about her death." Frankie allowed the opening comment to hang there, waiting to see his reaction. She had caught the doctor off guard for certain.

"Oh, well, yes, it was unexpected." He looked uncomfortable, shifted his feet, and looked around the room, perhaps for an escape route.

Frankie quickly switched gears. "I'm sorry. I'm sure you weren't expecting to discuss Emily. How do you like Deep Lakes? Have you lived here long?"

"Deep Lakes is charming. Of course, my practice is in Madison, but I used to come here often when I was growing up, so it's like a second home to me. And it's full of history and architectural treasures worth preserving and highlighting." Frankie contrived to steer the conversation to get some answers to her questions.

"Can I ask you a few questions about Emily, please?" Frankie sounded sad and a little desperate, so Dr. Barnard nodded, leading her by the arm onto the back deck, overlooking the creek. Frankie continued. "I know Emily had kidney disease, and I know she was on several medications. Was dialysis inevitable?"

Dr. Barnard sighed and hesitated, as if to answer her would be a violation of patient-doctor privacy. "Well, with any kidney disease, dialysis is almost always inevitable." He chose the safe detached answer.

"Yes," Frankie prodded, "I suppose. Does that mean the medication wasn't effective?"

"Yes and no." There was that medical response again. "The medication just postponed dialysis for as long as possible. Emily was hoping for a more permanent solution."

Frankie was confused. "Permanent solution?"

"A kidney transplant would have potentially allowed her to live a fairly normal life without dialysis," the doctor stated, as if giving a lecture to a first-year class. Frankie tried to disguise her amazement, filing away the potential clue for later.

"Can you tell me why Emily would call you the night she died, instead of calling 911?" Frankie asked, boldly, not choosing a careful path.

Dr. Barnard's face flashed anger initially, then serious consideration. "Why would you ask that? How did you know that?" He demanded. Frankie regretted her question. She didn't want to reveal her intentions.

"I was at the press conference earlier today. Any information you can give me will help me understand better what happened to Emily. You know her death is suspicious. You know it's being investigated, Doctor." Frankie had to be an honest operator. It wasn't in her nature to be underhanded.

The doctor's expression was narrowed and grim. "So, I guess this means I'm going to have the press at my door until this is wrapped up, huh? Look, I'm not too happy about this, Ms. Champagne. I don't think I should say anything to you or any reporter." He turned to walk back into the dining room. Frankie ventured an opinion.

"Emily was reclusive. She wouldn't have liked going to Madison for doctor appointments or dialysis. That's why she had the equipment set up at her home. Did you come to the mansion for appointments?" Dr. Barnard nodded. Frankie continued. "Did you bring an assistant, a nurse? I can't imagine a busy doctor would have time to sit through dialysis; someone else would be administering that." Frankie hoped the doctor would be flattered she considered him too important to spend that much time away from his practice.

"Well, you're right, of course. I only came to the mansion because I live just outside of town. It was easy for me to come at the end of my work day. And, yes, I was training Emily's assistant for dialysis procedures." Frankie was getting somewhere.

"Do you mean Alana West?"

"Of course. She is an LPN and perfectly equipped to assist with dialysis."

Then Dr. Barnard was gone, leaving Frankie alone on the deck, gazing at the dark ripples on the creek. Frankie glowed inwardly at the discovery of another potential clue. Frankie hadn't known Alana was an LPN, but that meant she would have detailed knowledge about Emily's illness, medications, and treatment. Alana may also know why Emily took a laxative the night she passed away.

And the kidney transplant? Well, that was one good reason for Emily to locate her cousin Cordelia, a potential donor.

The Golden One tsked, weighing in on the thought. "I thought you were fond of Emily. Now you're practically accusing her of having an ulterior motive for reuniting with her cousin! Hmph!"

Frankie wanted to think the best of Emily, of course, but what was so wrong with having two reasons to reunite with Cordelia? Besides, Cordelia broke ties with Emily in the first place, didn't she?

Peggy's hand on Frankie's arm interrupted her musings. "Well, how did it go, dear? Did you find out anything useful?"

Frankie nodded and sighed. "I believe I did, Mother,

but I may have hurt your position in the society. I don't think Dr. Barnard was happy at all with my questions or my impertinence." Frankie meant what she said but couldn't help letting out a little laugh. To her surprise, Peggy let out a laugh of her own.

"You don't need to worry about me. I can hold my own with Fitz Barnard. I have experience on my side, plus I know everyone in Deep Lakes. I helped him get elected president. Once I saw how ambitious he was and how often his ego needed feeding, it seemed like a good fit for the society's future. My guess is that Dr. Barnard will feather his nest in Deep Lakes, then seek out larger, greener pastures elsewhere."

Peggy's comments made Frankie wonder if Dr. Barnard's ambitions included some shady behavior toward Emily. After all, gaining the Granite Mansion and its contents for the historical society would certainly help the doctor make a name for himself. Perhaps the upcoming art auction fundraiser would feature items from the mansion. The society was going to need all the money it could raise for the aspiring projects Barnard had in mind. Frankie intended to add a Post-it note with Fitz Barnard's name on it to her suspect board when she got home.

Chapter 14

Geologists have a saying – rocks remember.
- Neil Armstrong

Beware of the scorpion that rests under the rock.
- Greek Proverb

Frankie woke up from a sound sleep to her singing phone. The call was from Bountiful Fruits, and her heart started thumping in her chest.

"Hello!" her voice held a note of panic.

"Good morning, Frankie. It's just Zane. Nothing to worry about here." At least Zane Casey was able to detect worry and fear in the human voice, something Nelson may have missed.

"Then why are you calling this early, Zane? Don't you have a class this morning?" Frankie managed a glance at her bedroom clock radio - 5:00 a.m. "What are you doing out at the lab at five in the morning anyway?"

Zane laughed nonchalantly. "I fell asleep here last night, looking for digital dirt on that Grant Foster dude."

"And I'm guessing you found something, Zane?"

"You bet I did. Talk about a poser; this guy's a gambool

fool with a supposed list of fame names in his pocket, but he's a real fakey." Frankie wondered if she was dreaming because she had no idea what Zane just said.

"Zane, are you drinking those energy shots again? Could you please repeat that, only in English for the middle-aged."

Zane explained that there was no Grant Foster. In fact, it was hard to discern Foster's real name. It appeared during his maybe two-year history with Cordelia, he was using the name Rex Findlay and Grant Foster; both men posed as attorneys for a potentially fake law firm in Philadelphia. Foster was reportedly a gambler and a grifter, careful to avoid the spotlight or any camera equipment.

Zane had patched together bits and pieces from the last several years using "a friend's" hacking skills, a fact Frankie filed away for later to question whether the "hacking skills" were legal and traceable. Most of Foster's traces were found in Atlantic City.

"From what I'm seeing here, though, Frankie, I think Cordelia knows who Foster is. I'm sure they're working together to get some big green."

Frankie understood, but when pressed, Zane admitted he had no proof. So, Cordelia might just think Foster is a real lawyer. Still, she added the information to her Post-it note board. It was time for Frankie to visit her old bosses at Dickens and Probst to ask about Emily's will.

After spending the next two hours in the bakery

kitchen, Frankie left Bubble and Bake in the capable hands of Aunt CeCe doing front-of-house sales. Tía Pepita and Jovie manned the kitchen baking for what was certain to be a big Saturday morning. Tess would be in later to work the wine lounge along with Frankie and Carmen.

Frankie headed East on the familiar Highway 40 to the small town of Gibson, where she had worked as a legal assistant several years while raising Sophie and Violet. Mostly a blue-collar community, Gibson was home to two large factories and a few small ones, but the downtown was unremarkable, except for a seasonal flea and farmers' market.

Turning from Main Street onto Henry Street made Frankie perk up, however. The old large homes on Henry Street were now mostly turned into boutique shops, artist galleries, and B and B's. Her bosses had started the trend, turning a classic Victorian boarding house into the law firm Frankie called her favorite job . . . before running Bubble and Bake, that is.

She parked on the street and bounded up the front steps to the painted wooden wrap-around porch, and pushed heavily on the varnished oak and stained glass door to enter the reception area. Since her last visit here, the area had been updated, but carefully, so as to remain in the Victorian tradition. A new receptionist, Brenda, greeted Frankie with a smile and offer of help.

"I'm Frankie Champagne. I used to work for Dickens and Probst. I was hoping I could speak with one of them?"

Frankie smiled at Brenda and hoped she wasn't being too forward.

Brenda beamed as if the First Lady had just walked into the office. She came out from behind her desk to shake Frankie's hand warmly. "Oh, Ms. Champagne. It's so nice to meet you. You're a legend in this office. I'll tell Mr. Dickens you're here."

Brenda was back in a flash with Ward Dickens two steps behind her. Frankie had seen Ward now and then at community events, and she honestly believed he'd never aged a day since she'd left the law firm. He was still athletically built with perfect posture, and his dark hair had a little graying on the sides, but his eyes still sparkled a deep gray, sharp as ever. The only sign of aging was where the silver mustache and goatee had overtaken the dark hair.

He smiled warmly at Frankie and held both of her hands in his. Ward Dickens had helped Frankie out of many scrapes, handled her real estate sale, and set up her business plan. He also handled Frankie's father's estate and the settlement of her house fire with the neighbor's insurance company. For all of these reasons, Ward held hero status in Frankie's eyes.

"Come on. Let's go talk in my office, Frankie," Ward offered, gesturing with one hand to lead the way. Frankie left bakery treats with Brenda, who promised to set them out in the office kitchen.

Ward's office hadn't changed much since Frankie left the firm. It was still bright with a bay window overlooking the cottage garden. The whole office had a beach vibe, decorated in sea green, dark blue and cream, not the typical masculine colors of most law offices Frankie had seen. Frankie noticed Ward was dressed in cream slacks and sky blue golf shirt, so he wouldn't be in court today.

Frankie began the banter. "What's this 'Frankie is a legend around here' business, anyway, Ward?"

He chuckled. "We still use many of your documents as examples for the new paralegals to follow, Frankie. What can I say? You're a good writer. Anyway, what's on your mind? I get the feeling you're here for some information." Ward's eyes crinkled to match his smile.

Frankie didn't intend to waste his time with small talk. "I saw Emily Spurgeon's will and noticed it was prepared here." Ward didn't look surprised.

"So, you have questions. Shoot. I'll see if I can help."

Frankie knew she'd have to ask the right questions worded just so, or Ward wouldn't be able to answer. "I get the feeling this will replaced an older one, seeing that a new trust fund was established for Alana West in 2016."

Ward nodded, adding nothing. Frankie continued. "So, tell me what The Ranch in Texas is. I mean, all of Emily's estate is tied to Wisconsin in some way except for this Texas Ranch. Why?"

Ward looked serious. "You're sharp, Frankie, and you're asking the right questions, but I have to protect the privacy of that particular trustee, so I can't tell you."

"You know that Emily's death is looking like homicide,

right? Come on, Ward. I want to help Emily." Frankie explained the recent connection she'd made with Emily, along with her suspicions about Cordelia and Foster. She confided to Ward she wasn't certain about Mack Perry's or Alana's innocence either. "Can't you give me anything useful?"

Ward leaned back in his leather armchair and sighed. "Having money makes life more complicated most of the time, that's for sure. What I can tell you is this: you might find some answers in the old lawsuit files in the attic. We represented the plaintiffs with quarry sickness in 1985. I can have Brenda take you upstairs, if you have the time."

Frankie nodded enthusiastically. It was worth a shot. Before she followed Brenda up the back hall staircase, Ward threw out one last comment. "About The Ranch, Frankie. Open your mind up to other possibilities. It's not a horse or cattle ranch."

"So, some other kind of animal then?" Frankie threw back.

Ward shook his head. "Other things need care, too." Then Ward was gone.

Frankie was not amused. Why did it have to be so difficult to get straight answers anyway?

She entered a large attic area in the house that was largely unfinished. The room smelled like an old library, which was one of Frankie's favorite comfy smells, so she didn't mind. One dormer window overlooked Henry Street. Against the back wall, file boxes were stacked by year, some by case name if the case was a big enough one. A large work desk and black office chair sat on the unfinished floorboards along with a goose-neck adjustable floor lamp. A yellow legal pad sat on the desktop, hanging out with a few pens and paper clips.

"I hope you find what you're looking for," Brenda shrugged, having no idea what Frankie might be doing with decades-old file boxes. "We close at four, but I'll check on you if you like. Can I bring you some coffee? We've got an excellent machine." Brenda brightened as Frankie agreed that coffee would be welcome.

Frankie located the "Quarry Sickness" files with no difficulty and began looking for helpful labels. There were medical records and depositions, which she skipped for the present, hoping to find a case summary file that would name the plaintiffs.

The fourth manilla file was thin and labeled, "Complaint." Yes, this would give Frankie the names of the plaintiffs and description of the suit.

There were three plaintiffs named on the complaint: The Estate of Fritz Kuhn, The Estate of José Gomez, and The Estate of Iain Perry. Frankie drew in a sharp breath. She had heard Tía Pepita and Carmen talk of the Gomez family, but now she wondered if Iain Perry was related to Mack Perry?

The Defendants in the complaint were listed as not only Deep Lakes Granite Works Quarry but also the owners, Elmer Spurgeon and Edgar McCoy. Filing suit against a business is normal, but to include the owners by name made it personal, and it meant, if found liable, the owners could lose their fortunes as well as their assets. Frankie took a picture of the document's pages.

The complaint claimed the quarry and its owners were directly responsible for the deaths of the three named men due to the negligent practices and disregard for the use of safety equipment and safety standards in place for industries at the time of their deaths or diagnosed illnesses.

The medical records file was thicker, but that was because all three men's records were contained in one file. Although it was the 1980s, doctors were reluctant to tie lung diseases to workplaces in many cases. Silicosis, caused by inhaling crystalline silica dust, was a known disease for centuries, even mentioned in ancient documents as miner's disease.

Skimming the medical records, Frankie found much of the same information. Symptoms of the disease included chronic respiratory issues, chronic cough, shortness of breath, labored breathing, fatigue, chest pain, and fever. Little to no treatment existed. None of the physicians would go on record stating that the quarry work was the cause of the chronic lung condition, and none of the records ever used the term "quarry sickness."

While Mr. Perry and Mr. Gomez continued to work at the quarry, even after getting sick, Mr. Kuhn died within weeks of being diagnosed. Gomez and Perry were not diagnosed until after the quarry closed. In fact, Mr.

Gomez was diagnosed post-mortem, after dying from injuries in an explosion at the quarry right before it closed for good. Mr. Perry died in 1984, the same year the quarry shut down.

Frankie next reviewed the testimonies given by each of the three wives at formal depositions. Heart-wrenchingly, Mrs. Kuhn, Gomez, and Perry were asked about and then delivered the gruesome details of their husbands' suffering: the painful coughing spells, which were drawn-out and often bloody episodes, lack of sleep due to discomfort, weight loss, and constant fatigue.

All three men showed little interest in daily life or family activities. The women described activities the men couldn't do with their children, birthdays and holidays the men missed from being too sick, and the physical and emotional changes witnessed in the men they loved.

The wives further testified to extra expenses as a direct result of the illness, including repair work on houses, cars, and property that had to be hired out since their husbands were too ill to do the work themselves. Sadly, the women also testified the men were cigarette smokers, a factor that would lead to the dismissal of their claims.

Another deposition from a state safety expert explained that it was common for quarry stonecutters to lack adequate respiratory equipment to use on the job, although such equipment existed.

Spurgeon and McCoy each admitted their stonecutters did not use respiratory equipment, nor did they provide said equipment. But, neither of them admitted to knowing said equipment existed either. Still, this testimony must have weighed heavily against the quarry owners, yet it wasn't enough for the Court to grant relief to the families.

The physicians' testimonies did not aid the families either. Silicosis is often latent, appearing years later, meaning it's hard to directly connect it to an event, location, or specific time period. Spurgeon's and McCoy's lawyers knew which questions to ask and how to ask them, so the doctors could not specifically state that prolonged exposure to silica dust was the cause of the men's deaths, especially since the plaintiffs were smokers.

Silicosis generally progresses faster when accompanied by smoking, so the sick person bears a good deal of personal liability. It's impossible to separate the disease into proportional causes: how much is the fault of smoking, and how much is the fault of the quarry dust?

If the case had gone to trial, a jury would have had the task of determining a percentage of blame and assigning a number to the men and to the quarry. Only then could relief be awarded in proportion to the quarry's negligence.

Dicky Bryant, who represented the families, must have seen the odds were stacked against them and accepted dismissal of the claims before the added expense of a trial. Frankie smiled thinly to see that the law firm had waived all of its legal fees for the families, a small compensation of sorts, she supposed.

Feeling weary and downtrodden about the three families, Frankie skipped a few files in the box, looking for the final judgment. There it was in the last thin manilla file: two pieces of paper dismissing the claims of the three families with prejudice based on the findings of fact made in discovery. There would be no monetary award to the families, no medical payments, and no future legal recourse. The cases against Deep Lakes Granite Works, Elmer Spurgeon, and Edgar McCoy were a dead end.

Not until 1996 did the International Agency for Cancer Research classify crystalline silica as a carcinogen to humans. Frankie's eyes welled with tears thinking about the three families, a small representation of who knows how many others, who died from work-related diseases.

By now it was almost noon. A passing cloud blotted the sun briefly. Frankie began stuffing files back into the box on the wooden floor, accidentally pulling out an unread folder as she stuffed another into it. This file was titled "family members," causing gears in her brain to click sharply. *How dumb could I be to almost miss this file? Survivors would certainly have motive to want Emily Spurgeon dead.*

She practically ripped the folder with shaking hands as if she might discover definitive answers in black and white. Ignoring pangs of tightness in her knees, she began reading lists of names under each family title, including dates of birth.

The Kuhns had a daughter, Anna, born in 1964. Frankie calculated her age at 20 when her father died. Adult children over the age of 18 did not have a claim since they reached what the law termed "age of majority."

She moved on to the Perry family. There it was in black and white: a son, Mackenzie, born in 1959. Well, Mack Perry had no claim for relief under the law either. No other children were listed under the Perry name.

On to the Gomez family. A son, José Jr., was born in 1970. That information jibed with Tía Pepita's story that José Jr. was 15 when he went to work at the quarry after his father died. There were also two daughters listed under the Gomez family: Amelia, born in 1979, and Marta, born in 1984.

Frankie tried to imagine Mrs. Gomez coping with losing her husband and, soon after, her son, while raising two young girls alone - one, just a baby. The Gomez children would legally all have claims for relief against the quarry, if the case had been successful. She wondered where the daughters were now.

Rising from her sore, cracking knees, she laid the list of names on the desk and snapped a photo. Her bouncy spring mindset had been replaced by gloom, and she felt oddly alone and cold in the warm attic. It seemed as if the fireflies had left her to her own devices, too. She looked at the phone. It was 12:10 p.m. She needed to leave behind the file box and reset her mood. She hadn't recorded a single word on paper or her tablet, just taken photos of documents and immersed her silent mind into the contents of the files.

Walking stiffly down the attic's narrow stairs to the curving, wide, grand staircase, Frankie found the law office was strangely quiet. She went to the front desk to thank Brenda, but she wasn't there.

About to exit the front door, she mechanically reached for her SUV keys, but they weren't in the familiar front pocket of her bag. She hoped she hadn't left them in the attic; her body winced in pain at the thought of a second three-story climb. *I'll just check in Ward's office first.*

She headed back down the hallway to the large corner office and poked her head around the door. It was empty, and her keys were right where she'd set them on Ward's large walnut desk. Some magical, or possibly nosey, instinct kicked Frankie's senses into high gear as she looked at the files lying on Ward's desktop.

The Golden One had returned from lunch apparently. "This is not your desk, Miss BusyBody."

Frankie employed the warning she had used on her children many times: it's okay to look, but don't touch. Obviously not an adequate excuse for Goldie, she continued buzzing in Frankie's ear.

Thank goodness The Pirate countered, cheering Frankie on. "Go ahead, chérie, you might find something helpful."

That was enough encouragement for the moment. Frankie noticed a document lying on the top, which she scanned, but didn't pick up. It was a codicil to a will, and not just any will either: Emily Spurgeon's will. A yellow Post-it was stuck to the margin with a note. Frankie didn't pause but instead pulled her phone from her pocket and clicked a photo.

"Well, you're obviously headed for a life of crime, Francine," Goldie spoke harshly.

"I'm leaving, and I'm not even going to look under that paper. See? I didn't *touch* anything!" Frankie found herself speaking out loud and stomping her foot.

At that moment Brenda appeared in the office doorway. "Did you say something?" she asked, followed by, "What are you doing in Mr. Dickens' office anyway?"

A guilty Frankie muddled up her response by making Brenda believe it was her fault. "You weren't out front at your desk . . . and I left my car keys here." She held up the keys in one hand, giving them a little shake.

Brenda looked contrite. "Oh, sorry. I was warming up my lunch in the kitchen. Are you staying for lunch, or can I get you something to eat?" Brenda certainly was good at providing customer service, Frankie thought.

"No, thank you. I was coming to tell you that I'm finished. I need to get back to my shop. Friday night, you know . . . very busy." Frankie thanked Brenda again for her time, assuring her she left the file box and attic in good order. Frankie drove the 12 miles back to Deep Lakes, resisting the urge to look at the photo of that codicil all the way back.

*   *   *

Summer-like weather in April brought people out of their winter doldrums in droves, making for brisk business Friday night that sprawled into all day Saturday. The Bubble and Bake pastry case was bare except for crumbs and stray icing, and the wine lounge needed restocking from the shop basement before Sunday.

Frankie felt exhausted for the first time in months, but it was a good exhaustion. The shop made money Friday night and Saturday, and that's what business was all about.

Highlighting Frankie's evening, Garrett showed up with grilled chicken and Mediterranean vegetable skewers from the new bistro on Sunset and an inviting smile to boot. He'd guessed correctly that Frankie'd had little time to eat during business hours.

They finished off the evening on the Bubble and Bake deck, crooner tunes playing softly in the background as they ate, sipped glasses of Two Pear Chardonnay (Garrett's particular favorite wine), and chatted. Knowing Frankie would be busy Sunday afternoon and helping at Emily Spurgeon's funeral on Monday, he invited her to dinner Monday night.

"What do you say we get out of Deep Lakes for a change of scenery?" His smile suggested he had a plan.

"Ok by me. Got something in mind, Mr. G?" Frankie teased.

"There's a new restaurant in Madison called The Nook. Supposed to be a hot ticket. Lots of creativity by the young chef and locally sourced products. So?"

Garrett had used all the right buzz words on Frankie's checklist, so she nodded enthusiastically but couldn't resist another teasing response.

"Here I was hoping you were going to invite me to the Prairie Chicken Festival in Wisconsin Rapids." Garrett had to admit ignorance of such an event. Bird enthusiast Frankie explained how the once prevalent species could now only be found in central Wisconsin grasslands where they were carefully managed.

"In April, the males make this booming noise, stamping their feet and puffing out jowls that look like brown eggs as they compete for territory; then they do a wild dance for potential mates. It's really quite a site, although I've only seen it on video. Their Latin name translates to 'drummer of love.'"

Seeing Frankie's genuine interest, Garrett responded. "Well, that sounds romantic, Francine; maybe we should go to the Prairie Chicken Festival instead." Garrett's sincerity, pretended or not, made Frankie laugh out loud.

"Well, we should go one day for sure but not this time. Let's go to The Nook," Frankie countered.

Garrett held up a warning finger. "Save your appetite, though, Miss Francine. They serve a six course dinner, no menu options."

Frankie promised she would, mentally noting that

funeral fare wasn't usually her favorite food, and she'd need a nice break after this particular funeral. She leaned over Garrett for a long good night kiss before languidly padding up the steps to her apartment, Liberace in tow, admonishing her in tiny meows that it was way past their bedtime.

Chapter 15

*As for the bitter herbs . . . To see everyone with tears
coursing down their faces, laughing and gasping at the
same time, is fun and also makes the point – bitter herbs
must be really bitter to experience the suffering.*
– Julia Neuberger, Baroness Neuberger

Betrayed by her roaming thoughts, Frankie rose at
1:00 a.m., mindlessly looked out the front window at the
quiet street, and poured a tall glass of cold water from the
refrigerator. Her feet were chilly, so she returned to her
room for the fleece socks she often wore to bed during
the winter months, then headed to her kitchen counter,
perched on a stool, and opened her phone.

She sent the quarry document photos to her email so
she could open them on the tablet and view them on a larger
screen. Right now, she only cared about the document that
wouldn't allow her to get a peaceful sleep: the codicil.

She read the short paper, eyes growing wider line
by line, shook her head, and read it again to be certain
she was awake and reading coherently. The codicil was
drafted by none other than a law firm in Philadelphia
where Grant Foster was the drafting attorney.

The codicil laid out the items that would be transferred to Cordelia McCoy upon the death of her first cousin, Emily Spurgeon. The language was carefully framed, and Frankie imagined Emily sitting at her desk, penning the words personally: *To my darling and only remaining family member, Cordelia McCoy, who made the unselfish sacrifice in donating a kidney to extend my life: I entrust to her the management of Granite Mansion and its contents, along with the trust funds described herein.*

Frankie gasped. So, the donated kidney was a transaction between Emily and Cordelia. She knew the wealthy could be quirky in their desires and plans, but she couldn't imagine such a strange quid pro quo tied to an inheritance. Well, now she understood why Cordelia might agree to a reunion and why Emily sought out her cousin through a legal representative.

Except, Grant Foster wasn't a real lawyer, was he? According to Frankie's intern, he wasn't. If that was true, this codicil wouldn't hold up in court even if the transplant had occurred, which it hadn't. Is that why Cordelia called the clerk to say she would be contesting the will? Frankie looked at the Post-it note on the codicil. In Ward's handwriting it said: *Is Cordelia's kidney a match? Test results pending.*

Her brain continued to pound, unable to focus on a single thought. She wondered if anyone else knew about the codicil. Alana? Mack? If so, both would have something to lose if Cordelia inherited and gained control over trust fund payments that were supposed to be awarded for years to both employees. Under Cordelia's management, would Mack be allowed to stay in the gatehouse?

Then she recalled that the Historical Society would lose a lot, too: instead of a fully furnished mansion that was part of the National Historic Register, the Society would only gain some of the antiquities, not the greatest consolation prize. Did Dr. Fitz Barnard know this?

And what about Cordelia? Would she honestly agree to donate a kidney to prolong the life of her cousin, only to wait years for the money she seemed to be craving right now?

Frankie quickly captured her questions on her suspect board of notes before she lost them in the mind maze she was currently wandering around. Sleep: that was what she needed most, but her brain was on high alert with a pool full of thoughts swimming laps back and forth, up and down.

Remembering the empty bakery case, she decided *might as well get up and bake*. Liberace, who had crept out to the kitchen to see if Frankie was in her right mind since she'd left a perfectly warm bed, stretched, yawned, and peered into his dish under the breakfast bar. Finding it empty, he meowed weakly and padded back to Frankie's bedroom.

Promising to bring Liberace downstairs later, Frankie donned a clean shop apron right over her pj's and began assessing the cooler. She was thrilled to find five empty pie shells, which would make enough quiches for Sunday, since the bakery was closed and the wine shop only opened from noon until six.

Her brain still half asleep, she slogged around the kitchen in slow circles, coming back to the cooler time and time again for forgotten ingredients. Finally, The Golden One ripped off her sleep mask in a huff and told Frankie to make some coffee before she completely ruined the quiches. Goldie did have good ideas once in a while.

Double Shot Latte in hand, Frankie strode over to the portable speaker, turned it on and up, then punched in a playlist from her tablet labeled "wake up tunes." Katrina and The Waves sang "Walking on Sunshine," and Frankie was bouncing along happily to the beat. Now she could tackle those quiches.

Soon, two of Frankie's signature Springtime Quiches with asparagus were sending umami waves of their own throughout the kitchen. She'd prepared one traditionally with bacon but left the bacon out of the second one and swapped the cheddar cheese for gouda. Quiche number three was her This Little Piggy quiche, strictly for meat lovers. She made the last two with cheese and chives, one with garlic cheddar and swiss, the other with havarti dill. By 6:00 a.m., all five were cooling.

She only had about an hour left to prepare a dessert for the funeral tomorrow. She'd already pulled out her grandmother's recipe for Rum Raisin Cake, and raisins, along with some craisins, were already soaking in pineapple rum. Frankie couldn't leave most recipes alone - she loved to experiment - and this one was no different. She used half raisins, half dried cranberries. She used flavored rum in place of the dark rum and coconut cream in place of evaporated milk. She usually iced the cake with a pineapple or coconut frosting she adapted from the tried and true buttercream frosting.

What seemed like just minutes later, Frankie lifted her head off the kitchen counter and stared into the amused faces of Carmen, her mother, and Aunt CeCe. Frankie's cheek was sticky from a bit of stray cake batter, while the cake recipe was stuck to her forehead.

"What are you all doing here? We don't open until noon today," Frankie said in a thick voice while reaching for her phone to check the time.

All three women laughed out loud simultaneously, looking at one another. Frankie felt like she was the only one left out of a good joke. Peggy pretended to sound outraged. "We came to check on you, Frankie. You missed church!"

Frankie was astonished. Hadn't she just taken the cakes out of the oven to cool for 15 minutes, thinking she'd grab a catnap until the timer went off? "I set the timer . . ." she began.

"Oh, we know. It was still going off when we got here." It was Carmen's turn to poke fun at her friend. "Guess you were tired. By the looks of things here, you didn't sleep much last night." Carmen gestured at the dirty dishes and the finished quiches.

Now Frankie was more alert and upset about her cakes. "Oh no! I didn't take the cakes out of the pans. I'm not sure how I'm going to get them out now - they're rum cakes and they needed a soak while they were still warm."

Aunt CeCe came to the rescue. "Never mind, dear. I already have the oven on low so you can put them back in to warm them just a little. You'll be able to get them out of the pan then and pour the rum over them. Why don't I take care of it for you?"

Frankie excused herself for a shower, hoping Choir Director Steve wouldn't be too displeased that she'd missed mass. Since she wasn't even in hot water with her mother, she figured it didn't matter what anyone else thought.

Peggy followed her daughter up the stairs to her apartment, though, so maybe, Frankie thought, she was in trouble after all. Yes, Peggy stood in Frankie's kitchen, hands on her hips, lips pursed. "Well, any special reason you didn't sleep well last night?"

Frankie believed her mother had a direct connection to The Golden One: they could realistically share one mind, Frankie thought. She knew better than to pretend around her mother; Peggy could read her daughter like a three-step recipe. Frankie shared the new information she found out Friday about Grant Foster's identity, the quarry case file, and grudgingly, even the snapshot of the codicil.

Peggy sat down and took one of her daughter's hands in her own well-manicured one. "Good work, Frankie," Peggy said matter-of-factly, her icy blue eyes dancing with pride. "Now, you should go to Alonzo with what you have. There's too much at stake here to try to go it alone, dear."

Frankie nodded in agreement. "I plan to talk to Shirley Lazaar tomorrow, either at or after the funeral. It's too hard to talk to Alonzo. He treats me like a little girl, a little girl who needs a spanking," Frankie amended. "Besides, Shirley is decent about *sharing information* as long as I know how to ask the right questions. Alonzo, well, he just gets irritated with me."

Peggy patted her daughter's hand and excused herself to go home and change clothes. "I'll see you at noon. Or, are you taking the day off? Maybe you have a better place to be . . . like a date, perhaps?" Peggy was never subtle in conversations with Frankie. Being the only daughter in a family with four brothers was highly inconvenient, Frankie decided. Someone was always in her personal business, it seemed.

"Not today. But I do have a hot dinner date tomorrow night," she responded brightly.

Peggy smiled at that bit of information, then tossed a final suggestion over her shoulder. "Put some lotion on those hands, dear. Your job is a hazard to soft skin."

*   *   *

Frankie was back downstairs just after noon. Carmen surprised her with a lunch salad she'd picked up at Festival Foods after church, and the two sat at the back counter together, while Carmen proofed pastry dough for Tuesday.

Both women tried not to do kitchen work on Mondays, especially if they worked on Sunday. It was a good day to get ahead of schedule by making dough and letting it rest in the cooler until Tuesday.

Typically, Carmen shopped for the bakery on Mondays, while Frankie opened neglected mail, worked on accounts, and wrote feature articles for the newspaper. For now the bakery was still closed on Sunday, Monday and Tuesday, but during the summer, it would be open Tuesday through Saturday. The Wine Lounge closed early Sunday but reopened Wednesday at 11:00 a.m. It, too, would be open longer hours for the tourist season. So, no time like the present to try to stay ahead.

Carmen raised a large cucumber chunk to eye level, deciding whether she could manage it all in one bite. "Tell me what you've been up to, Frankie. You must have news about the quarry lady's case, or you wouldn't have baked half the night," Carmen commented, cutting the cuke in half.

Frankie shared the same information she'd just told

her mother with a serious warning. "You absolutely can't tell anyone what I found out. I don't even know if all of it's real or accurate," she finished. Carmen promised not to breathe a word of it, then looked at her friend, conspiratorially. "What is it?" Frankie asked.

"I have an idea! Let's team up at the funeral and do some investigating! You know, like we did at the pastor's funeral last winter?"

Frankie couldn't believe what she was hearing. Carmen wanted to investigate at the funeral? She remembered the last time she wanted Carmen's help investigating: she'd had to drag her to the funeral service. "You, Carmen? You want to help investigate?" Frankie laughed, and Carmen pouted a little, turning back toward her salad. Frankie was immediately sorry.

"I think it's a spectacular idea. Let's see who's there tomorrow, and we can make a plan. Two heads are definitely better than one!" Frankie's words brought a beaming smile back to Carmen's face.

With lunch over, Frankie headed out to the lounge area, admiring the dark wooden plank floors polished to a glossy sheen and took in the view of all the nooks and alcoves filled with Scandinavian designed sofas and chairs sporting colorful, oversized cushions and pillows, perfect for nibbles and conversation.

In one corner, she spied the Buzzards, her Sunday group of older men who gathered to put puzzles together, or play Scrabble, Pinochle, or other card games.

Sometimes they filled two or three tables. Today, there were seven men: three with a barely-begun Scrabble board and four playing Uno with Aunt CeCe. Peggy was picking up empty beer bottles and asking if they needed anything.

Frankie noticed the men were somber today and wondered what was up. She approached Gordy "Red" Robbins, a long-time local barber, who usually teased Frankie mercilessly. "Hey, Red, how's your hair growing these days?" Frankie threw the first punch, poking fun at Red's renowned bald head. Red barely acknowledged Frankie, staring at his cards, his mind evidently in some far-off space.

"Oh, hello, Frankie. Yeah, business is pretty good, I guess," Red managed.

Peggy jabbed Frankie's hip and led her back to the bar area with a couple of empty glasses. She spoke in a low whisper to her daughter.

"They've all been talking about the Spurgeons and the good old days of the quarry operating in town. It seems nostalgia has made them all melancholy. Why don't you change the music to something more modern?"

Frankie nodded, studying the men. She always played Big Band tunes, crooners from the 1950s or traditional country-western music for the Buzzards. But now, she switched to oldies - jukebox and pop hits.

Frankie saw no change on their faces, despite The Big Bopper's booming voice singing "Chantilly Lace." Each man looked far away, deep in his own thoughts. Frankie went back over to the Scrabble game, intent on changing the atmosphere. She did the unthinkable.

"Hey, Hoot! Why don't you play on this "u" tile and make the word *jukebox*?" Frankie suggested, looking at Hoot Tilly's tiles as she leaned over his shoulder. The Buzzards hated interference of any kind in their games, especially anything they considered cheating. Hoot raised watery brown eyes and knotted his bushy brows together in a perfect glare at Frankie. Then, he tipped over his Scrabble tiles and stood up a full foot or more above her.

"Dang it anyway, girl!" Hoot's voice was more of a warbling cry than a bark. "I was saving those tiles for something really big," Hoot announced, then tromped off to the restroom.

Frankie's initial reaction was puzzlement. "I mean the word *jukebox* is worth 77 points." She looked around the table, making a perfectly logical statement. Kurt Schneider raised his neatly trimmed dark gray head, looking a bit forlornly at Frankie over his wire glasses.

"You have to excuse Hoot, Frankie. He's all torn up about Emily Spurgeon's death. Hoot used to be sweet on her," Kurt gave Frankie his version of an encouraging smile, lips curved more downward than upward.

It turned out Kurt had been the crane crew supervisor at the quarry during the 1970s until it closed. Hoot was one of his crew, also a crane operator. Hoot admired Emily, even though he knew he never had a chance to date her. Frankie was intrigued and wondered if the Buzzards could be an untapped source. Maybe they could fill in some details about the Spurgeons and the families who lost loved ones to the quarry.

Hoot returned from the restroom, looking contrite and grateful for the free beer Frankie offered in apology for outing his Scrabble tiles. Yes, both Hoot and Kurt knew Iain Perry, Fritz Kuhn, and José Gomez. Kurt weighed in about the quarry sickness.

"I don't know of any stonecutter or paver that didn't get some kind of sickness from breathing in that granite dust. Even the ones who wore the masks coughed and hacked every day."

Frankie wanted to know more. "What do you mean, wore masks? What kind of masks? I thought the quarry didn't have masks for the men."

Kurt explained the masks were made of paper-like fabric, "Sorta like the ones you see doctors wear or the ones you can buy at the True Value if you're going to do any sanding." Frankie understood.

Kurt added, "They weren't respirators or anything. They didn't do any good keeping the dust away."

"Didn't Elmer Spurgeon and Edgar McCoy know about respirators? Didn't they see how the men were coughing and wheezing from the dust?" Frankie wondered.

Red decided to take up the story. "I remember one time when I was cutting Mr. Spurgeon's hair, we were talking about some of the cutters and pavers. I told him how I wouldn't ever want to work in all that dust, no matter how pretty the granite turned out. Mr. Spurgeon agreed but said he was mighty glad to have such skilled men like Iain, Fritz, and José. He said they were the best workers he had ever had." Frankie didn't think Red's memory was much of a help.

She prodded onward. "That's great, but don't you think the quarry could afford to buy respirators for the cutters?"

Kurt jumped back in to offer his viewpoint. "You see, the problem is that the equipment was expensive, especially for all the men who were exposed to the dust. Then, there are other factors, too. All the jobs at the quarry needed better safety measures and apparatuses. In order to get everything up to standards, it would cost lots of money. It wouldn't be worth it to run the quarry at all. And, that's why it eventually closed."

Frankie frowned. Somehow, even though the reasoning made sense, it still wasn't fair. Throughout the conversation, Hoot looked like a stew pot on a hot burner. Now, he found an entry point in the discussion, and red-faced, his words came out in wet sputters.

"You all don't know how much this hurt Miss Emily her whole life. She felt terrible about those ladies who lost their men. She knew about loss, too. First her mother, then her father. She paid a big price for inheriting that quarry fortune. Her whole life she suffered, felt guilty.

Her whole life," Hoot's words sounded like a haunted echo around the cheerful shop. He sat down, exhausted.

Kurt patted his friend's shoulder. "There, there. It's okay, Hoot. Her suffering's over now. It's all over now."

But Frankie wondered if it was all over now. There was still Cordelia and Mack Perry. Both of them were directly tied to the quarry and its sometimes painful history. Still, she'd heard enough from the Buzzards and decided to check out the other side of the fence to see if the grass was any greener.

She headed next door to Rachel Engebretsen's shop, Bead Me, I'm Yours. The shop was a crafting haven where the Knit Witches met on Sunday afternoons while the men in their lives were playing games at Bubble and Bake. Well, most of the Knit Witches were connected to a Buzzard, that is. The two corresponding Sunday afternoon meetings were the brainstorm of Frankie and Rachel and provided much-needed business for both shops during the usual inactivity of a small town Sunday.

Frankie brought wine or beer over to Rachel's shop for the ladies and took their food orders as well. Unlike the dour atmosphere produced by the Buzzards, the Knit Witches were chatting as fast as their needles were clicking, with three or more conversations going at once.

Esther Brockton looked up from the granny square she was crocheting, a lovely combination of autumn colors. She gave Frankie a little wave, asking if she'd brought any fresh coffee and bakery with her. In her younger years, Esther had been the town's meter maid, writing out parking tickets like a madwoman, decked out in a crisply pressed dark blue skirt and tailored shirt.

The citizens of Deep Lakes knew better than to try to argue their way out of a ticket with Esther. She stood taller than most, especially with her stacked hairdo and patent leather platform boots. In her older years now, Esther had acquired a dowager's hump and walked with a cane, but her mouth was as sassy as ever.

"I'll bring some fresh coffee over in a while and see what I have in the cooler for bakery. It's been a big couple of days, Esther, and the fresh bakery sold out, I'm afraid." Frankie meant to sound congenial, but she had come to Rachel's store on a mission, and she wasn't going to be deterred. So, she ignored the humph and muttering of Esther and sought out the company of Wilma Schneider, Kurt's wife.

Wilma was the retired Whitman County Register of Deeds and knew a little about everything and everyone in the county. Since Kurt had worked so long at Granite Works Quarry, she might be able to share some important information.

"Hi, Wilma. Looks like someone you know is having a baby?" Frankie asked, leaning over Wilma's shoulder to look at the pretty lilac sweater she was knitting.

Wilma smiled broadly, holding up the almost-completed sweater for a better view. "Yes, indeed. My niece is going to be having a baby girl in June. Once this is done, I have a bonnet and booties to add to the set."

Wilma's hands were nimble as ever, a fact Frankie found remarkable, considering she was in her 70s. With the handiwork required of a baker, Frankie imagined her fingers would be gnarled with arthritis by the time she reached 60. She complimented Wilma's knitting skills, the perfectly matched stitches in a lovely honeycomb pattern. Wilma fished beautiful pearl buttons from her knitting bag for Frankie to admire, the finishing touch for the sweater. Baby sweater sets were an old-fashioned tradition, yes, but still a prized possession for most mothers.

"Wilma, can I ask you some questions about Emily Spurgeon?" Frankie pulled up a spare chair, nudging her way between Wilma and Gertie Powell, who appeared to be knitting a scarf for a giant, perhaps? Frankie wanted to ask Gertie what in the world that mass of colorful yarn blocks that hung to the floor and wrapped under her chair could possibly be, but she didn't want to hurt her feelings.

Wilma looked at Frankie, questioning. "What brought that subject up?" she wanted to know. Frankie relayed pieces of the Buzzards' conversation from next door. Wilma nodded. "So, ask away!" she said.

"Did you know Emily? I mean, when she was younger? I wonder what she was like," Frankie admitted.

Frankie conjured a new impression of Emily from Wilma's stories of her younger years when she was outgoing and carefree. "Emily was the hostess with the mostest, so to speak. The mansion had parties for every occasion. Emily sang and played the piano while people danced and sang along. There were board game nights and marathon card games, too. Those were some fun times," Wilma said.

"Of course that all ended after her beloved papa passed away. I think there was too much loss for Emily to handle." Wilma looked sad and thoughtful. The sadness was contagious, but other ladies had their own insights to add to Emily's history.

"Did any of you know Cordelia McCoy, Emily's cousin?" Frankie wondered.

Wearing various facial expressions, Wilma, Gertie, and Esther all said they knew her. All three were stumbling over one another's words until Frankie gestured for them to stop a second.

"Gertie, why don't you go first?" Frankie suggested. Gertie was married to Jim Powell, retired Army sergeant, and affectionately called Ol' Jim by his friends. Since Gertie and Jim were active at the American Legion, Frankie thought her viewpoint might represent a collective opinion.

Gertie's lovely unwrinkled face, belying her true age, was a mask of disgust. "Cordelia McCoy was a spoiled brat. She got anything she wanted or threw a conniption about it. I used to see them around town and church, too. Her parents just gave her everything." Gertie ended with a grunt of disapproval, then began rifling through her bag for a new yarn color to add to the colossal trail she was knitting.

Esther responded to Gertie's assessment of Cordelia. "You have to remember, Gertie, she was just a little girl when she left Deep Lakes. I remember that she followed Emily Spurgeon around like a little lost lamb. They went everywhere together even though Emily was maybe 10 years older than Cordelia. She was almost a second mother to her."

Esther picked up her coffee mug, remembered it was empty, and set it back on the nearby stand, giving Frankie a half-frown. "Besides, Mrs. McCoy wasn't exactly the motherly type. She thought she'd come here from the city and make everything just so. But, you can't change small town folks into cultured city snobs."

Frankie giggled at the stereotypes she encountered time and time again about small town people versus city people. Inwardly, however, she was making plenty of mental notes to add to her profile of Emily and Cordelia.

"What do you think, Wilma?" Frankie asked.

Wilma looked sad and thoughtful again. "I'm not going to say anything about Cordelia, but I know that when she moved away, Emily was not just heartbroken but broken in other ways, too. She wasn't the carefree girl I used to see at social events. And after her father died, she sort of shut herself up in that rock mansion for good."

"Hmm." Frankie paused to let that sink in. "What about Mack Perry? Did Emily spend time with him?"

Wilma raised both brows sharply. "What an odd question, Francine! Of course, she hired Mack Perry and gave him a home in the gatehouse, but that was out of guilt, nothing more." Wilma seemed defensive, and Frankie wanted to know more.

"Out of guilt? What do you mean?" she queried.

Wilma lowered her voice as if sharing a secret. "After that bad business with the sick men and the lawsuits, Emily was heartsick. The quarry was closed. She lost her father a few years later, and she was left all alone to carry the burden of those tragedies. I think she stayed in the house because she thought the whole town had passed judgment on her family. She couldn't bear it." Wilma's voice quavered. Esther, Gertie, and a couple of the other Knit Witches nodded in a chorus of agreement with Wilma.

Frankie decided it was time to shift gears, but she needed to ask one more question. "Does anyone know Alana West, Emily's personal assistant?"

Again, a few women talked at once. Wilma, the perceived authority on Emily, spoke as the others hushed. "Alana was a replacement for a perfectly capable assistant, and I have no idea why Emily made the change," she proclaimed. A choir of nods and affirmative murmurs followed.

Well, this was interesting news. "Who was her former assistant?" Frankie asked, trying to sound nonchalant.

This time Esther, who knew the former assistant,

chimed in with the answer. "Lorna Ricks. She lives in Gibson. She has a reputation for being a wonderful caregiver, secretary, housekeeper - you name it! She's top notch." Esther finished her acclaim with a sidebar. "I got my Siamese cat Chester from her when he was a kitten."

Frankie was pleased to get this information. She wondered if Lorna Ricks had given Pearl to Emily. She made another mental note to find this woman for a chat.

But now, she needed to change the atmosphere in Rachel's shop. Frankie took responsibility for ruining the happy, cozy environments in two places that afternoon. She thanked the ladies for their help, told them she'd be back with coffee and pastry, and headed out the front door. It was there Frankie saw a sight she would not soon forget.

Kneeling on the sidewalk between the two shop entrances were her mother and Aunt CeCe, coloring in a spring scene drawn with sidewalk chalk! Peggy looked up at her daughter, beaming, holding a piece of yellow chalk.

"I never realized yellow was such a cheerful color before," Peggy announced like someone who had never seen yellow. Then, smiling, she resumed coloring a big sun in the picture.

Aunt CeCe nodded her approval, smiled larger than necessary at Frankie, and held up her blue chalk. "No more gray skies today!" Aunt CeCe exclaimed.

Frankie was certain she had made a wrong turn into the Twilight Zone. "Alright, you two, what in the hell is going on?" Frankie saved her swears for specific occasions and felt like this occasion warranted one. She knew her mother disapproved wholeheartedly of swearing, so she was sure Peggy would snap out of whatever world she was in to admonish her daughter. It was Sunday, after all.

Peggy looked up at Frankie, tried to glare, but couldn't somehow find the expression or words she wanted to use, so she began laughing uncontrollably, which spilled over onto Aunt CeCe, who laughed with her. The women leaned on each other and nearly lost their balance on the sidewalk.

"Oh. My. Goodness. You're drunk!" Frankie's accusation came out like a nail gun. She needed help, stepped over the two, and hustled up the steps through the front door of Bubble and Bake.

But her strange afternoon was about to get stranger. Inside the shop, the Buzzards were singing to the oldies, missing words, and laughing like little kids. *This is just super. They're all drunk*, Frankie thought. She scooted around the men and strode into the kitchen where Carmen was measuring ingredients for a batch of lemon bars to take to the funeral tomorrow.

"Do you have any idea what's going on out there?" Frankie pointed toward the door to the lounge, accusingly. Carmen shook her head, her expression blank. "My gosh, Carmen, I leave the shop for less than an hour, and everyone is drunk!" Frankie's volume rose markedly on the last word. Carmen stopped measuring abruptly.

"What do you mean, drunk? You weren't gone long enough for everyone to get drunk. Where's your mother, Frankie? She wouldn't let that happen."

Frankie shook her head. "That's what you think. She's drunk, too. She and my Aunt CeCe are, at this very minute, out in front of our shop, coloring sidewalk chalk pictures!" Frankie spat the words out, still in disbelief. "You have to help me get them inside before someone sees them, Carmen."

Unable to respond, Carmen decided to see for herself, first witnessing the Buzzards' sloppy singing. But, Carmen didn't have time to let that spectacle register, as another more incredible one was waiting outside the front door. Seeing the properly dressed, conservative person of Peggy Champagne on her knees coloring a rainbow on the front walk made Carmen freeze, then begin laughing.

"Oh no you don't, Carmen. Not you, too. Don't you dare laugh. You have to help me, right now!" Frankie shouted the last words at her friend.

First, Carmen and Frankie each took one of Peggy's arms and lifted her to a standing position, while the older woman pouted like a three-year-old. Frankie took on a motherly tone. "Come on, Mother. Let's get you inside for some coffee," she coaxed. The two women guided Peggy to a sofa on the opposite side of the lounge away from the Buzzards, who waved flirtatiously at Peggy when she was brought through the door.

After retrieving Aunt CeCe, depositing her on a large

floor cushion near Peggy, Carmen and Frankie looked in bewilderment at each other.

"We have to close the shop. I can't let anyone see them like this." Frankie checked the clock. It would be another hour before the Knit Witches would conclude their meeting to come and collect their menfolk. "Let's turn the open sign off and make some strong coffee."

A sudden dawning came across Carmen's face as she poked around the bar area to count the empty bottles consumed by the Buzzards, Peggy, and Aunt CeCe.

"Wait a minute, Frankie. There are only a few empty bottles here. But I remember Aunt CeCe came into the kitchen for cookies. Look, here's the container." Carmen held up a small Tupperware square with several cookies inside and opened the lid. "You better get over here, Frankie."

Thinking the whole world was crazy, Frankie considered going back to Rachel's shop to try leaving a second time, since the shop must be a secret portal to another world that Frankie was trapped in.

"Okay, so they were eating cookies . . ." Frankie began, peering at the dark chocolate cookies, loaded with chocolate chips and smelling of fresh mint from the herb garden.

Carmen overlooked Frankie's dim-witted comment. "Take another whiff. Can't you smell something off in these cookies? Aunt CeCe mumbled something in the kitchen when she came in to get them. Something about her special cure for sorrow. I'd bet my last dollar these cookies are laced with pot."

"Pot?! Oh, Hell, Carmen, we have to close the shop - NOW!" Frankie felt like she was drowning. She didn't know how to deal with a situation like this one.

Carmen switched off the open sign and locked the shop door. "Okay, we can keep other customers out, but we still have to take care of the Buzzards. Ideas?"

Frankie began brewing two pots of strong coffee, remembering she had promised to bring coffee and treats to the Knit Witches, too. She unearthed a third coffee carafe used on busy days and started another brew of milder coffee for next door.

Together, she and Carmen began doing internet searches about bringing people down from a high, hoping their computers would never be confiscated by the authorities for their search histories. After several minutes, Frankie handed out cups of coffee, while Carmen gave each person a glass of water loaded with lemon.

Carmen agreed to monitor the situation while Frankie hurried next door with a quickly defrosted batch of lemon basil scones and a pot of coffee. She barely caught Esther's comment, "Took you long enough" before she was out the door again, telling the ladies the shop was pretty busy at the moment.

Some of the Buzzards seemed a bit more coherent. At least the singing had ceased. They looked lethargic, however, and ready for naps. Peggy and Aunt CeCe were quietly sipping coffee and drinking water, staring at some random knick-knack or spot of sunlight crossing the plank floors.

A few minutes later, Carmen announced it was time for stage two of Operation Sober, and she brought out a container of freshly ground black pepper, offering it around the table for the men to smell. Acting as if they were hypnotized, each one took a big sniff of pepper followed by a blitz of sneezes and hacking coughs.

Frankie and Carmen couldn't hold back their laughter at the ridiculous situation of two middle-aged women trying to help these men out of a stupor they'd succumbed to purely by accident. The men were like puppets, doing anything Frankie and Carmen suggested, which only added to the absurdity.

Leaving the Buzzards to continue drinking coffee and water, Carmen offered Peggy and Aunt CeCe the ground pepper, which caused both women to sneeze violently and begin to cry.

"Come on, Carmen. Let's get my mom and Aunt CeCe upstairs to my place, where they can sleep it off," Frankie suggested. Getting the women up the stairs was a much more difficult task, but at least Aunt CeCe could help a litte. Perhaps the effects of the cookies wore off faster on someone who obviously imbibed more frequently, Frankie surmised.

Back in the shop, Frankie assessed the situation. Red, Hoot, and two of the other men were sound asleep, face down on the card table. Kurt was perched in a loveseat next to Ol' Jim Powell reading a book . It was a book of tall tales from the Old West, and Kurt was reading a story to Ol' Jim, as if he were a child.

The final Buzzard, Stu Shepard, generally referred to as Shep, was walking slowly out of the restroom. He peered quizzically at Frankie and Carmen, grinned broadly, and remarked, "Well, that was quite the afternoon, wasn't it? I think this meeting of the Buzzards is one for the history books." Stu Shepard was a retired railroad union boss from Chicago. Frankie figured he must have been exposed to pot and recognized its effects.

"Let's just keep this little event out of the books, shall we, Shep? I mean, what happens at Bubble and Bake, stays at Bubble and Bake?" Frankie wanted to wish this whole episode away. Shep nodded, winked at the women, and sat down in a chair by the window.

"Got anything to eat?" Shep asked. "I'm pretty hungry."

Carmen rolled her eyes and was off to the kitchen to retrieve a couple of extra scones. It was more than an hour later when the Knit Witches tucked away their projects and walked into Bubble and Bake to collect their men. Frankie and Carmen were grateful the knitters had lingered to drink coffee, nibble on scones, and tell more stories prompted by Frankie's questions about Emily.

By now, the Buzzards were alert and eating quiche. Since the shop had been closed, sales were dismal but perked up with the Buzzards' appetites. The women had to wait anyway, so most of them ordered slices of quiche, too, and glasses of wine.

"Guess I won't have to cook tonight," Gertie exclaimed happily to repeated echoes of the same by the other ladies. Frankie and Carmen smiled. It was certainly an unconventional way to sell quiche, but it worked.

Still, neither one wanted a repeat of this Sunday, and they put their heads together to discuss their course of action with Aunt CeCe later or tomorrow, whichever was most reasonable.

Chapter 16

April is the cruelest month, breeding lilacs out
of the dead land, mixing memory and desire,
stirring dull roots with spring rain.
– T. S. Eliot

Outside Bubble and Bake, snowflakes were spitting as the business day came to a close. The changing April weather reminded Frankie of just how delicate Wisconsin springs are - and fickle, too, since the day had started out sunny and warm.

The snow drops made Frankie wonder if she should check the vineyards in the morning to see how the grape blossoms were faring, but right now, she and Carmen needed to handle a more delicate matter: Aunt CeCe and her special cookies. The Knit Witches seemed none the wiser about the unauthorized consumption their men were part of that afternoon. Frankie and Carmen breathed sighs of relief, mounted the stairs to Frankie's apartment to check on the other women, and prepared to deliver a stern warning to Aunt CeCe.

Peggy was taking a shower, and Frankie couldn't imagine what her mother would have to say about today's recreation, but she could imagine it wasn't going to be pretty. Aunt CeCe was sitting on the sofa, staring into a tea cup, looking like she'd lost her last friend. The look reminded Frankie that her aunt had just lost a dear friend and that she might need to be a little gentler with her scolding.

The Golden One disapproved of that thought, reminding Frankie that her business and entire reputation were at stake. Goldie urged her to stay strong.

Frankie chose a seat across from her aunt, keeping a cool distance to help her maintain her stern composure. Carmen chose to stand near Aunt CeCe, looming over her with crossed arms and a killer look mothers reserve for a naughty child. Giving Frankie a sharp look, Carmen decided to start the lecture without delay.

"What in the name of heaven were you thinking today, Cecile, feeding those cookies to our customers? Are you crazy or something?" Carmen wasn't mincing words. "You could make the shop lose its license, or worse, we could get arrested. Dios mío!" Aunt CeCe continued to stare into her cup.

It was Frankie's turn to launch a second volley. "Honestly, Aunt CeCe, you promised to behave yourself. First the quarry pond, then the nude sunbathing, and now this - this illegal baking!"

Frankie was losing her grasp of language. "Carmen's one hundred percent correct. This could get us in a lot of legal trouble. We could be forced to close our doors, maybe even go to prison." Frankie wondered if all of that could be a real consequence of her aunt's actions, and saying it out loud made it much more serious. Frankie was incensed.

Carmen resumed probing. "Well, what do you have to say for yourself? Why did you give those men cookies with pot in them?"

CeCe raised her eyes to Carmen, then Frankie, and began to cry. "Everyone was so sad. I just wanted to fix things, you know, to help them," she began.

"Don't you know marijuana is illegal in Wisconsin? You shouldn't even have that stuff on you! Geez, Aunt CeCe," Frankie huffed, annoyed.

"But I have a prescription for it," CeCe said in her defense.

Carmen blew out an audible breath. "Great, Cecile. You know you can't share prescriptions of any kind with anyone else. That's just common sense."

Frankie wanted to know what the prescription was for. Did her aunt have cancer or some other illness that warranted it?

"It's for my anxiety. It helps . . . a lot. I don't use it all the time, Frankie, only when things get to be overwhelming. Today, everyone in the shop was overwhelmed. I wanted to do what I could," Aunt CeCe said.

Frankie considered backing down, seeing her aunt looking so fragile, but Goldie began fluttering in her ear, reminding her of the gravity of the situation. No, Frankie decided, anxiety or not, Aunt CeCe needed to follow Wisconsin laws and shop rules or else.

Prodded on by the possibility of losing her precious business, Frankie spoke quietly but seriously. "Maybe it's time you returned to California, since you seem to have trouble adjusting to Wisconsin ways." Inside, Frankie's stomach was in knots, and her heart ached at giving a voice to those terrible words.

Peggy emerged from the bathroom freshly showered just in time to hear Frankie's statement. She was surprised, not unpleasantly, at her daughter's fierceness.

"Well, Cecile, what do you think? Can you follow our rules, or is it time to return home?" Peggy had Frankie's back, an action that diminished the sting Frankie felt for saying those words to her aunt.

Outnumbered, Aunt CeCe sank back into the sofa cushions and studied her tea cup once more. Nobody said anything for what seemed like an eternity. It looked like a stalemate, leaving Frankie to wonder if there was any resolution at all. But then Aunt CeCe stood up and looked all three women in the eye.

"I'm so sorry. I would never want to cause you any trouble. You've all been so kind to take me in. I love the shop. I don't want to go back to California; it's too hard there," her voice faltered. "Please give me another chance?"

Frankie was ready to cross the room and squeeze Aunt CeCe, but Carmen and Peggy both shot her a look of restraint.

Carmen spoke first. "We will give you one last chance, Aunt CeCe, but you have to keep your prescription out of the shop. No more illegal baking of any kind. No more nudity. No more funny business. Got it?" Aunt CeCe nodded, crossing her heart.

Peggy added, "I'm not comfortable with you having that prescription of yours in my house. I think it's time for you to see a Wisconsin doctor, Cecile. I'll make an appointment for you straightaway. Got it?"

Aunt CeCe didn't look pleased but acquiesced. After all, she had to have somewhere to live, and for now, that was at Peggy's. Aunt CeCe looked expectantly at Frankie for further demands, but Frankie didn't have anything left to offer. Her anger had passed, and upon a second apology from her aunt, she gave her a small tight hug.

Before the three women left Frankie's home, she pulled aside her mother. "Are you okay, Mom?" Frankie was concerned about her proper mother's descent into a taboo activity. Peggy patted her shoulder and smiled.

"I'm fine, Frankie. Thanks for your concern, though, honey. What a weird day." Peggy followed Aunt CeCe and Carmen down the stairs.

Lacking sleep the past couple of days, Frankie fell into bed early after logging the particulars shared by the Buzzards and Knit Witches onto her suspect board. Were one of these people truly cold-blooded enough to kill Emily Spurgeon?

Cordelia McCoy - her own cousin?

Mack Perry - who adored the woman?

Alana West - who had a well-paying position that seemed relatively easy?

Fitz Barnard - a medical doctor who saves lives?

Grant Foster? Well, Frankie could see the phony Grant Foster having a role in Emily's death, but how? And now she added a new name to the list - Lorna Ricks, with the motive of revenge. After all, Lorna had had a good position with Emily, only to be suddenly replaced by Alana West.

*   *   *

Monday dawned cold with a bracing wind, but not a trace of last night's snow could be found, which Frankie found comforting as she thought about her grapevines. Still, she watched out the window as her spring birds shivered and struggled to fly straight. She was glad to see them take advantage of the suet cakes and other chow she offered at feeders posted along the creek and garden edges. The robins looked determined to find worms as they prodded the ground with their feet. Frankie reminded herself to take some dried mealworms out to them until the fresh wriggling variety began emerging from the cold earth again.

Donning black trousers and a white blouse for the funeral service luncheon, Frankie noted the weather seemed right for a somber occasion. Two coffees, a pile of blueberries, and a couple of scrambled eggs later, Frankie was ready to meet Carmen at Prince of Peace Lutheran Church on Pine Tree Avenue, a long, wide street where almost all of the Deep Lakes churches resided.

Prince of Peace was at the corner of Pine Tree and Wisconsin Avenue, two major thoroughfares in town. The funeral was at 10:00 a.m., but the luncheon volunteers were arriving at eight to set up and receive dishes to pass.

Rum Raisin Cake in tow, Frankie entered the back door leading to the kitchen and fellowship hall. She could hear a couple of ladies at work in the kitchen and walked in carefully. Prince of Peace was not Frankie's church, and she was a little uncertain if these ladies would consider her an intruder. After all, Frankie was Catholic, a lifelong member of St. Anthony's down the street, and at times, the two denominations didn't see eye to eye.

She was relieved to see Adele Lundgren organizing casserole dishes and salad containers in the commercial fridge, pulling out the casseroles to place in ovens that were pre-heating.

"Oh, hello, Frankie. We were happy to hear you and Carmen volunteered to help with the luncheon. I think we'll need all the help we can muster. Speaking of mustering, did you get Cordelia McCoy to agree to give the presentation at the festival?"

Good old Adele, jumping from topic to topic as usual. Frankie shook her head and said she was still working on it, which wasn't exactly true. She hadn't made any set plans to speak with Cordelia again, but it was on her radar.

"Hello. I'm Eleanor Brickerson. My husband and I used to own the gift shop on Meriwether. Brickerson's? Of course, now it's a travel agency."

Frankie remembered the gift shop, which was also a year-round variety store. As a child, Frankie had bought her mother a pretty blue glass fruit basket there. She remembered how proud she'd been to use her own allowance money when her father, Charlie, took her to Brickerson's to pick out something for Peggy's birthday. She guessed Eleanor must be in the neighborhood of 80 or so, but she looked healthy and moved with ease, wrangling industrial-sized jars of pickles and salad dressing.

"I do remember your store, Mrs. Brickerson, from when I was growing up. Deep Lakes was lucky to have it during the winter months when so many other businesses shut down and their owners headed South," Frankie remarked, making Eleanor grin.

"Please: call me Eleanor, and give me a hand with these king-sized jars, would you? My grip isn't what it used to be. You can set your yummy-looking cake over on that countertop by the other desserts." Eleanor gestured behind her where Frankie saw a lovely line-up of desserts already in place. Frankie felt at home in the church kitchen; really most kitchens were alike, and, thankfully, were a universal place of companionship no matter what one's beliefs were.

Carmen arrived a little later and settled into small talk with the other women, now totaling six. Since the other ladies knew the luncheon layout at their home church, Frankie and Carmen went out to the dining area to set up tables with linens and flatware. They also wheeled out the giant percolators and got coffee brewing, both regular and unleaded.

Two more volunteers showed up, the husbands of a couple of the women, who went to work setting up folding chairs from storage. Frankie and Carmen pitched in on that activity as well. Preparations wrapped up early. The men left to change into funeral clothes, while the women gathered in the kitchen to perk up with some coffee and conversation.

Standing by the dessert counter, Adele chirped, "Now which one of these desserts should we break into to have with our coffee, ladies?" Frankie and Carmen laughed. It appeared every church kitchen was the same. When women worked around food, taste testing was standard operating procedure. Eleanor winked at Adele, nodding eagerly as she picked up the Rum Raisin Cake.

"I vote for this cake. After all, it was made by our local baker. It has to be good. It smells like paradise." Eleanor removed the cover, offering the women a whiff of pineapple, rum, and coconut as she passed by.

Kathy Schwen, an assistant to the county clerk, gave an audible sigh. "I love coconut. My family hates it, so I can never bake with it. I'll take a piece of that."

Eleanor carved out thin slices of the triple layer cake, but it was rich, buttery and rummy, so small slices sufficed. She cut several more slices and placed them on dessert plates for the luncheon.

The women chatted about everything except Emily Spurgeon and the quarry, which was a welcome reprieve for Frankie, who needed to steel herself to complete the plan she and Carmen had concocted for investigating later.

The ladies left the kitchen and proceeded into the church sanctuary, which was filling up fast. Carmen and Frankie took seats in the last pew on the left side, a place where few people tended to look and a place where they could view the attendees.

Cordelia McCoy made a dramatic procession to the front pew, dressed in a skin-tight black sheath and shiny black pumps. She was on the arm of none other than Grant Foster, who looked uncomfortable in the role of consoler, but he managed to put an arm around Cordelia's shoulder as she raised a black lacy handkerchief to her teary face. Carmen and Frankie exchanged eye rolls, each wondering if this was an Oscar-winning performance or something more sincere.

Dr. Fitz Barnard, dressed in a business suit and looking dapper, strutted to a pew near the front, a voluptuous brunette on his arm. "I assume that's Mrs. Dr. Barnard?" Carmen asked.

"I assume so, too, but I've not had the pleasure. She wasn't at the Historical Society meeting. I thought you knew everyone in town, Carmen." Frankie giggled quietly.

"Nope. I don't travel in the right circles. Besides,

they're fairly new in town; didn't you say that?" Frankie nodded in response.

To Mrs. Barnard's credit, she was dressed for church, unlike Cordelia, who looked ready to go out for cocktails. *And maybe she is ready. After all, things aren't exactly going to be easy for her in Deep Lakes*, Frankie thought.

Just before the service began, Alana West walked in quietly with her husband, Jeremy. Jeremy was dressed in his Fleet Delivery uniform, so Frankie assumed he was working today and took time off just for the funeral. Alana held onto Jeremy's hand tightly, and she looked down at the carpet the entire walk. She and Jeremy chose a seat on the side near the middle.

"Hey, doesn't that guy do deliveries to the shop, Frankie?" Carmen whispered.

Yes, Frankie recognized Jeremy. She'd had many small talk interactions with him the past few years, but she didn't know his full name so never associated him with Alana.

"Doesn't he look much older than Alana? Do you know him, Carmen?"

Carmen shook her head to the second question. "I only know him the same way you do. I don't know. He looks like he could be almost 40, huh? How old is Alana? I didn't get a good look at her," Carmen wondered.

Frankie wasn't sure. When she first met Alana, she guessed she was probably a recent college graduate, maybe 25, since she had worked less than three years for Emily.

Her musings were interrupted by Mack Perry's arrival. Poor Mack was dressed in a brown corduroy suit with black elbow patches, probably the best thing in his closet since he didn't have much cause to dress up in a suit. He looked uncomfortable at best, and his worn black dress shoes didn't help him out much.

He slid into the same pew as Frankie and Carmen, to their disappointment. Frankie hoped she and Carmen would be able to take notes during the service, even though they were queasy about the disrespectful nature of doing so. Now, with Mack close by, they'd have to curb their activity. Frankie felt even worse when Mack reached over, grabbed Frankie's hand in his gnarled one, and gave it a tight squeeze.

"I'm glad you came, Frankie. Emily liked you. She would be happy that you're here." Mack pulled out a white handkerchief as tears rolled out of the corners of his eyes. He blew his nose unceremoniously. Then he picked up something wrapped in layers of brown paper and walked up the side aisle to Emily's closed coffin at the front. Frankie and Carmen were shocked when Mack unwrapped the package, revealing a bouquet of French lilacs, and laid them on Emily's coffin, right on top of the large funeral spray of lilies, to be exact. He bowed his head for a moment, then returned to the back pew.

By the time Mack was in his seat, Frankie had recovered enough from the gesture to give Mack's hand a little squeeze, bringing fresh tears to all three of them seated there. Frankie recalled that lilacs were Emily's favorite, and she had no idea where Mack found any since it was about a month too early. His action was so humble, yet so powerful and real that Frankie was afraid she may not be able to stop her tears. But now the players were all in their places, and, unbeknownst to them, the game would begin in about an hour.

The music began, and Pastor Schinkel entered the sanctuary as his organist wife, Ruth, played "How Great Thou Art," and the congregation did its level best to fill the church with the hymn.

Frankie was surprised to hear that Emily had been a long-time member of the church, having not missed a Sunday service in 30 years. So, Emily got out more than Frankie realized.

The reverend spoke about Emily's generosity, her contributions to charities and the community, and her witty nature. Frankie admired Pastor Schinkel for his sincere and personal delivery during the service, something that was often lacking at many funerals she'd attended. "A Closer Walk With Thee" hummed from the organ, closing the service as six able-bodied men in dark suits processed out of the church doors with Emily.

The only notes Frankie made were mental ones. She'd noticed Cordelia making a public display of sorrow, perfectly timed when Pastor Schinkel gave an example of Emily's kindness and charity.

She also noticed that Alana West stared straight

ahead for much of the service, looking much like a stone statue. Other than that, nothing else seemed out of sync.

Mack hung on every word the minister uttered, dabbing his eyes on and off throughout the service and finally blowing his nose again as the final hymn drew to a close. He choked a little as Emily's casket passed their pew and looked as if he might fall over to boot, so Frankie grabbed his arm to steady him. She wanted to talk to Mack right away, but he hurried out the front doors, and headed for his car to follow the procession to the cemetery.

As Grant Foster led Cordelia down the aisle, he paused and leaned down toward Alana West. Frankie craned her neck to see the exchange. It looked as if Foster had handed something small to Alana. If Alana had dropped something, Frankie missed seeing it. Suddenly, things seemed out of sync, and Frankie couldn't wait to leave the pew so she could write down what she saw. Had Foster handed Alana something important or just something she'd dropped? Either way, what could it be?

Chapter 17

Whatever hysteria exists is inflamed by mystery,
suspicion and secrecy. Hard and exact facts will cool it.
- Elia Kazan

Frankie and Carmen made a pit stop at the restroom, then headed to the kitchen before the mourners started parading into the dining hall. Speaking in hushed voices, the women quickly exchanged impressions.

"If you ask me, that Cordelia is a fake. No way was that real crying. If she was so shook up about Emily's death, where has she been all these years? I think it was all show." Carmen was adamant in her belief.

Frankie agreed, having seen Cordelia in action at the mansion. "What do you make of Alana though? She was stiff as a board and showed no emotion at all. She wasn't like that the day Emily died; that's for sure." Alana's behavior made Frankie wonder if she'd taken some medication.

"Maybe she's just cried herself out, Frankie. Hard to say. But, yeah, she looked like an ice queen today," Carmen shivered a little thinking about it. "Mack Perry, though. Dios mío, Frankie; there's a man in love. Total devotion to that woman, I bet. He made me cry, Frankie."

"I'm with you, Carmen. You can't fake that kind of emotion. I think what he did with the lilacs will stay with me forever. Poor Mack," Frankie finished.

Switching gears, the luncheon was in full swing, keeping the church volunteers on their toes replacing empty casseroles and salad bowls several times during the next half hour. With so many suspects gathered in one location, it was now or never; Frankie and Carmen knew people would only linger so long after they had their dessert. The two excused themselves from the kitchen to commence Mission Mayhem.

Frankie made a beeline for Fitz Barnard, hoping to take another swing at his cool exterior. When the doctor saw Frankie coming his way, he looked for a pathway out of the dining hall but was waylaid by an older man pushing a wobbly metal cart filled with dirty dishes. The two connected, forcing Barnard to apologize to the man and see if he was okay from the collision.

"That was a close one. Those darn carts are unpredictable, aren't they, Dr. Barnard?" Frankie was smiling in a good-natured manner. "Looks like no harm done." The older man resumed his way toward the kitchen, leaving Frankie facing Dr. Barnard squarely with nowhere to escape.

"Nice to see you again, Ms. Champagne," he said warily. "It was a nice service, wasn't it?" The doctor's eyes were surveying the fellowship hall, its pathways and visitors, possibly looking for a distraction.

"Please call me Frankie, Doctor. I'm afraid we got off on the wrong foot the other night. I'm so sorry," Frankie began, smiling a little at the effect she had on him.

The doctor relaxed a little. "No harm done. I guess you felt the same way about Emily as I did: protective." Dr. Barnard was testing the waters.

"Mmhmm," Frankie murmured, looking around the room noncommittally. "Fitz is such an unusual name. How did you come by it?"

The doctor was puzzled by the bend in the conversation. He reached one hand up and ran it through his dark hair. "Uh, it's a family name. A variation of my grandfather's first name, actually."

Barnard resumed perusing the room, and gave a wave at someone out of Frankie's sight line. "Well, if you'll excuse me, I see my wife over there looking in need of rescue from one of the church ladies. Take care, Frankie."

Fitz Barnard was gone, but Frankie was ready to fish in other waters. The fact that she made the doctor uncomfortable was enough for Frankie to keep him on her suspect list. She needed to talk to her mother; then she planned to corner Dr. Barnard again, hopefully before he left.

Meanwhile, Carmen followed Cordelia and Grant Foster to one of the Sunday school classrooms. Making herself as small as possible, she jammed herself into the supply closet just inside the door on the right, taking advantage of the dark room so as not to be noticed by Cordelia or Grant, who stayed in the shadows.

"Dios mío," Carmen whispered to herself. "I hope they didn't come here to make out. That would be gross." Carmen pushed the door open a smidge as they began talking so she could hear a little better.

The two were standing near the window so she could see their profiles clearly. Cordelia was angry, saying something about a codicil. Carmen's ears pricked up. This was likely the codicil to Emily's will Frankie had told her about.

"I can't believe you didn't get the codicil filed before she died, Grant. That was your one job, your one job." Cordelia's voice was low but spiteful.

"I didn't think we were in that much of a hurry. We didn't know she was that sick," Foster's voice was low and even. "Anyway, the codicil is no good without the kidney transplant. You would have had to go through with it, Delia." He sounded impatient, as if he'd said all of this before.

Cordelia said something Carmen couldn't hear, but Grant's response was clear. "I'm telling you we just need to wait things out. The court is going to take your side. You're her only living relative, and the mansion belonged to the McCoys first. The codicil will help, too. You'll see."

Grant reached over to run his fingers through a tendril of Cordelia's hair. He brushed his face against her cheek and pulled her in close.

Carmen truly hoped this was the end of the tête-à-tête. She had heard enough and certainly didn't want to see anything further either. Her leg, pinned against a vacuum cleaner, was cramping, and she didn't dare move for fear the vacuum would topple over. Luckily, Cordelia pulled away from Grant at that moment, walked quickly to open the door, and exited in a huff. Grant was in hot pursuit behind her.

Carmen let out a long breath and was about to open the closet door when she saw movement from the back corner of the room. Her heart pounded so loudly in her chest that she was certain the culprit could hear it.

Someone was creeping toward the front door or the supply closet, and Carmen said a fervent prayer in her head that it was not the latter. That someone was also having trouble with breath control and paused near the door to breathe in and out a couple of times purposefully before opening the classroom door and leaving.

Carmen pushed the closet door open just in time to see the backside of Alana West walking down the hallway. Apparently, Carmen and Frankie were not the only ones doing investigative work at the funeral today.

Carmen took a detour to the restroom before she could be seen by Alana and found Frankie and Peggy huddled in the mother's nursing area in close conversation. Mother and daughter paused and looked up expectantly at Carmen when she walked in. Carmen relayed the strange meeting between Cordelia and Grant, which included Alana lurking in the opposite corner of the classroom. Carmen guessed that Alana must have been in the classroom before the pair got there, but she couldn't be certain.

"Excellent work, Watson," Frankie said to her friend, twisting her lips. Carmen giggled but shuddered at the same time.

"I don't know about this sleuthing stuff, Frankie. I was scared out of my wits in that closet," Carmen admitted. "So what were you two discussing, if I may ask?"

"Dr. Fitz Barnard. I was just about to ask Mom a question about him." Turning toward Peggy, she asked, "Isn't there some sort of rule that you have to be connected to a Deep Lakes relative to be on the Historical Society Board?" Frankie sounded like Perry Mason, making Peggy sit up a little straighter.

"Why are you so interested in the doctor, honey? He's a married man, Frankie," Peggy said in a stage whisper, her hand curved against her cheek. Frankie shook her head in disbelief, frowning. She continued looking at Peggy, waiting.

"Okay, well, of course that is a Society bylaw. Good catch, dear. However, Dr. Barnard's mother was born in Deep Lakes. She lived here until she was a teenager, I believe."

Frankie's interest was piqued. "I knew you would be a good source of information, Mom. How about a name to go with Dr. Barnard's mother?"

Peggy's mind was turning, trying to access the information. "Oh yes, Anna Kuhn."

Jackpot! Frankie could barely sit still. "What does that mean, Francine? Obviously it struck a chord."

"It means," Frankie stated matter-of-factly, "the doctor has moved up a rung on my suspect board. His grandfather was Fritz Kuhn. Fritz Kuhn died of Silicosis, aka Quarry Sickness. I need to talk to the doctor again." Frankie strung out each point, allowing it to register. Carmen let out a low whistle, but Peggy was skeptical.

"Fitz Barnard may be an ambitious social climber, Francine, but that's no crime. I can't believe he'd be involved in murder. He's a doctor. He saves lives, not ends them," Peggy proclaimed.

"We'll just see about that. Besides, he's not the only one with something to gain from Emily's death, but he's still on the list. Gotta run." Frankie rose and left. She wasn't sure whom to pursue next - there were so many to talk to - but she decided to take Carmen up on her offer to chat with Alana, since her business partner had a sly plan that might work.

Perched in the doorway, like a cat about to pounce, Frankie noticed Ward Dickens for the first time that day. He was chatting with Judge Holman (the other Whitman County magistrate) and Virginia Busby.

Frankie wasn't surprised to see Virginia there, probably gleaning gossip to share at the appropriate occasion. This thought provoked Goldie to chirp in Frankie's ear, "Well, what a hypocrite you are, Frankie. Aren't you doing the same thing?"

Frankie noticed that lately The Pirate seemed to be noticeably absent from all firefly appearances. She didn't have time to think about the reason for it right now, but she would examine recent firefly conversations at a later time. Speaking of absence, Frankie noticed Dicky Bryant hadn't come to the funeral or luncheon.

Near the kitchen, the mayor was having a one-sided animated conversation with Cordelia McCoy, which produced a wry smile from Frankie. Adele was like a dancing puppet, waving her hands around, unaware of the volume or tone of her voice. Cordelia looked like a chalk stick plastered to a blackboard - her fair skin stark against the backdrop of the tight black dress. She was virtually immobilized by Adele - such was the effect of an Adele conversation.

Frankie gazed toward the back tables where people lingered to catch up with one another or reminisce. At one table she spied Carmen, sitting close to Alana, looking very chummy. She hoped Carmen's chit-chat would yield some new information. At least, she would get Carmen's perspective, which was golden in Frankie's mind.

Dr. Barnard was still sitting at a table, too, surrounded by notable Deep Lakes citizens, including, oddly enough, Sheriff Alonzo Goodman. The doctor's wife, unfortunately, looked like a prop, disengaged from the conversation, perusing her cell phone. Barnard looked up momentarily, locked eyes with Frankie and shifted uncomfortably in his chair. Trying to avoid a scene, Frankie decided to sidle up to Ward and pull him away from the Judge and Virginia.

Ward smiled warmly as Frankie walked over to the little group. "Frankie Champagne! Good to see you! It's been awhile." Ward was practically gushing, and Frankie took the cue that he needed rescuing from the conversation, since the two had just seen each other the other day at the law office.

"I was hoping to talk to you, Ward. Do you have a few minutes right now, by chance?" Frankie smiled at Virginia and Judge Holman, greeting each one. Ward nodded affirmatively, and the two headed off to a table in the opposite direction.

"Thank you, Frankie. I just didn't feel like talking shop today. You know, I'm looking forward to retiring," Ward said, wanly. Frankie noticed for the first time that Ward was getting older and suddenly felt guilty that she approached him to ask a legal question. She supposed it must be a nuisance to always be seen in one dimension. She loved baking and wine-making, but she didn't always want to chat about recipes and grape cultivation.

"What's on your mind, Frankie? I can tell you want to talk shop, too. Might as well get on with it." Ward's winning smile made him endearing, and won over many juries, Frankie thought.

"Let's go get some coffee and dessert, first, Ward," Frankie said. "I know what you like. I'll be right back."

Frankie sprinted to the dessert table and grabbed two of Carmen's famous lemon bars, while she flagged down a volunteer to bring them coffee. "Here you go, Counselor. Now I don't feel quite so bad about my questions."

Frankie always knew how to work around Ward Dickens. She was closer to him than her other boss, Jonah Probst, who was much more professional in nature. Ward was like another uncle to Frankie, and she knew how to charm him. Chalk it up to having four brothers and being a daddy's girl.

"I might have seen a copy of a codicil to Emily Spurgeon's will yesterday on your desk, when I went back in to get my car keys," she admitted.

"Well, isn't that a lucky accident?" Ward chuckled. "And, is there a question here?"

"What was your advice to Emily about signing such an agreement?" Frankie cut to the chase, and Ward was surprised by the question.

"Hmm. I always told you that law was a good profession for you, Frankie. I guess I can tell you that I warned Emily not to change the will, that is, not until I could meet Cordelia personally and her lawyer, too. My gut told me it may cause Emily more harm than good."

"So the codicil was never filed. I'm guessing the meeting you wanted never happened."

Ward nodded. "Right on both counts. Emily died

before anything was finalized. Of course, now Cordelia is contesting the original will, holding up the proposed codicil as proof Emily intended to change her will. And, as the only surviving relative, she has a viable claim. I suspect the estate will be tied up for some time in probate court."

"Where does that leave Mack Perry and Alana West?" Frankie asked.

"In limbo. If Cordelia stays camped at the mansion, Mack and Alana may get tired of waiting and move on. She could make life difficult for them." Ward was forthright, confirming one of Frankie's own ideas.

Finishing their dessert and coffee, Frankie asked Ward about life, golf, and possible retirement plans, easing her conscience a little and appeasing The Golden One, who gave her a small golf clap for taking the extra time for small talk.

Ward left, and Frankie was about to make a trip to the ladies' room when Mack Perry sat down opposite Frankie, a chocolate frosted brownie and coffee cup in tow. Frankie greeted him affectionately. "I thought the lilacs were the perfect touch, Mack. Where did you ever find them this time of year?"

"When you've been gardening and landscaping as long as I have, you make a lot of connections. I know where to get pretty much anything in the gardening department." Mack smiled back at Frankie.

"How long have you known Emily, Mack?"

Mack said he knew Emily practically his whole life, and since his father worked at the quarry, their paths often crossed. However, Mack had left home during his father's illness so he could learn a trade, which is how he came to know the landscaping business inside and outside from his uncle.

"It's clear you were invaluable to Emily at the mansion. The grounds are perfect; you give them all that TLC. She was lucky to have you there, and I'm sure she told you so." Frankie hoped this recognition would lighten Mack's sorrow, but it had the opposite effect.

"Emily hired me after her father died . . . out of guilt. I wanted to take her out when we were in high school, but I was never grand enough for the Spurgeons, just a lowly son of a quarryman." Mack's gaze drifted off into a memory.

"I even took a swing at her father once, after he insulted my family. My father was dead, and all Elmer Spurgeon could say was that he couldn't help us any further." Mack was becoming more irritated with every word. Frankie was sure he'd never voiced these feelings before.

"Didn't things change for you and Emily after her father passed away, Mack?" Frankie offered.

"You'd think so, wouldn't you? After 29 years working at the mansion, I was just an employee after all. I don't think Emily ever forgave me for trying to punch her father. Elmer may have been gone, but his ideas were like fertilizer. They were embedded in her roots. She couldn't get over our class differences no matter how much time passed." Mack shrugged. "When she hired me, she told me I'd always have a home there, so I guess that's something."

Mack picked up his plate and cup, leaving Frankie alone to absorb Mack's feelings. This was a new side of Mack, and Frankie noted the anger, disappointment, and injustice Mack presented. She sat another minute in silence, then noticed Dr. and Mrs. Barnard making their way out of the dining hall.

Not wasting a second, Frankie chased them down, catching up with them in the parking lot. But, as she called out the doctor's name, Frankie's shoe caught on a loose stone, causing her to roll her ankle and fall. She cried out, prompting Fitz Barnard to look behind him and retrace his steps to a sprawling Frankie.

"Are you alright? What happened?" the doctor asked, examining Frankie's ankle, as he kneeled down beside her, never mind his suit and dress shoes.

Mortified, Frankie didn't want help from Fitz Barnard of all people, and she tried to dismiss the throbbing ankle. "I just want to know why you prescribed Emily Spurgeon a laxative, Dr. Barnard!" she stammered between clenched teeth.

Fitz Barnard dropped the rapidly swollen ankle on the pavement and rose from a squatted position. "You're unbelievable, Ms. Champagne. I'm trying to help you!"

Frankie's manners recovered themselves briefly. "I

know you are, but I'm okay. I just need to know about that prescription. Why would you prescribe a laxative to a woman with kidney disease?" Frankie's stubbornness resumed the upper hand.

"Look, I don't know why I should answer that question, but since you're obviously not going to leave me alone, here it is. Barnard looked down at Frankie, who had managed to prop herself up on her seat. He used the voice of an instructor to a silly child.

"The experimental medication Ms. Spurgeon took often caused, hmm, bowel difficulty. The laxative was only to be used in severe cases of constipation. Anyway, she never filled it. If you knew Emily at all, you knew she always looked for natural ways to deal with side effects. She didn't want to take any more medications."

Frankie looked up at Fitz Barnard apologetically. She suspected she had crossed a line maybe. But, she'd asked a perfectly legitimate question, and she knew the police had probably asked him the same thing. Instead of apologizing, however, she settled for, "I didn't mean to offend you, Doctor; I'm just doing my job." She raised her chin a little in defiance, ready to burst into tears at the pain in her ankle.

"Are you sure you're okay? Can I help you get up?" Frankie shook her head, making no attempt to raise herself upward.

"Just please go," she sputtered.

Fitz Barnard couldn't believe what he'd just witnessed.

He stomped indignantly toward his waiting wife and car but turned back with a warning. "Please leave me alone, Ms. Champagne, before I file harassment charges."

Before Frankie attempted to get up, she saw a shadow looming behind her. A woman dressed in a robin's egg blue skirt and blouse held out a meaty arm to help Frankie rise. "It's okay. I'm a nurse. Let's get you inside and get some ice on that ankle."

Frankie gratefully accepted the proffered hand, finding she needed it for support as she hobbled back into the church. The woman settled Frankie into the first chair she found in an empty office area just inside the door. "I'll be right back with ice. Don't try to stand up." The sturdy woman returned with ice, a towel, a glass of water, and a couple ibuprofen. She was clearly practiced at handling such situations.

"You said you're a nurse?" Frankie asked.

"Yes, sorry. I'm Lorna Ricks. And you are?" Lorna asked.

"Frankie Champagne. What do you think about the ankle?"

Lorna was carefully examining the ankle's color and condition. "I think we'll sit tight for 20 minutes and see how it looks after some icing. So, you didn't seem to be getting on too well with Dr. Barnard."

Frankie felt embarrassed that her bad behavior had been witnessed by someone and wondered if others had seen or heard it, too. But she also decided it was her good fortune to be aided by a nurse and none other than the same nurse who used to work for Emily Spurgeon. With 20 minutes to kill, she decided to break the ice, so to speak. "Lorna Ricks. You used to be Emily's assistant, didn't you?" Frankie began.

"That's right. How did you know Emily?" Lorna set her heavy shoulder bag on the carpet and dragged a second chair over to sit across from Frankie.

"I didn't know her very long. I was helping her organize photos and write a speech for a presentation at our upcoming Roots Festival. She was going to rededicate Spurgeon Park and all its new facilities. I was sorry she passed away before that could happen." Frankie's honesty struck a chord with Lorna, who nodded her agreement.

"I was sad to hear the news. I had hoped Emily would respond to the medication or maybe find a kidney donor." Lorna appeared to be telling the truth, Frankie decided.

"Why did you quit working for Emily?" Frankie asked bluntly.

Lorna tilted her blonde head, probing Frankie with serious brown eyes. Frankie guessed she was in her mid to late 30s and was a practical woman. Her shoulder-length hair was straight and unfussy, and she didn't bother with make-up. Frankie noticed she wore dark, orthopedic flats and imagined she had a pair for every occasion.

"It's nice to meet someone who doesn't mince words. I didn't quit. Matter of fact, I was let go, so Emily could hire Ms. West." Before Frankie could ask a follow-up question, Lorna added, "It turned out fine for me. Emily found a client for me in Green Lake, a wealthy woman who requires minimal care and pays very well. It's only a couple miles from my house, too."

It didn't seem like Lorna Ricks held a grudge against Emily. Quite the opposite: she seemed grateful. Frankie took the conversation in a new direction, probing into the topic of Pearl the Siamese. "Esther Brockton tells me she got a Siamese cat from you. Do you raise them?"

"Odd question. Yes, I do. I've been raising Blue Point exclusively for years." Lorna must have figured out the connection, adding, "I assume you must have met Pearl?"

"Yes," Frankie nodded. "But this Pearl is not a Blue Point. She's a Chocolate Point, according to the vet." Frankie added no other explanation.

Lorna said she had given Pearl to Emily as a gift eight years ago when Pearl was a kitten, a Blue Point kitten. Frankie said she found it strange that a second cat was also named Pearl and had never been to the vet, until Frankie took the sick kitty there the day Emily died.

"I find it odd that Emily never said this was the second Pearl, especially as Pearl was her constant companion, according to the vet." Lorna knitted her brows together. She, too, found that strange, confirming Emily's attachment to the Blue Point.

"I have a friend who breeds Chocolate Points. She lives in Gibson. Maybe this Pearl is one of hers. You might ask her just to see if she knows anything." Lorna produced a shopping receipt from her bag and wrote down the name and number of the woman.

"Thank you. I'll check it out. And thank you for helping me in the parking lot. My ankle feels much better." Lorna removed the ice bag and concluded the ankle probably wasn't broken.

"But you should ice it every hour or two and don't do any acrobatics or such for at least a couple of days," Lorna said, winking. "And, you're welcome. Nice to meet you, Frankie. Maybe I'll check out your shop sometime soon."

"Yes, please do," Frankie buzzed. "Hey, Lorna," she called out to the retreating nurse. "You never told me why Emily Spurgeon wanted to hire Alana West."

Lorna smirked a little. "No, I didn't," she stated firmly and left Frankie to ponder that.

Frankie gathered up her purse, looked sadly at the hole she had torn in the right knee of her dress pants from the fall, and proceeded gingerly back to the fellowship hall to find Carmen.

As bad luck would have it, Abe Arnold, editor of *The Whitman Watch*, was coming toward her, and she had nowhere to hide. Abe was carrying his reporter's notebook, his old-school way of investigating, and he was grinning smugly at Frankie.

"Couldn't help but notice you were busy making the rounds around the room today, Frankie," Abe pulled open his notebook and thumbed to a blank page. "Care to share anything?"

Frankie did her best not to reveal anything, so she offered him a large disingenuous smile. "Nope, nothing. How about you, Abe?"

The editor closed his notebook, looking squarely down into Frankie's face. Abe stood a full foot plus a few inches taller than Frankie. He was impossible to miss anywhere he turned up. "I thought you agreed we would share information on this case, Frankie. You know, help each other out. Whad'ya say?"

Part of Frankie knew that Abe was right. The two were not enemies, after all. They worked for different newspapers, and each had their own style and could put their own spin on the story. Still, in the deep recesses of Frankie's ego, she bore the marks of Abe's dismissal of her when she wanted a part-time reporting job a few years back. This part of Frankie controlled her voice at the moment. "I don't think so, Abe. Sorry, I'm not ready."

Abe appreciated Frankie's sincerity as much as it disappointed him. He waved both hands in surrender. "Okay, okay. Come and see me if you change your mind. Honestly, Frankie, there are things I can teach you." Frankie didn't doubt that for a second.

The fellowship hall was all but empty now, and Frankie found Carmen in the kitchen, stacking dishes on the countertop with other donated items. She looked up at Frankie, an expression of annoyance mixed with concern. "I was about to file a missing person's report on you," Carmen said huffily.

"Let's talk in the parking lot. It's time to go." Frankie took her empty cake plate and Carmen's equally empty bar pan and did a slow walk down the hallway, favoring her right leg. She intended to spend the rest of her day talking with Shirley Lazaar and making a call to the Chocolate Siamese cat woman. First, she filled Carmen in on her conversations with Fitz Barnard and Lorna Ricks, sharing the ankle mishap as well.

"Yep, I see you're living up to your middle name again, Francine Grace." Carmen ribbed her friend, simultaneously grabbing the two pans from Frankie so she could concentrate on walking. Frankie often bumped into things without any provocation and even tripped over imaginary obstacles. She frequently told others her middle name was Grace, but that's where her gracefulness began and ended.

"What can I say? I was in a hurry." Frankie often reminded herself to slow down. It always seemed like she injured herself whenever she was on a mission.

Carmen told Frankie she didn't have much luck trying to make friends with Alana. She introduced herself to the young woman, beginning with a remark that she looked familiar and that wondered where she might have seen her. The comment didn't go anywhere, though, as Alana said she wasn't from Deep Lakes, only moving to the area three years ago to take the job as Ms. Spurgeon's assistant.

Carmen tried to ask questions about what it was like to work for Emily, offering her sympathy about her loss, but Alana just looked around the room and switched topics to Carmen's occupation. Since Alana didn't care a jot about sheep farming, she sat in silence. Carmen prodded her about college - where she went and when, but again, Alana was closed off, only saying she was a LPN and had taken some business classes at Mid State Tech. "Sorry I didn't do a better job, Frankie. I'm not that great at interrogating."

But Frankie smiled warmly at her partner and squeezed her shoulder. "On the contrary, Carmen. Your chat with Alana makes me wonder why she would look for a job in Deep Lakes in the first place. Emily wasn't advertising. She already had a good employee in Lorna. At least that's what I think. Most people would look in the city for a job like Alana's. So, why Deep Lakes?" She arched her brows up and down rapidly, making Carmen laugh.

"Okay, Sherlock. You investigate. I'll go back to the shop and see what's happening for tomorrow." Carmen's silver mini-van headed one direction, while Frankie's SUV headed another, toward the sheriff's department.

Chapter 18

In the spring, I have counted 136 different
kinds of weather inside of 24 hours.
– Mark Twain

Spring is when you feel like whistling,
even with a shoe full of slush.
– Doug Larson

Frankie hadn't even driven a block when her cell phone jangled. It was Adele Lundgren. "Frankie, glad I caught you. I cornered Cordelia McCoy at the luncheon and told her the Roots Fest needed her to make that presentation. What a nice gesture it would be to take Emily's place, leave a legacy, and all that." Adele was speed talking, of course.

Before Frankie could ask if Cordelia agreed, Adele jumped back in. "Bottom line, she said she's waiting for you to come to her with the presentation. She wants to see it before she'll agree. So hop to it, okay? Great PR for the town to have a family member do it. Okay, gotta go. Bye-ye." Adele finished with her signature melodic goodbye.

Frankie was chomping at the bit to have another reason to return to the mansion and now she had one; she would be expected, and she decided to call Cordelia in the morning to get on her agenda.

By now she was in the Sheriff's department lot. Once in Shirley Lazaar's office, Frankie realized she hadn't brought a bakery offering, as was normal, and she almost turned around and left again before Shirley caught her.

"Well, Francine, it's about time you showed up. Been expecting you for days." Shirley pursed her lips together, but her eyes twinkled. "What new information did you dig up, Hot Shot?" Shirley ushered her into one of the conference rooms for privacy.

Frankie began by apologizing she'd arrived sans baked goods, which made Shirley laugh. Then she proceeded to share as much as she could remember or cared to reveal about Fitz Barnard, Cordelia McCoy, Grant Foster, Alana West, Mack Perry, and even Lorna Ricks.

Shirley made just a few notes, so Frankie figured that the police already knew most of what she shared. Shirley leaned forward, though, when Frankie repeated the conversation between Cordelia and Grant as overheard by Carmen.

Frowning, she said, "I don't like second-hand hearsay, Frankie, but I'll take it for now. This could give us enough cause to search the phones of Ms. McCoy and Mr. Foster. Tell your friend Carmen that we may need to take her statement unless Ms. West comes forward to tell us what she heard." Frankie wondered if the reticent Alana would. It would be in Alana's best interest to reveal that conversation, as it pointed a potentially guilty finger at the pair.

"What can you share from your investigation? Who are your suspects?" Frankie probed. Shirley opened an accordion file and pulled out some papers, careful not to show too much. Frankie was surprised and disappointed to hear that Mack was under investigation.

"Your idea to talk to Alan Christensen about herbs paid off. Turns out Mack is growing all kinds of potentially harmful herbs, if used in the wrong way. He's the one who made all the teas for Emily we found in the house." Frankie frowned. She was under the impression Alana had made the loose teas, recalling the computer tab opened to herbs in the library.

"Perry even had a tansy marker in the garden, although the plant isn't up yet. And his garden shed has a number of insecticides and herbicides . . . lots of poisons." Shirley didn't seem to mind sharing details with Frankie, who wondered if she should tell the officer about Mack's outburst at the funeral lunch. But a nagging rumble in her gut made her pause before revealing that story.

"Anyone else?" Frankie was a little undone from being informed about Mack. "What about Cordelia and Foster?" She sounded defensive.

"Yes, we're looking. They are also persons of interest, for sure. Especially Ms. McCoy. She has a lot to gain from her cousin's death. The only problem is: she wasn't here before Emily died or the day she died. She has an iron-clad alibi."

Frankie sprang forward in her seat. "Sure, but that's where Grant Foster comes in. He could have done her dirty work for her, you know. Does he have an alibi?"

Shirley smiled like the Cheshire Cat. "Nope, he doesn't. He had a plane ticket back to Philly the morning Emily was discovered. But, we need to find evidence he was at the mansion on Sunday. It was Alana's day off. Mack Perry didn't see Foster on Sunday. That only leaves Emily, and she isn't talking."

Frankie marveled that Shirley could have a sense of cool humor about the dead but knew that after 30 years of working as a Chicago PD detective, murder and other ghastly stuff were part of the mundane. But Shirley's words only made Frankie feel worse. If Alana, Cordelia, and Foster were not at the mansion Sunday, that only left Mack, who lived there. Mack certainly had the opportunity to poison Emily.

Frankie promised to keep Shirley apprised of any other juicy tidbits and even informed her of her upcoming visit to the mansion to see Cordelia about the Roots Festival presentation. Shirley scowled a bit. "Make sure you're careful. I don't want to have to rescue you - or worse - Francine."

Frankie held her right hand over her heart as a promise. "Be sure you come by the bakery so I can give you a treat, or if you're in the mood for something stronger, come at night for a glass of wine." Frankie exited, hoping she could keep her promise to be careful.

What Frankie didn't know was that Shirley Lazaar intended to fill in Alonzo on every detail Frankie shared, including her visit to the mansion. Shirley was serious about the risk Frankie was taking entering that hornet's nest, not certain which person there had the lethal stinger.

* * *

The drive back to Bubble and Bake only took a few minutes, but Frankie needed to make one more call, so she pulled over to the curb at the corner of LaFollette and Meriwether, close to the new beauty salon, Bloom Studio, where Frankie would soon be a customer.

Her hairdresser, Janie, sold the business and moved to New Glarus to help take care of her ailing father. New owners Kris and Heidi were busy painting and redecorating to make the place boho chic before opening sometime next month.

Frankie glanced in the rearview mirror at her hair and rapidly growing bangs, hoping she could make it that long, or else she'd have to return to Henrietta's House of Hair. Henrietta was nice enough, but she always made Frankie's head into a hair helmet, not the style she was going for.

Back to the matter at hand, Frankie pulled the

shopping receipt from Lorna Ricks out of her purse and pressed in the number of Carly Bennett. A loud, slightly nasal voice picked up. "Carly's Cattery. This is Carly."

"Hi, Carly. This is Francine Champagne from Deep Lakes. Lorna Ricks gave me your number. I'm trying to track down the origins of a Chocolate Point Siamese cat named Pearl. She's about eight months old. If I send you a photo, would you recognize her?" Frankie had taken a photo of Pearl the same time Sadie the vet had, just in case.

Carly was helpful. "You bet I'll recognize her. I have photos of all my cats and who they were sold to. Text it to me and I'll look through my photos from the past year to see what comes up." Apparently cat breeders didn't find this kind of inquiry to be unusual. Frankie imagined cats changed owners often enough that breeders were used to the question.

Frankie zapped the photo to Carly, hoping she would hear back sooner than later. Then, she was off to Bubble and Bake, checking the time. Three o'clock. She wondered what she could accomplish the rest of the day, knowing she had at least three orders for pick-up tomorrow, when her phone rang. Thinking it was a speedy return from Carly, she chirped an excited hello.

Carmen's voice on the line wasn't quite as chirpy. "Frankie, where are you?"

"What's wrong, Carmen?" Her mind immediately wondered what she'd forgotten this time. "I'm almost to the shop. Be there in a minute."

"Well, that's good because Garrett is picking you up in two hours, remember?" When things became hectic, Carmen frequently served as Frankie's calendar alarm. This fact made Frankie feel guilty for not having better time management skills.

"Oh gee, I'm glad you called. I was just organizing the rest of my day according to bakery orders. How am I supposed to go on a date? Maybe…" Frankie was calculating, but Carmen cut in.

"Oh no you don't, Frankie Champagne! You are not cancelling this date. We'll finish this conversation when you get here." Carmen hung up.

A couple minutes later, Frankie breezed through the back door like her hair was on fire, wincing from the reminder her sore ankle produced when she hurried up the steps. But she paused when she spied all the activity in the kitchen. One baker's rack held pans of tarts in sour cherry, apricot, Italian lemon, and custard flavors.

Tess had pulled out shortbread dough from the freezer and created peanut butter, butterscotch, and honey almond cookies that were cooling on the counter. Carmen was filling bismarks with pastry cream in vanilla or chocolate, then would shove them in the walk-in cooler until Wednesday morning when they would get a fresh coat of icing.

"You see, Frankie, everything is under control here. Jovie is making scone dough for mini scones. We'll bake them up tomorrow and add flavors then. Come out here.

I want to show you something." Carmen gestured to the hallway that led to the front of the shop, and Frankie followed.

"Okay, I don't have anything to show you but I just had to tell you. Tía Pepita had to talk your aunt into coming back here. She went to your mom's house to get her a couple of hours ago. I think she's embarrassed, Frankie."

Back in the kitchen, Frankie saw Aunt CeCe was dressed in a somber shade of gray and black yoga pants. Frankie didn't know her aunt owned anything that wasn't colorful or patterned. She eyed her carefully, noticed she was preparing Frankie's pull-apart cinnamon rolls for Adele's order, and reached out to her, patting her hand delicately. "Oh thank you, Aunt CeCe, for working on the mayor's order for tomorrow morning."

Aunt CeCe smiled weakly at first, then a little brighter. "And look, Frankie. The other pull-aparts are finished. I'll ice them after they cool. Once these are in the oven, I'm going to put the other order together. So, you just go have a good time with Mr. Handsome." Frankie couldn't resist pulling Aunt CeCe in for a warm hug.

Once again, Frankie's crew had come to her rescue. "Okay, everyone. Take a break. I mean it. I can work on cookies and bismarks for an hour or so." But everyone shook their heads. Carmen said she'd only been there an hour herself and was picking up where Jovie left off. Tess was finishing up the last of the honey almond cookies and going home.

"Tía, Aunt CeCe, and I will finish the orders for tomorrow and call it a day. You can come in early tomorrow, Frankie, if you're worried about it." Carmen was teasing, though.

Frankie could relax, enjoy a special dinner with Garrett, and come in around seven tomorrow since Adele would be picking up her order at 8:30 a.m. Someone from Deep Lakes High School would be picking up cookies and tarts later that morning for the Spring Band and Choir Concert.

An hour later, Frankie passed judgment on her appearance with a satisfied approval. She was saving an aqua dress she'd snagged during a rare shopping excursion with her mother for such an occasion as tonight's dinner with Garrett at a five-star restaurant. A flattering empire style with a sweetheart neckline and pearl button placket, the dress hung in pleats, making Frankie look taller than her five feet.

She wore cascading earrings of silver seashells and a pair of muted silver criss-cross sandals with a short heel. Her mother had insisted she get a complete ensemble, so the earrings and sandals were purchased specifically for the dress. Looking over herself at every angle, she reminded herself to thank her mother for being so bossy. Then, she parked herself on a chair and iced her ankle before Garrett arrived.

Garrett was one hundred percent right: Frankie needed the royal treatment after the day she'd had. She brought along a portable ice pack for her ankle, but that didn't chill the date in any way. Dinner and conversation were cheerful and filled with laughter. The Nook measured up in spades to its online reviews. Frankie and Garrett were still talking about the quail dish made with rhubarb and the shrimp and banana curry on the way back to Deep Lakes.

But Frankie's favorite part of the evening was a surprise stop after dinner at The Blue Velvet Lounge where people danced the night away to the sultry tunes of a Latin quartet. The couple were lost in the music and finally departed at midnight, reluctant to call it an evening.

"I just thought those silver slippers deserved a few turns on the dance floor, Miss Francine," Garrett had said with a wink. "You're as beautiful as a warm spring day," he added, gliding her across the floor, practically carrying her so her ankle wouldn't get any worse.

When Garrett suggested a rest, Frankie used ice from her drink, wrapped in a napkin, on her ankle, making both of them giggle like kids. This would be an evening for Frankie's memory book, she decided. She was growing closer to Garrett with every date but was determined not to do any soul searching until it was necessary.

Why spoil a good thing by over-analyzing it? Frankie wasn't sure if the thought belonged to her or was planted by The Golden One, but she didn't care; good advice was good advice. Falling into bed after one in the morning, she set two different alarms, just in case.

* * *

Rising at 5:30 a.m., Frankie made a mental note that a date ending at 1:00 a.m. was not conducive to an early alarm at her age. Still, she awoke smiling, stretched, and looked out on a world still bathed in darkness for at least another half hour. Doing an automatic phone check, she noticed a text from Carly Bennett and clicked on it without hesitation. It was time stamped last evening at 7:00 p.m.

I have the information you asked for. Call me and I'll tell you what I remember about the buyer. Frankie almost started hitting the call button before remembering not everyone gets up at 5:30 a.m.. She would have to cool her jets until 8:00 a.m., a time she deemed reasonable for making a call to a stranger.

By 5:45, she was out of the shower and downstairs, putting tuna in Liberace's bowl and setting the coffee maker to "strong" for her first mug. She smiled proudly at the boxes of pull-apart morning rolls for Adele's order: one a classic cinnamon, the other a cherry-apricot concoction with added spices and orange zest. Next to those boxes was the stack for the school.

Everything was ready to go, and Frankie could focus on tomorrow's bakery day. First she checked the order board, finding a larger than normal order from Alonzo. *Maybe the department was hosting a regional meeting of some kind*, Frankie thought, searching her memory bank from last spring as to whether this was a recurring order.

Onward. She needed to prepare four coffee cakes for Alonzo, so she began gathering ingredients for the basic yeast dough, then retrieved the yeast cake from the cooler and the thermometer for the milk, which she began heating in a kettle.

It had been quite some time, maybe a couple of weeks, since she had a personal chit-chat with Lon, which prompted Frankie to want to make at least one special coffee cake in his honor. Alonzo had been a pillar of support for Frankie after her marriage broke apart. He often fixed things around her house before the fire and would even show up to blow snow in the winter and plow out her driveway. Frankie felt a pang of guilt again that their friendship had taken a backseat to her investigating ventures and her romance with Garrett.

"C'est la vie, chérie!" Well, at last The Pirate Firefly was back on duty and speaking French with an Italian accent, making Frankie giggle. "You deserve some romance in your life, chérie. Don't knock it, eh!"

Still, she searched her recipes, looking for the coffee cakes she made for holidays, and located the pistachio chocolate cake that was always a hit and frequently requested. Along with that delicious green cake, she would make monkey bread, balls of dough stacked in an angel food cake pan with melted dark brown sugar and butter poured over it in layers, nuts tucked in between.

The other coffee cakes would be fruity: one cherry and one apple. Lucky for her, that was the only order that needed filling for Wednesday.

By seven, the kitchen was bustling with chatter, clanking pans, and whirring mixers. Tess arrived early, giving time for her and Frankie to catch up with each other. Jovie was working at the florist's to help with arrangements for an upcoming funeral at the Methodist church, and Carmen was shopping at the Madison Market, something she did most Mondays, except that Emily's funeral forced a change in plans. She dropped off Tía Pepita and Aunt CeCe together since neither aunt much liked to drive.

The aunts were busy with their customary empanadas and macarons. Tess was making mini scones from yesterday's dough, putting her own African twist to a couple of batches; one featured yams, and another was made with cardamom, plantains, and coconut. Their scents wafting from the oven transformed the kitchen into an exotic place.

Two coffee cakes were in the oven by eight, so Frankie excused herself to call Carly Bennett. Carly picked up almost immediately and sounded a nasally buoyant hello into Frankie's ear.

"This is Frankie Champagne. I got your text message about the cat we talked about yesterday."

"Sure, yeah. Just a minute, let me grab that info." Carly was back in moments. "Okay. I remember selling this cat because the woman specifically asked for an adult cat, which is unusual because most people want kittens. The only cat I had was a five-month-old, but she didn't look like a kitten anymore, so . . ."

"And what do you remember about the buyer?" Frankie prodded.

"She was kind of young, I mean, maybe late 20s. Dark hair, I think she was Latino."

"Are you sure, I mean about her being Latino?" Frankie hadn't noticed any particular ethnic features in Alana. Maybe Frankie was barking up the wrong tree, assuming Alana had purchased Pearl.

Carly said she was pretty certain. "That was only three months ago, and I have a pretty good memory. Let's see here. Well, I have her name as Rona Gomez, so that sounds Latino. I guess with her dark hair and eyes, I just assumed . . ."

"Did you say Rona Gomez?" Frankie wanted to be sure she'd heard correctly.

"Uh huh. Do you know her?" Carly asked.

"I sure don't," Frankie admitted, "but I've heard the name. Thank you for the information; I owe you, Carly. What kind of bakery do you like? I'll drop by with some next time I come to Gibson."

Carly's information floored Frankie. The widow of José Gomez, the man who had died from an explosion at the quarry and victim of silicosis, buying a cat for Emily Spurgeon? That Rona Gomez would be at least sixty or older by now. Was Rona Gomez living around Deep Lakes and conspiring with Alana to off Emily?

She had to think. She needed a picture of Alana to show Carly. Maybe social media could provide one. Frankie did a quick search on her tablet, but the name Alana West turned up nothing.

She tried Alana's maiden name: Brophy. *The Whitman Watch* had published her marriage license with Jeremy West in 2015. Nothing else emerged, though. Then she remembered the information Carmen scraped together from Alana at the funeral.

Frankie searched "Alana Brophy" under the Mid State Technical School archives, choosing a ten year time period. To her amazement, a photo and obituary appeared on the screen. A food service employee of Mid State Tech, Alana Brophy, died in 2010. The photo of a robust, middle-aged woman, regaled for her kindness to students, revealed this was not the woman Frankie was searching for. *Huh, what a weird coincidence.*

Frankie remembered she needed to contact Cordelia McCoy to make an appointment to see her. Alana picked up that call. "Spurgeon residence. May I help you?" The melodic lilt to Alana's voice was replaced with fatigue and a hint of irritation.

"Hello, Alana. It's Frankie Champagne. I'm supposed to set up a time to see Cordelia with the presentation information for the park dedication. The sooner the better, please." Frankie's voice was perky and firm.

"Okay, but Ms. McCoy keeps her own schedule, so I don't have anything concrete. Why don't you come over tomorrow morning? Will ten o'clock work? She's not an early riser." Frankie said 10:00 a.m. was fine. That would give her time to work in the shop until the bakery closed.

On her way back to the kitchen, she turned toward a loud rapping at the front door of the shop. She could see Adele peering through the window as she ran over to unlock the front door. "Sorry I had to use the front door, Frankie. The New Glarus beer truck is blocking the alley."

"That's okay, Adele. People around here just love their Spotted Cow, you know." New Glarus beer was popular all over the state, but people in Frankie's area loved the Spotted Cow brew the best. Now that summer was on the horizon, Frankie would need to place a beer order, too. Maybe she could waylay the New Glarus guy before he finished his delivery. To Adele, she said, "Just wait here, and I'll grab your order."

"Thanks, Frankie. Be sure to send the bill to my office. It's budget time, so I'll need something for next week, same time. Just change it up, okay?"

Adele was ready to fly but turned at the last second. "By the way, I love the sidewalk chalk drawing you have in front of the shop. Do you know who made it? It gave me a good idea for the Roots Festival." Frankie jumped in before Adele was off and running with her next thought.

"My Aunt CeCe actually drew and colored it," Frankie said, uncertain where the conversation would go from there. She purposely left out her mother's contribution to the artwork.

"How would your aunt like to lead a sidewalk drawing activity for kids at the Roots Festival? She can show them some ideas, then they can each have a sidewalk square to draw something related to Deep Lakes. Maybe even make it into a contest . . . hmm." Adele's head was twisting and curving in multiple directions.

"I'll run it past her, Adele, and give you a call, okay?" Frankie's offer was minimally acknowledged before Adele was out the door. Frankie had to laugh that the chalk drawing amounted to something positive for her aunt, since it was crafted in mischief.

Entering the kitchen, Frankie walked over to Aunt CeCe, who was dressed today in her typical floral garb. She repeated what the mayor had said and asked her aunt if she would lead the activity. Aunt CeCe beamed and agreed immediately. Frankie thought her artistic aunt must miss using her talents; even though she baked works of art in her macarons, it wasn't the same as drawing or painting. She was happy Aunt CeCe would have something else to showcase her talents and occupy her time.

By lunchtime, all of the bakery was ready for tomorrow, except for finishing touches that would be done before opening time in the morning. Carmen arrived with a van full of market goods, honking from the alley for anyone left at the shop to help her unload. Frankie was alone in the kitchen, but dashed out the back door to meet her business partner, her ankle reminding her it was still sore. Opening the basement overhead door, the two women grabbed dollies and made fast work of hauling the boxes inside and up the basement ramp Frankie's brother James had built to ease an aching back.

"Anything good at the market today?" Frankie asked, knowing Carmen always found some quality produce she hadn't expected.

"I got some gorgeous spring onions and plump asparagus. I also snagged some early peas, rhubarb, and leaf lettuces, along with the usual." Frankie had a rhubarb pie recipe that, in her opinion, was heaven-sent, and she intended to make it for her friends and Garrett. The spring onions and asparagus would be essentials for her signature quiche but would also make great flatbread pizzas for the wine lounge.

The two used some of the leaf lettuces, early peas, and other fresh veggies to make a quick salad for lunch, while Frankie filled in Carmen on the phone call with Carly, the cattery lady.

"That Rona Gomez story freaks me out a little, Frankie. I wonder what it means and who's behind it. Weird, huh?" Carmen was trying to piece the information together.

"Two Alana Brophys: that's just as weird. And at the same college! Too bad you couldn't come up with a photo of Alana." Carmen looked at Frankie, who was smiling slyly, and added, "Oh no, Frankie. I hope you're not going to try to take her picture tomorrow at the mansion. Don't do it." Frankie admitted that Carmen had read her mind.

But Carmen was on to a different subject. "What I really want to know, Frankie, is how was your dinner with Garrett?" Carmen gave her friend a curious side-eye, inwardly delighted at the expression of excitement she saw on Frankie's face.

"I don't know how it could have been more perfect, and it was just what I needed after the funeral escapades," Frankie sighed, like a teenager, and filled in all the details for Carmen, who was impressed the two had gone dancing to cap off the evening.

After filling out inventory sheets, Frankie sitting with her sore ankle propped up and icing, they called it a day. Carmen left out the back, and Frankie decided to make a run out to the vineyard, followed by a careful workout at the Wellness Center, when she heard a thump coming from the lounge.

Thinking Liberace had knocked over something, she headed through the shop to see what trouble the kitty had caused. But Liberace was curled up in a ball in the sunny window, softly snoring.

Near the corner coffee table, Frankie found a book on the floor, *Tales and Legends of the Old West*. It was the same book Kurt was reading to Ol' Jim on fiasco Sunday (as Frankie called it), and it was the same book she'd put away Sunday after the Buzzards went home. She remembered how tightly it fit into the slot on the bookshelf. "Okay, who's messing with me?" Frankie said aloud to scare away the heebie-jeebies she was feeling.

* * *

Instead of taking the traditional route to Bountiful Fruits, Frankie drove Lake Road to see if the ice had melted. She picked up the road where Lake Loki came into view and noticed the ice was all but gone, and the formerly naked trees were dressed in wispy lime green leaves.

Hopeful fishermen lined the shore here and there, ready to reel in walleyes, a tasty white fish abundant in the spring during their annual "run" from the Fox River. The cold waters of Deep Lakes produced delicious fish most of the year, but the walleye were highly prized for their size and the sport in catching them.

At Bountiful Fruits, spring looked like it had unpacked its glad rags and was ready to settle in to stay. Most of the trees were in some stage of budding, ready to display flowers or leaves.

The grapevines looked healthy and lively. The sound of birds singing out calls to potential mates made Frankie smile affectionately in the direction of the melodies. Inside the wine lab, Zane and Nelson were busy with spreadsheets and measurements.

"Nice to see you, Ms. Champagne," Nelson said, then

turned to his lab partner. "May I tell her, Zane?" Zane nodded, somewhat absently. "The new chardonnay is tasting marvelous. I think the investment will pay off."

Frankie had gambled, trying to entice new customers to the winery by making some traditional wines that were less sweet. She'd bought the grape juice from New York, and it wasn't cheap. Because her facility didn't have the luxury of aging wines, she added apricots to the Chardonnay juices to boost production.

The grape variety grew in many areas of the U.S., but the juice varied with climate. The New York region produced a complex flavor profile with higher sugar content, whereas California was known for its rich, buttery flavor.

"Would you like a taste?" Nelson was already getting a sample glass from the rack. He poured out a finger-full for Frankie. Like an expert, she swirled it, took in its floral citrus fragrance mixed with the heady apricot, then sipped, swirling it around her mouth, before swallowing and taking intentional breaths.

"You're right, Nelson, as usual. I like the harmony of the grape with the apricots. Now we just need a name for it." Secretly, Frankie anticipated naming the wine after the aunts in some way. "When do you anticipate it will be ready to bottle?"

Nelson opened the calendar tab on his computer to consult and count the days. "I think ten days more would be beneficial. So anywhere in the 10- to 17-day range,

Ms. Champagne. Frankie opened her phone to block off the dates for bottling. "Would you like to taste any of the other batches?" Nelson asked.

"I'd better not, thank you. I'm going to the Wellness Center, and I better go sober," Frankie laughed and headed to the door before Zane stopped her.

"Wait a minute, Frankie. I did a little poking around and found some more information on your Granite Mansion people. There's not much out there, but I printed off what I found today." Zane handed Frankie two sheets of paper.

Frankie was surprised that Zane had done some freelance snooping. Frankie folded the papers, tucked them into her purse, and left with a wave. She breathed in the fresh spring air before opening the SUV door and driving away.

Late afternoon at the Wellness Center brought a different crowd to classes. The early morning workout warriors were mostly gray-haired women and men, trying to stay active in retirement or working on physical therapy per their doctors' orders. The late afternoon schedule brought in people just finished with work for the day, trying to cram in a workout before going home for the evening.

Before spying Peggy by a locker, Frankie stopped at the reception desk to catch up with Taylor. "How's your dog doing, Taylor? I remember you said something about him having surgery." Jameson, a chocolate lab, was recovering well from having an ear tumor removed but now needed to return to the vet for anxiety. *What dog parents wouldn't do for their dogs*, Frankie thought.

"Maybe Jameson just needs a shot of Jameson for his anxiety," Frankie quipped, hoping not to offend. Taylor just laughed and talked about recent fishing excursions she'd been enjoying in recent weeks with her hubby, Jake, and plans for a number of short summer getaways.

Frankie excused herself to catch up with Peggy before their classes began. She knew her mother would not be joining her for WERQ, a cardio dance class, although some days Peggy could dance circles around Frankie. Frankie was reminded of her wobbly ankle again and wondered if she was able enough for a cardio dance class.

"Hey, Mom." Frankie caught Peggy at the bubbler, filling her water bottle.

"How is my ace detective doing today?" Peggy wanted to know. Frankie looked at her to see if she was being sarcastic but decided the comment was her mother's form of approval instead. Before Peggy could remind her about the need to talk to the police again, Frankie filled her in on her talk with Shirley, including the department's investigation of Mack Perry. Since her mom had lived through the quarry lawsuit and much of its history, she shared the cat story, too, featuring someone named Rona Gomez.

Peggy's jaw was set, and her lips were one grim line. "The Rona Gomez story is a mystery all on its own. I just don't know. But, I'm glad you've decided to give Fitz Barnard a rest, dear. You're barking up the wrong tree on that one; the only thing Fitz is guilty of is being ambitious."

Peggy was sad to hear about Mack Perry being treated as a suspect. "Just because a person grows herbs, doesn't mean they plan to poison someone. If you ask me, the department is barking up the wrong tree, too!"

She huffed and strutted off to a Strength and Balance class. Frankie agreed with her mother but knew that Alonzo would instruct his investigators to follow all viable leads in the case.

An hour later, Frankie felt better for having danced off some of last night's 5-course feast, although some of her moves were a little off-kilter. She happily shared memories of the evening with her mother over a protein-powered smoothie in the Wellness Center cafe. Her daughter's willingness to share personal information without being prompted brightened Peggy's mood.

"All I can say is I'm happy you're taking some time for yourself . . . that your life isn't all work." Frankie had to admit that her mother was right. Before parting ways, Frankie told Peggy about the mayor's offer for Aunt CeCe to teach sidewalk drawing. To her surprise, Peggy laughed out loud.

"Well, isn't that something? That will be good for CeCe, doing something artistic. But you have to admit, it's pretty amusing how it came about." Frankie was shocked her mother would make light of the event. After all, Sunday was only a couple of days past, and Frankie hadn't recovered from the memory of Aunt CeCe's shenanigans. She was still worried the police might somehow get wind of it, too.

Chapter 19

Manipulation, fueled with good intent,
can be a blessing. But when used wickedly, it is
the beginning of a magician's karmic calamity.
- T.F. Hodge

On a whim, Frankie headed to the shop kitchen an hour early and decided to make a gluten-free quiche to bring to Cordelia McCoy that morning. She had coconut flour, which she combined with cauliflower for the crust, then used three kinds of cheeses, onion, and garlic powders and paprika for spices. It was Frankie's first attempt at a gluten-free quiche, and she thought it smelled good baking in the oven.

She also made a flourless chocolate cake, pouring the batter into four small pans, so she could freeze the others. She knew a couple other Deep Lakes citizens who would appreciate the gluten-free chocolate cakes, so a small cake would have to do for Cordelia. Honestly, Frankie wasn't sure why she was going through the trouble for a murder suspect. "Because: you know you can catch more flies with honey than vinegar," The Golden One quoted.

It was Carmen's traditional day to help Ryan with farmwork, so Tess and Frankie had charge of the business while the aunts baked. Frankie decided to run retail this morning, so she could catch up with customers, hoping she would get to chat a little with Alonzo. Tess orchestrated kitchen business, icing Carmen's bismarks for the bakery case, then readying dough for tomorrow.

Between 6:30 a.m. and 7:00 a.m., the bakery was bustling with regular customers picking up their favorites with coffees to go. Promptly at 7:00 a.m., the bell jangled louder than usual, and Frankie stared into the unwelcome face of Donavan Pflug.

"Morning. The sheriff said it was my turn to pick up the bakery order." Pflug looked just about as happy to see Frankie as she was to see him.

Frankie picked up two large boxes from the bar. "Here you go. Everything's ready. It's a bigger order than usual. You must have a big meeting today." Frankie attempted small talk.

"Yes," Pflug said, not elaborating. Then he lifted his index finger to signal he was about to make a point.

"By the way, I need to let you know that your aunt gave away some herbs last week." Frankie's heart grew stone cold, and she held her breath. Here it was, the moment she'd dreaded. The cops knew about Aunt CeCe's extracurricular habit. She couldn't reply, but Pflug wasn't finished anyway.

"As I told your aunt, it's okay to give away herbs from

your garden, but you can't make it part of your business here, not without a permit to sell them."

Had Frankie heard Pflug correctly? Herbs from the shop garden? Herbs from plants Frankie was growing in her make-shift greenhouse behind Bubble and Bake? She almost did a little victory dance, then caught herself, but she couldn't help but smile at Pflug.

"Just a minute," Frankie said, then reached into the bakery case to carefully settle several macarons into a bag and handed them to the officer.

Pflug looked dumbstruck. "What's this, Mrs. Champagne, a bribe? I mean it about the herbs. You can't just include them in your business." Pflug's tone was flat and stern. It was his tone and the use of the word "Mrs." that darkened Frankie's mood.

"No, these are not a bribe, Officer. They are the best macarons you'll find outside a French patisserie. I'm trying to be nice," she said crisply.

Pflug's expression indicated he didn't comprehend what she said, but he turned toward the door, boxes stacked in his arms, the bag of macarons balanced on top. Frankie knew he couldn't open the door without help, so she pranced around the counter, beating him to the shop door. As she opened it, her better judgment to keep quiet lost out. "You should try it sometime. Being nice, I mean." Then she shut the door firmly behind him to cheers from both fireflies.

* * *

Alana ushered Frankie into the mansion's familiar library while she summoned Cordelia McCoy. Alana wore a yellow uniform today with athletic shoes that were the same color. Her dark hair was pulled into a ponytail, revealing a face that looked tired.

Frankie studied Alana with scrutiny, wondering if she was Latino, wondering how old she was, wondering if she gave the name Rona Gomez to the cat lady. She also wondered how she was going to take a photo of Alana without her knowing it. Alana looked at Frankie with the same scrutiny.

"I don't know what's in those boxes, but *she* will never eat it. You can bet on that," Alana said with disgust, then left the room.

Frankie didn't waste any time sitting around. She went to the large mahogany desk to see if the medical records were still stacked there. The pile was gone. The desk looked like it had been recently cleared. The mansion tablet was sitting on the blotter. Beside it was the giant book of North American trees. A blank pad of paper sat next to the tablet with a pen laying atop.

Frankie poked the tablet to see if it was on. It came to life, revealing a screen open to Wisconsin statutes on estates. There were a couple of other open tabs, too. She grabbed her own tablet to take a photo of the estate page, clicked the camera button, then dropped the tablet in her haste, where it skidded underneath the desk. At the sound of approaching feet, Frankie scooted back to the sofa without the tablet.

Alana opened the door, motioning for Frankie to follow her. "Ms. McCoy is in the solarium." Frankie was surprised at Alana's use of solarium rather than sunroom, which it was called before Emily died. She was even more surprised to be meeting Cordelia there. Cordelia's pale skin looked like it never saw any sunlight. Alana gestured to the entrance then left without checking to see if either woman wanted anything.

Cordelia was dressed in black lounging pants and an oversized black and gray striped sweater. She was curled into a ball in a corner of the wicker sofa, her feet tucked under her bottom. Her hands were wrapped into the overly long sleeves of the sweater, and she cradled a steaming mug of coffee. Cordelia looked just awful.

She presented a pitiful face to Frankie. "I have a terrible headache, Ms. Champagne. The only reason I agreed to see you is to get that crazy mayor lady off my case."

Frankie laughed inwardly at the assessment of Adele. She set both bakery boxes on the glass coffee table and opened each.

"Look, Ms. McCoy, you can't live on caffeine alone. You have to eat something. That's probably why you have a headache. I brought you a quiche and a cake. Both are gluten-free. Should I get Alana to bring you a plate and fork?" Frankie actually felt sorry for Cordelia for some reason. It was Frankie's nature to care, to show kindness; she had been raised that way.

Cordelia shook her head, rose off the sofa, and slipped on the black ballet flats nearby. "Let's not bother Elaine. Come with me to the kitchen. And bring the boxes. Let's see how good of a baker you really are."

Frankie was surprised but followed Cordelia down a short hallway leading to the kitchen. She opened a cupboard, took down a cake plate, then produced a fork and knife from one drawer. She cut a slice from the chocolate cake and took a bite, lingering over the flavor.

"Oh my, this is heaven, Ms. Champagne." Cordelia pointed to the coffee maker in the corner. "Please help yourself. The coffee pods are in the drawer below. Mugs are up above."

Frankie was beside herself at this new version of Cordelia, one that was almost amiable instead of condescending. A little chocolate cake offering went a long way, apparently. Frankie made a dark roast brew from a well-known chain, while Cordelia cut another slice of cake. "May I get some cream from your fridge?" Cordelia nodded, unable to speak with a large chunk of cake in her mouth.

Just then, in walked Alana, looking unpleasantly surprised at the two women camped in her space. "What are you doing in here?" She glowered at both of them.

"If you wanted something, you should have rang for me."
Alana turned and stomped out of the kitchen. Getting
Alana to stay in one place long enough for a clear photo
wasn't going to be easy today.

"She doesn't like me at all," Cordelia said in a low
voice. Frankie wanted to respond by saying Cordelia
could start by calling her the right name but decided
against that tack since she was finally connecting with
her. Instead, she changed topics.

"You know, people in Deep Lakes remember you
as the little girl who adored her cousin, following her
around, keeping her company," Frankie began.

Cordelia stiffened a little. "Things changed. It's not
that simple."

"You never forgave Emily because of Taffy," Frankie
stated directly. "She told me as much."

Cordelia's reaction was a bitter snort. "That's what she
told you? Come with me, Ms. Champagne." Cordelia set
the cake plate on the counter and headed out the back
door with Frankie in tow, following her toward the lake.

Frankie saw Mack working in the perennial beds and
made a point of throwing out an exaggerated wave. If
this woman was going to push her into the lake, Frankie
wanted someone to know where she was. Mack waved
back, stood up, and stared in the direction they were
going.

A small path of granite pavers suddenly appeared
in the grass, leading to a square space surrounded by

evergreen hedges. Cordelia walked through the narrow opening in the hedges, and Frankie followed, throwing caution to the wind.

Inside the hedges, Frankie was amazed to see a tall granite monument marker in the center with the name Spurgeon and the name McCoy on it. On either side of the monument were headstones. There were three of them. The first two headstones belonged to Cordelia and Elmer Spurgeon. Cordelia's headstone included an inscription for the infant she lost. The third one, where Cordelia stood, was engraved "Bryan McCoy. Born: March 1976. Died: May 1978."

"My little brother. I absolutely adored him. He died of pneumonia. A week later, Taffy was hit by a car and killed. I lost everything I loved, Ms. Champagne." Cordelia's voice was soft and broken. She gazed into the distance, looking like a ghost who might disappear in a puff of wind.

"You didn't lose everyone. You still had Emily. She loved you, too." Frankie tried to help Cordelia see the truth in the situation.

"I was just a little girl. In my mind, it was all Emily's fault. She helped take care of my little brother when he was sick. She was taking care of Taffy when she was killed. It all made sense at the time."

"Then after your brother died, your parents decided to move. Your mother must have been heartbroken," Frankie offered.

"Yes. Mother wanted to get as far away from Deep Lakes as possible. She wanted to go back home to her family. We never looked back." The verdict against Deep Lakes and the Spurgeons appeared to be final for the McCoys.

The April wind had picked up, and rain clouds loomed overhead. "Come on; let's go back inside, Ms. McCoy." As they exited the little cemetery, Frankie noticed Mack was examining a tree within earshot of the hedges. He nodded at Frankie as the women headed to the back door.

Alana was in the kitchen. She didn't look busy, and Frankie wondered if she'd been snooping out the window at them. "Are you finished with this food, Ms. McCoy. I'll clean up if you are."

Alana had adopted a more contrite tone. In reply, Cordelia picked up the chocolate cake tin and a fork and left the kitchen without a word. Frankie shrugged and followed her back to the solarium, where Cordelia proceeded to finish the rest of the chocolate cake, handing Frankie the empty pan.

"Thank you. That was delicious. As long as I'm staying in Deep Lakes, you can make that my weekly order, Ms. Champagne." Cordelia actually produced a small smile.

"It's a deal on one condition. You agree to do the presentation for the park?" Frankie thought the cake might give her a tiny bit of leverage.

"Oh, I might as well do it. Here." Cordelia handed Frankie a slip of paper with her personal email on it.

"Send the speech and the presentation to this address. I'll let you know if I have questions or changes." Cordelia was suddenly astute and business-like.

Frankie nodded, ready to leave, satisfied she'd made a little progress with Cordelia. Then she remembered that her tablet was still under the library desk. She retraced her steps, opened the double doors and closed them as quietly as possible behind her. Right away she noticed both tablets were sitting on the desktop, and neither one responded when swiped. Both tablets were in sleep mode. They were identical.

Anxious to be on her way before another awkward encounter with Alana, she grabbed the one on the left, hoping that Alana had seen it on the floor and simply picked it up without thinking. Then Frankie slipped quietly out the front door.

Frankie barely greeted her kitchen crew when she breezed through the back door of the shop and scampered up the stairs to her apartment, still a little wobbly on her tender ankle. Marveling that Cordelia managed to eat an entire chocolate cake but not a bite of the nutritious quiche, Frankie pressed the on button of the tablet so she could add information to her Post-it suspect board.

With slow internet connections in her small town, Frankie grabbed some leftover chicken casserole her mother gave her on Sunday, sniffed it, decided it was perfectly edible, and reheated it while she waited. The home screen appeared with the numeric keypad, and

Frankie tapped in the password, once, twice, a third time. No luck.

Oh crap, she thought, *I grabbed the wrong tablet. This is just great.* Her only consolation was that Alana wouldn't be able to get into her tablet, so at least her notes and suspect board were safe. Then a perfectly terrible idea occurred to Frankie. She could take this tablet out to Nelson and Zane to see if they could unlock it.

Eating the casserole, she chewed over the idea of breaking into the tablet, but her conscience got the better of her, and she set the tablet aside, trading it for her phone. She could access her tablet files on her cell, but they would be much smaller and harder to work with. Still, it was better than nothing.

"Oh for Pete's sake, why don't you just drive back to the mansion and get your tablet? It's not that big of a deal." The Golden One seemed perplexed by Frankie's alleged dilemma. Frankie shushed Goldie, trying to think about how unethical it would be to hack into the mansion's tablet.

"If you have to think that hard about it, you already know the answer, Francine," Goldie admonished.

With difficulty, Frankie managed to add the newfound information about Cordelia's little brother under Cordelia's name. Under Fitz Barnard, Frankie added the name of the doctor's mother, Anna Kuhn, and Fritz Kuhn, the grandfather who died of quarry disease and whose family received zero compensation. She wasn't one hundred percent ready to let Barnard off the hook, a thought that made her turn to Mack Perry's name to sadly add the investigation notes about his herbs and pesticides.

She also made a new note with questions about who bought the Chocolate Point Siamese, Pearl Two, and who gave the name Rona Gomez to Carly Bennett, and why use that name? If only she had a photo of Alana to send to Carly.

The questions triggered Frankie's memory of the folded printouts from Zane. When she opened them, she realized he'd been looking into Alana. Zane didn't have much luck, but there was a brief profile that included her date of birth, current address, and listed her LPN degree from Mid State Technical College. It also listed her name with "also known as" Alana Brophy, but no other details. No birthplace, no list of family members.

Frankie stared at the paper absent-mindedly, then she gasped as she recognized something. She quickly opened her phone and thumbed through document photos until she found what she was looking for. *It couldn't be, could it?*

Chapter 20

A cat has absolute emotional honesty:
human beings, for one reason or another,
may hide their feelings, but a cat does not."
– Ernest Hemingway

They are like the clue in the labyrinth,
or the compass in the night.
– Joseph Joubert

Frankie had to do something; every fiber of her being was prickly, electrified by scraps of information gelling into a concrete form. She needed to be alone, so baking in the shop kitchen was impossible. She grabbed her fleece jacket and headed out the shop's front door, bypassing the kitchen altogether.

She walked down Granite Street toward the quarry; a jumble of ideas skipped along various pathways in her mind as she tried to capture them and pin them in place. Frankie stopped when she reached Spurgeon Park. Green grass was sprouting upward. Large mounds of mulch had been dumped near the construction site to spread around the landscape once the buildings were completed.

The place was loud with the hubbub of equipment - not the quiet atmosphere Frankie was hoping for to aid her thought process. She found herself looking around as if she were lost, then saw someone coming toward her wearing a neon yellow vest and helmet, carrying a clipboard; it was her brother, James.

"Frankie, what brings you out here?" James shouted over the din of crunching and scraping backhoe loaders. Frankie didn't answer, still caught up in her swirling thoughts, disoriented by the noise. James hooked his arm in hers and led her toward the gazebo area. Somewhat sheltered by a border of tall trees, the area was quieter.

"Hey, I want to show you something." James pulled his sister into a concealed entrance inside the covered gazebo. Here it was even quieter. "I'm not supposed to do this - the gazebo is supposed to be top secret, you know, but I'm itching to show this design to someone. Look at the top; walk around it."

James pointed to the octagonal roof, which was edged in solid decorative cedar. Cemented onto the cedar edging were brightly polished granite tiles, each carved with compass points.

"Isn't it clever, Frankie? We wanted it to match the courthouse dome with its directional points. And of course, it had to feature our local granite."

James was proud of the idea. But there was more. Also carved onto each granite face was a constellation, visible to the viewer who looked in that particular direction of the night sky. The gazebo served as a map for stargazers.

The artistry and thoughtfulness that had gone into the design made Frankie tear up. Their father, Charlie, would have swelled with pride. James gave his sister a tight, one-armed hug.

"I knew you would appreciate this, Frankie. Here I was thinking that I just had to show someone, and you showed up!" James left Frankie to return to work, saying she could stay as long as she wanted.

Frankie gazed with wonder at each polished slab with its compass point and corresponding constellation. She immediately recognized Ursa Major on the North tile as the Great Bear, easily spotted in the sky as it included the Big Dipper. She knew the Hydra on the South tile, too, since it was one of the largest constellations: a horizontal sea serpent stretching across that section of sky. The East tile depicted both Cancer the Crab and Leo the Lion, memorable because of their home in the Zodiac.

The West tile, however, gave Frankie pause. She knew Virgo the maiden, even though she couldn't always find it in the sky, but the constellation Boötes was unfamiliar. It looked like a large kite with stick legs and arms holding a small kite. She made a note to herself to look it up when she got home or when she got her tablet back. The thought of the tablet brought Frankie back to her senses for the moment, and she exited the concealed gazebo, feeling oddly detached from the world.

Walking back toward Bubble and Bake, Frankie tried to work out how she was going to get her tablet back. Should she call first or show up unannounced? Was it even a wise idea to go back there; a house full of suspects in Emily Spurgeon's death? Oddly enough, Frankie was spurred on by the two fireflies.

"You might as well finish what you started, Frankie. No turning back now," The Golden One weighed in.

"We're with you all the way!" The Pirate enthused, clacking the heels of his big pirate boots together.

Frankie wished she felt the bravado the two fireflies imparted. She wasn't in the mood to procrastinate, knowing her mind would never let her rest until she exchanged tablets. But, she needed to make a phone call first. She walked through the back alley to the sitting area along Sterling Creek and sat on a bench where she hoped she wouldn't be disturbed.

"Dickens and Probst. How may I help you?" Brenda's voice greeted Frankie pleasantly.

"Hello, Brenda. This is Frankie Champagne. I was wondering if anyone else has called or come in recently to ask about the quarry case files? You know, the ones I looked through, up in the attic?"

Brenda was quick to reply. "Yes, as a matter of fact. Just hold on a minute while I look at the guest log. We keep a record of everyone who inquires about cases ... but I'm sure you knew that already."

Brenda set the phone down, and Frankie could hear a

little background shuffle going on. Obviously organized, Brenda was back in a matter of moments. "Here we are. Abe Arnold from *The Whitman Watch* came in yesterday. Mr. Probst escorted him to the attic, and he was there about a half hour. "

Darn that Abe! He must have talked to Ward at the funeral, or he's just a good investigator. Frankie knew Abe would likely go down the same trails as Frankie; after all, he was an excellent journalist.

Brenda was speaking again, and this time her tone shifted to one of uncertainty. "Well, this is weird," she began. Prompted by Frankie, she went on, half speaking to herself. "There's an inquiry here from over a month ago. I don't remember this man. I wonder who recorded this." Brenda was clearly searching her own memory bank and coming up empty.

"Brenda, who was it? Do you have a name?" Frankie prodded.

"Yes, sure. The name is Rex Findlay, but it doesn't say where he's from." Frankie gasped, and she almost dropped her phone into the creek. She had not expected that name, but new realization was beginning to tick into her already addled mind.

"Oh, do you recognize the name, Frankie?" Brenda wondered. Boy, did she. So, Grant Foster had gone to Dickens and Probst to poke around the quarry case files. And he obviously didn't want anyone to know it, so he used his other name.

"I think I do, Brenda. What's the date of that inquiry, please?" Brenda said it was March 4th. That seemed to match the timeframe of Emily's search for her cousin. "Brenda, please leave a message with Ward Dickens. Tell him that Rex Findlay is Grant Foster. He'll know what I mean. And point out Rex Findlay's visit and inquiry, too."

Feeling more motivated than before, Frankie climbed into her SUV and drove toward the Spurgeon mansion. First though, she decided to text Carmen that she was going into the "den of serpents" just in case she found herself in trouble. Although, she couldn't imagine how Carmen would help her if anything went awry. Somehow, just knowing that someone else knew where she was made her feel more at ease.

Frankie parked in the driveway near the front entrance, where her SUV could be seen from the street. As she got out, though, she spied Mack Perry in the side yard, pulling the last of the tappers from trees and looking a little flustered. The afternoon sun warmed the day, but a westerly wind carried Frankie's greeting away. She called out again to Mack when she got closer. He had a large pail perched inside the garden wagon, half filled with tree tappers.

"Hey, Mack. Sugaring season must be officially over, huh?" Frankie remembered how much Mack looked forward to making maple syrup from Emily's trees every year.

"Blooming idiot!" Mack growled as he pulled out the tapper from the tree. Frankie noticed it wasn't a maple, however, but birch.

"Are you tapping birches too, Mack?" Frankie asked.

Mack flushed red as he yanked out the tap and deposited it robustly into the pail. "No, I'm not tapping birches, but some other fool was. That's the second tap I found today in a birch. What idiot doesn't know the difference between a maple and a birch?" Mack continued to mutter under his breath.

"You mean you're not the only person tapping trees on the property?" Frankie asked.

Mack shook his head and informed Frankie that the Garden Club has volunteers who tap the trees and monitor them as a learning activity. "But they're supposed to be supervised by someone who knows what they're doing," he growled.

"Well, I hope it doesn't hurt the birch trees," Frankie offered.

"Me, too," Mack grumbled. "Whoever tapped the birch trees didn't know a thing about tree tapping."

Frankie switched topics. "Anything coming up yet in the herb garden?" It was an innocent enough question, and Mack didn't seem a bit bothered by it.

"A few things. We need more warm days. But, soon, everything will be up," Mack seemed to brighten a little at the mention of gardening.

"Yes, and then the bugs will come out, too. Just another

gardening challenge," Frankie hoped Mack would give her some helpful pest control ideas, ideas that would also help dismiss suspicions the police had about him.

"Well, I don't use chemicals on anything. I got a lot of old ones that I need to dispose of, though. But, with the herbs, I don't want anything on them when we're going to be cooking with them," Mack sounded adamant.

"So, did all the teas in the house come from the herbs you grow here, Mack? I thought Alana made the tea blends. She seems knowledgeable about them."

Mack scoffed a little. "I make the tea blends. Alana is interested, but she has a lot to learn. That's not *her area*. Well, I have to get this finished. The police are on their way over to look at trail camera footage at the gatehouse."

The news caused Frankie to stand up like a cat perched by the aquarium. "What do you suppose they're looking for?" She tried to sound nonchalant but knew Mack was pretty sharp.

"They want to look at the weekend before Miss Emily was found dead that Monday. I hope they find something that clears my name; that's what I'm hoping." Mack looked away then down at the ground.

Frankie reached out and laid a firm hand on his shoulder. Obviously, Mack was aware he was a suspect, and she wondered if he knew more than he revealed. "Have you looked at the footage?" Mack had not, indicating it hadn't crossed his mind to do so.

"Would you do me a favor and let me know if you

find anything worthwhile? I have to see Alana about something." Mack promised to keep Frankie posted.

Frankie crossed the lawn back to the front entrance, carrying the tablet in her totebag where it couldn't be seen. Alana didn't answer the door until the third knock. "Hello, Ms. Champagne. I saw you talking with Mack Perry, so I brewed some tea. Would you like to wait in the library or the solarium?"

"The library is fine," Frankie said, noting that Alana hadn't asked her the reason for her return. When Alana disappeared down the hall, Frankie looked at the library desk, but her tablet wasn't there. She pulled the other tablet from her tote, placed it on the desk, and began opening drawers to locate her own tablet. She didn't find it so started looking around the library shelves, noticing the North American Trees book had been returned to one shelf, although it was sticking out like it didn't belong there.

Frankie noticed that all the large books were located on a bottom shelf and decided that this book was filed hastily or carelessly. *"Alana has a lot to learn."* Mack's words came back to Frankie like a small wave.

Frankie opened the tree book to a spot where a corner had been turned down and the spine was flattened. The chapter was entitled "Toxic Trees." Frankie became nauseated as her brain pulsed a rapid firing of facts she had recorded on her suspect board, rendering her motionless, staring at the open tree book.

Just then, Alana walked in with the tea service and

looked curiously at Frankie and the book. "Is there something I can help you find?" Alana asked, her voice tight and shrill.

Frankie quickly decided what avenue to take in the conversation, knowing she couldn't turn back whichever direction she pursued.

"Actually, I was looking for my tablet. I accidentally grabbed the wrong one earlier. I put Emily's back on the desk. I thought that's where I left mine. Have you seen it?" Frankie willed her voice to sound normal and even.

Alana, expressionless, shook her head no. "I'll check the solarium for the tablet. Meanwhile, help yourself to some tea."

"Will Ms. McCoy be joining me soon?" Frankie asked.

Again, Alana shook her head. "She's indisposed. I'm afraid her headache got the better of her. She went to bed after you left. Perhaps she ate too much chocolate cake." This time, Alana's voice had an edge to it that sounded an alarm in Frankie's brain. Should she leave now, Frankie wondered, but she decided she just couldn't go without her tablet. She couldn't afford to have it in the wrong hands.

"Maybe it's already in the wrong hands, Francine," Goldie squawked in Frankie's ear. Simultaneously, The Pirate warned her not to drink the tea. *Alana has a lot to learn.* Just how indisposed was Cordelia? Had Alana made Cordelia sick?

Frankie pulled her phone out and sent a text to Carmen. *Please call the sheriff's department, and tell them where I am*, the text read. She wanted to elaborate, but Alana was back, holding Frankie's tablet. Frankie hoped the police were on their way to Mack's or already there.

"Well, look what I found," she said smugly. "You know the first rule of privacy is to have a locked screen on your tablet so nobody can see your information."

Frankie had a screen lock, but it was set to ten minutes because she'd been tired of entering the passcode so frequently. Alana had obviously found the tablet before the screen lock was activated. Frankie berated herself for not taking extra precautions. She knew Alana had seen something; whether it was photos of documents or her suspect board, she wasn't sure. One thing she knew for certain was that Alana had a motive for murder.

Frankie needed to buy some time, but she also wanted answers. Although her body was urging her to flee, her curious brain wasn't quite aligned.

"You knew about the codicil Emily planned to file, didn't you?" Frankie decided the more questions she could ask right now, the better, and she started with the more generic ones.

Alana nodded and shrugged. "I did, but it was never filed, so I guess it doesn't matter now."

Frankie guessed Alana was lying. She needed something that would rattle Alana. "No, it may not matter now, but then again, it might. It shows the court that Emily intended to change her will." Alana didn't react, leaving Frankie to try another approach.

"You and Dr. Barnard were the only ones who knew how sick Emily really was. That a kidney transplant wasn't likely to extend her life." Frankie was trying to toss out bread crumbs to see if Alana would follow.

"Why do you think I knew how sick she was?" Alana raised her chin in defiance.

"Well, you assisted at the doctor's home visits. He was teaching you how to administer dialysis. You had all the medical records at your disposal. You must have known the prognosis." Frankie knew part of what she said was true and the rest was conjecture, but she hoped she hit a nerve. Alana didn't respond.

"You know the police are looking at Grant Foster, checking his phone records. He was in town the day Emily died. I know Sunday is your day off, but try to think back, Alana. Was Grant Foster here on Saturday? That was the last day you saw Emily alive." Frankie hoped this line of questioning would give her some time to think and put Alana at ease.

It was becoming clearer by the minute that Alana had poisoned Emily, and she suspected that Grant Foster was in on it. That was why Alana was in the Sunday school classroom at the funeral; she knew Grant and Cordelia were going to talk because he had tipped her off when he handed her something - a note probably - as he was leaving church. But why? What was Alana supposed to get out of the conversation about the codicil? Frankie snapped back to the present when Alana spoke.

"The detectives already asked me this, Ms. Champagne. I don't remember anything more now than I did then. As far as I know, he wasn't here Saturday. Why? What do you think happened?" Alana was turning the tables, and Frankie tried to think fast on her feet.

"Well, you always made Emily's Sunday meals ahead of time. If Foster was here Saturday, he could have put something into her food or into her tea."

Once the words were out of Frankie's mouth, a large rock sunk to the bottom of her stomach. One, she shouldn't have referenced the tea, because there was Alana, staring at the tea service she brought for Frankie. And, two, Frankie was certain she knew why the refrigerator was empty the Monday morning Emily's body was discovered. Alana had no plan of cooking another meal for Emily Spurgeon.

Frankie was thinking back to the Saturday before Emily was found dead. Where had she been? Working at Bubble and Bake, no doubt. Saturdays were busy enough that Frankie rarely took a full day off. It was only three weeks ago. That was ancient history, though. She wished she could look at her phone calendar - it would surely jog her memory.

She figured she was likely out at the vineyard after working the bakery shift, checking on vines, checking in with Manny, checking the progress of new wine batches. That jarred loose a memory of a wet day when several inches of rain had fallen, causing flash floods a few counties over. Luckily Whitman County was mostly sand, and it could take the rain.

She recalled driving past Marjean Van Dyck, the insurance agency receptionist, who knew everyone in town. Frankie remembered laughing at the sight of her, looking like a giant construction cone in a bright orange vinyl raincoat with matching umbrella. Marjean was walking her yappy Papillon pup, Monarch, in front of the office. Like his owner, Monarch was dressed in a bright orange slicker, too. The memory was vivid, and it triggered another just as vivid.

She remembered Mack Perry's orange mud-caked boots by the back door the day of the investigation. At the time, Frankie was puzzled as to why Mack's boots were sitting in the kitchen when Monday was dry; the rains of Saturday were a distant memory. Surely Mack would be in garden clogs, or the boots would have lost the dried mud from the walk between the gatehouse and the mansion. It was a detail that bothered her then, but she lost that detail amidst all the other details that followed. Now she recalled that Mack's boots were green, not orange.

Alana interrupted Frankie's train of thought now. "Why don't you have some tea. Here, let me pour it for you, and you can tell me some of your other ideas about Grant Foster. I didn't trust him from the beginning, and I don't think Ms. McCoy's intentions were honorable either, but I'm curious about your ideas."

Alana's voice was smooth, silky, and calculating.

Frankie wished she could bolt out of the library, just grab her tablet and run, but Alana was still holding it under her arm as she poured a cup of tea for Frankie. The tea was still steaming, making Frankie wonder how long the two had been there, standing in silence.

Frankie sat down and tried to look calm. Inside, her heart beat wildly, and the fireflies were vigilant. She looked around the room, maybe for an escape route, maybe for a weapon if she needed one. The marble fireplace had tools in a stand that looked like brass. One of those would do the job, if she could get across the room fast enough, and if she had the intestinal fortitude to use one.

She picked up the tea cup and took a wary sniff. It smelled like a combination of herbs and something piney she couldn't identify. It didn't matter because there was no way she was going to drink it.

"Well . . . ?" Alana drew out the word as she stood across from the chair where Frankie was seated. "Your ideas?"

"Cordelia needed the money. She was used to a fancy lifestyle, and she lost that when her husband went bankrupt. She was doing all she could to get that lifestyle back. I think that's how she hooked up with Grant Foster; they were two of a kind."

Only now Frankie didn't think Cordelia and Foster were two of a kind. Then another realization struck her. Grant Foster read the quarry case files; he had something to hold over Alana. They were working together. But Frankie had to resume with her original idea.

"I think Foster and Cordelia hatched a plan to trick Emily into changing her will, then tried to kill her so she wouldn't have to follow through with the kidney transplant. But they could still use the codicil as leverage with the court." Frankie's brain admitted this was a logical scenario.

Alana looked impressed. "Okay, Ms. Champagne. But how did Grant Foster kill Emily? Cordelia wasn't even here, so that lets her off the hook."

Alana looked like a kettle about to boil over. If she was hoping for Frankie to provide the solution to the crime, she couldn't do it. She sincerely hoped the police had evidence she didn't know about, especially since Frankie was afraid she was in the room with the real murderer.

"I don't know how Grant Foster did it. But, the police are capable of figuring it out. And, you know, I really need to get going back to my business. My crew is waiting for me so they can leave for the day. So, I'll take my tablet now, please." Frankie hoped she sounded stronger than her gooey insides felt.

But Alana wasn't having it. She held onto the tablet more tightly and moved toward the door to block Frankie's exit. "I don't think so. You haven't even had any tea yet, and I think you have more to say. A lot more."

Frankie's skin prickled, and the fine hairs on her arms stood on end while the skin below glistened. Frankie had had enough of the conversation and enough of Alana's game playing. Maybe she was channeling her grandmother Felicity, for her Irish temper rallied an army of adrenaline-charged soldiers.

First, Frankie took the lid off the teapot, then rising to her full five feet, she launched the open pot at Alana's head, and watched as hot tainted tea streamed down her face.

Alana dropped the tablet and bounded after Frankie, flailing her arms, swearing, and trying to wipe her face. She caught Frankie's sore ankle with one of her feet, tripped her and brought her down to the floor, where Frankie tried not to react to the pain.

Frankie was several feet from the fireplace tools and began inching her way toward them on her bottom, while Alana was moaning, cursing, and clutching at Frankie's legs.

Frankie had enough of her senses to conclude that Alana couldn't see, at least not very well, and she hoped to use this to her advantage. Some bravado swelled within as she couldn't resist a verbal jab. "Oh shut up, Marta Gomez, just shut up."

Alana stopped her tantrum long enough to answer in a strained whisper, "How could you possibly know that?"

Alana had dropped her grip on Frankie's leg, so Frankie quickly slid to the fireplace, using the brass tool stand to rise up, unsteadily. She looked at Alana. She saw burns on her face, hands, and arms, and couldn't help but feel sad. Alana's eyes were swollen, and Frankie wasn't sure how much of her faculties she possessed. Frankie put her right hand over the end of the fire poker, on the ready.

"I read the quarry case files, Alana. It was easy to imagine that Emily wanted to make things right for the families in the lawsuit. That's why she hired Mack Perry and left him the gatehouse and a trust fund. That's why she took a chance on a young inexperienced doctor to assume her care." Frankie was in the moment now, no sense stopping the inevitable.

"But there was still the Gomez family. It didn't add up. You didn't add up, actually. Why would Emily replace Lorna Ricks, a very capable assistant? You must have been very convincing to get the job. You had to tell Emily who you were, and somehow still keep it a secret just between the two of you."

"That still doesn't explain how you figured out that I'm Marta." Alana was still seething, ready to fight.

"It was the simplest thing, actually. I wanted to find a photo of you so I could show it to Carly, the Siamese Cat breeder. You know, where you got Pearl the Second? So, I tried to look you up, but there was so little about you online. It was your date of birth that made me wonder. You look like a 20-something, but birthdates don't lie. You're 36."

Alana flinched at Frankie's accusation, but the litany went on.

"When I saw that, it was easy to put you into the right age for Marta Gomez or her sister. When I looked at the photos of the quarry documents, your birthdate matched Marta's. Maybe you can fill in some answers for me now."

Alana was still lying on the floor, and Frankie thought shock might be setting in, but she didn't take her hand off the poker.

"You were already in Emily's will. Why couldn't you just wait? You knew she was very sick. She was paying you well, I assume. Why not wait for the trust money?" Frankie felt emotional now, afraid she might lose the upper hand.

Alana's low gurgle of laughter sounded icy. "The Spurgeons took my whole family from me. My father first, then my brother. My mother married a man who didn't want me or my sister. My mother and stepfather made me guardian over my sister, then threw us out of the house when I turned 14. I wasn't about to wait for Cordelia McCoy to have her turn, taking even more away from me."

"So, you tried to poison Emily, but you didn't know what you were doing. Mack said you had a lot to learn." Frankie guessed Alana may have tried insecticides or pesticides, in small doses, maybe accidentally poisoning both Pearls.

"After you found out about the kidney transplant and the codicil, you had to act quickly. So, you tapped the birch trees and gathered the sap in the pouring rain, then made a lethal dinner for Emily's last supper." Frankie wasn't sure if she had the facts correct, but she struck a bitter chord in Alana.

"How could you know that? You think you're so smart, sticking your nose in other people's business."

Alana cocked one eye open and lunged at Frankie,

planning to knock her off balance. Just as Alana lunged, a ball of freaked out Siamese cat landed squarely on Alana's head, yowling and scratching. As Alana tried to wrestle the possessed Pearl off of her tortured head, Mack Perry burst into the room and loomed over Alana with a spade in hand, bidding her not to move.

"Thank God you're here, Mack. How did you know to come in?" Frankie marveled.

"That." Mack pointed to what looked like a nursery monitor on one of the shelves. "Miss Emily and I used that to communicate if she needed something. I have one in my house and one in the shed. There's one in the sunroom, too."

Frankie smiled, still holding the fireplace poker. Well, I'm grateful to you and to Pearl." Frankie hobbled over to Pearl and gingerly put her hand out. The kitty rubbed her head against it then calmly sat down on top of Frankie's feet.

Shirley Lazaar was just seconds behind Mack with her gun pulled. Sirens wailed up Whitman Avenue announcing Alonzo Goodman, who also entered, gun drawn. But when they surveyed the scene, Shirley called an ambulance for Alana, who was now deeply in shock. Frankie covered her with a blanket Mack provided from a linen closet, but she wasn't moving, and her breathing was shallow.

"Remind me not to go to any tea parties with you, Frankie!" There was Shirley with her gallows humor. "Any idea what might have been in there?" She pointed at the broken teapot that had left a bleached stain on the hardwood floor.

"I'm guessing it's the sanitizing cleaner I found under the sink the day Emily died. I remember thinking it was strange to see an industrial cleaner in a regular household . . . unless you need to clean up after your own dirty work like Pearl the cat and in Emily's bathroom and bedroom," Frankie offered.

Shirley patted Frankie on the shoulder, harder than Frankie would have liked. "Good guess, Hot Shot. I guess we better get you checked out, too. You've been through quite a lot today. Though it's your own fault." Shirley was shaking her head.

Alonzo knelt beside Frankie, who had laid down on the sofa, and measured her pulse. "Mack, you got any brandy or something along that order?"

When Mack brought a glass from the antique corner cabinet, Alonzo propped Frankie's head up with his sturdy arm and told her to drink. Frankie stared at the brown liquid, took a large sip, and made a face.

"Okay, good job. Now drink the rest," Alonzo instructed, but Frankie wanted answers first.

"What was on the trail cam footage, Shirley?"

Shirley laughed heartily, looked over at Alonzo, who nodded half-heartedly. "Delivery van showed up here Sunday night. A Fleet van. Ms. West was driving it. She had on orange boots and was carrying a bucket. Foster was with her, carrying a jug of laxative powder."

"Birch sap, I think, Shirley. In the bucket. It's toxic. I saw the page marked in the tree book over there." Frankie made a weak gesture toward the book shelf.

After the brandy, Frankie fell asleep, and she woke up in her own bedroom with her mother, Aunt CeCe, and Carmen sitting around the bed, staring at her.

"Dios mío, Frankie. You could have been killed! What were you thinking anyway?"

Frankie smiled weakly at Carmen. "Thanks for reading my text and calling the sheriff."

It was Peggy's turn to take up the butt-chewing. "Please don't put Carmen in that position ever again, Francine. Friends don't do that to friends."

Frankie couldn't help but laugh. Of all the things she expected from her mother, it wasn't a lesson on etiquette. "You're right, Mother. Next time I think my life is in danger, I'll text you first."

Carmen snickered, producing a little snort.

"That is not at all what I meant, and you know it." Peggy raised her voice a bit, then reached one hand over to smooth her daughter's hair. "Anyway, I'm glad you're okay." She surprised Frankie by giving her a gentle kiss on the forehead. "Now get some rest, and we'll see you tomorrow. I'm not going anywhere. I'll be in the living room if you need anything tonight."

Frankie's voice became softer. "I'm sorry I worried you."

Chapter 21

What we do for ourselves dies with us. What we do
for others and the world remains and is immortal.
- Albert Pine

When Frankie woke up, a smiling Garrett was sitting by her bed, sipping coffee, ready with a latte for Frankie. She grimaced a little when she sat up in bed, wondering how she could hurt in so many places from the day before.

"I guess the mansion's floor is harder than I thought, Garrett," Frankie let go a little giggle despite the body aches. What time is it, anyway?" Garrett helped prop her up with pillows, handed her the latte, and kissed her gently on the forehead. She breathed in its robust fragrance. "Just what the doctor ordered. Thank you."

Garrett informed her it was only 6:00 a.m., that Carmen, Tess, and Jovie were in the kitchen holding down the fort and that Peggy had gone home to take a shower. "How about some breakfast, Miss Francine? You missed dinner, so you're probably hungry. You know, trying to fend off a killer can work up an appetite, I hear."

Frankie laughed, even though she smirked at Garrett's sarcasm. "You know, you're right. It does. I am hungry, but first I just have to know what happened yesterday after the police called the ambulance."

Garrett raised his hands in surrender and sat back down. "Here's the short version. Alana will be taken into custody and charged with intentional homicide, once she's out of the hospital from the burns on her face and arms." Frankie nodded, already certain of this fact.

"The crime lab found residue in the oil diffuser, thanks to you pointing out that it had just been cleaned." Garrett was certain to give Frankie credit for her help, and he looked at her with admiration.

"Besides that toxin, they found more on Emily's pajama top, although it took a couple of days to find it. Shirley was suspicious after you told her how obsessed Emily was with order." Frankie arched one brow quizzically.

"Emily wasn't wearing matching pajamas when they found her, you see, so police searched for the matching top and found it washed up on the lakeshore south of town."

"Huh, there's one clue I missed," Frankie admitted, keeping a mental tally of things she still needed to learn in the detective world. Right now, though, another question needed answering.

"Did they catch Grant Foster?" Frankie asked.

Garrett showed his contempt for Foster, grimacing. "Yep. They found him staying at a hotel on 404, registered under another name, of course. But Cordelia helped the police with that."

Frankie began to relax a little, settled into the pillows, and sipped her latte, thoughtfully. "It's nice to hear Cordelia helped out. So, she wasn't in on it, then?"

Garrett said there was still a lot to sort out. It appeared Foster was trying to involve Cordelia, but she didn't want to be part of any scheme to hasten Emily's death. So Foster double-crossed her, chose to work with Alana instead, but pretended to go along with Cordelia's plan to wait out the court's decision about the estate. Since Foster had read the quarry files and figured out Alana's real identity, he figured Alana had motive for murder, and he could turn over the information to the police, or he and Alana could work together to get rid of Emily.

Frankie's head was beginning to hurt, trying to process all the details. She closed her eyes momentarily as Garrett held her hand tightly in his.

"Hold on there, Tiger. There's plenty of time to get all the facts. Right now, you need some rest. And, when you feel better, I'm going to chew you out for putting yourself in danger, by the way." When Frankie opened one eye to look at Garrett, she saw he was smiling.

* * *

A few days later, Frankie was compelled to pay a visit to Emily's grave, leaving a few daffodils she picked from behind Bubble and Bake. "They aren't lilacs, but I expect you will get your share of those from Mack Perry, Emily."

She offered a prayer that Emily would finally find peace and leave the guilt of her family behind her.

Frankie was happy to hear that Mack had been cleared of any wrongdoing. Of course, the same was true of Dr. Fitz Barnard. Frankie felt twinges of guilt for roughing him up at the funeral.

The police discovered that Emily had paid for Barnard's medical school tuition, compensation she felt was deserved to survivors of the quarry disease. Frankie had correctly guessed Emily's reason for hiring the young doctor as her provider, for taking care of Mack in her will, for hiring Alana to replace Lorna Ricks.

Alana returned to Deep Lakes with the sole purpose of getting something out of the Spurgeons. She changed her name, taking on the name of the deceased food service worker who died during Alana's time at the college, where she studied to become a LPN. She even had minor cosmetic alterations to look younger, so she couldn't be tied to the Gomezes. But, in order to get what she desired, she had to tell Emily the truth about herself.

Alana's sad story of abandonment at age 14 by her mother and step-father, and her guardianship over an older sister with Down syndrome, struck a chord deep in Emily's heart. She was compelled to compensate this woman for the injustices of life that began with losing family at the quarry.

So, Emily hired Alana and paid for her sister's care at The Ranch, a facility for adults with Down syndrome.

That's where Amelia Gomez had been living the past three years, in Texas at the state-of-the-art home that provided excellent care and warm ambience at a high price tag.

Somehow, Frankie had to admire Alana for ensuring her sister's care. Still, she had played upon Emily's guilt and compassion, a form of extortion. Frankie surmised she manipulated Emily into changing her will to include life-long compensation for Ameila and Alana. And then she did the unthinkable, poisoning Emily to preserve the contents of the will.

Frankie couldn't help but wonder if some guiding force urged her toward her deduction about Alana West. Given time to mull over the clues again, Frankie ruminated on bumping into the Old West tales book not once, but twice, in two days at the shop.

Then there was the North American Tree book at the mansion she saw first on the library desk, and again when it was misfiled on the shelf right under her nose, immediately after talking to Mack about tapping birch trees. When she saw the toxin Methyl Salicylate listed on the turned down page, she recognized it from the autopsy and concluded the tapped birch was the source. Furthermore, the book indicated the sap contained the same compound as Wintergreen oil.

And, was it a coincidence that she bumped into James at Spurgeon Park, that he simply had to show her the gazebo with its compass points, the direction west with the constellation she puzzled over and researched later?

Hadn't all of those things pointed West : straight to Alana? Frankie knew her imagination was running wild, but it was interesting to consider life's mysteries and to think that maybe Emily or someone was helping her from beyond.

Of course, Frankie's intuitions were only one piece of Emily's demise. Although Alana had been experimenting with poisonous substances for months, she only managed to murder Emily by tainting everything in her last meal with extraordinary doses of birch sap. The sap was found on Emily's slipper and her pajama shirt, which Alana had dumped into the lake.

But Alana's clean up of her crime was sloppy; she missed the honey jar and the slippers. Frankie guessed that somehow Pearl Two got into the birch sap concoction, making her sick. Alana had explained to Shirley Lazaar that the first Pearl met her demise ingesting an insecticide-laced tea spill in the kitchen. That tidbit made Frankie shudder.

Grant Foster simply added the laxative to Emily's last supper as a means of sealing her fate. Dr. Barnard's laxative prescription gave Alana the idea, but she didn't want to fill it, fearful of the damning evidence. So Foster simply found a large container of over-the-counter laxative to do the trick.

Thank goodness for Mack Perry's critter camera,

which clearly showed Alana and Foster's return to the mansion, poisons in hand. Talk about catching a couple of beastly critters in action!

What would happen to Granite Mansion now was a great unknown. Cordelia was still living there, trying to decide whether or not to continue her pursuit of Emily's estate. She seemed willing to keep Mack Perry employed and residing in the gatehouse, at least for now. Cordelia was also reportedly talking with the historical society, negotiating terms for a possible lease of the property and its antiquities. Maybe it would be enough for Cordelia to gain a partial inheritance.

* * *

One thing Frankie was certain about was that Mack Perry was the perfect person to rededicate Spurgeon Park in Emily's honor. Adele agreed, too, and Frankie began grooming the introverted Mack to deliver a speech of his own making at the Roots Festival.

The townspeople and visitors turned out in droves to the festival, enjoying a lovely, breezy spring day. Many took advantage of the free Kids' Fishing Weekend, where expert anglers from Deep Lakes were on hand to help kids learn the art of pan fishing: baiting a hook with a red worm or night crawler, casting out the line just right, watching the bobber for a bite, and pulling in perch and bluegills, just the right size for frying up in a pan.

The Bubble and Bake women sold out of kringles long before noon, leaving them plenty of time to enjoy the festivities. Watching Aunt CeCe teach a gaggle of children how to design spring scenes on sidewalk squares warmed Frankie's heart. She could see the joy that drawing and painting brought to her aunt and she began scheming about ways CeCe's creative side could be cultivated. Frankie pulled her aside after the festival to take a walk along Sterling Creek behind the shop.

"Aunt CeCe, I think it was time you met Coral Anders. She owns the lavender farm near the vineyard, and she's an artist. You two have a lot in common. Maybe you could offer some workshops out there; it's just a thought."

Frankie saw a faraway look of melancholy on her aunt's face and decided to take the plunge into her personal life. "Why did you come back to Deep Lakes?"

Aunt CeCe sighed heavily. Suddenly, she didn't look like the free spirit filled with youthful mischief that Frankie knew. "I was lost, Frankie. All I have left of my family is here . . . in Wisconsin. I hadn't thought about that in years. But after I lost my dear Nell, I felt more alone than I could remember, except . . ." Aunt CeCe trailed off and looked into the creek.

Now seemed like the right time to ask about Frankie's grandmother, Felicity, a woman whom Aunt CeCe knew in a much different way from how Frankie did. "Tell me why you left Wisconsin, Aunt CeCe."

Aunt CeCe looked frightened and childlike as she

wound back through a thorny past that didn't end happily. "Well, Frankie, I'm different, you see. When I went to college in Milwaukee, I met an art graduate assistant named Marie, and we fell in love. I tried to explain it to my mother, but she couldn't understand it. She made me quit school immediately and marry your uncle."

Frankie was stunned by her aunt's story. "But, you didn't stay married. So, what happened?"

"Marie became a professor at Berkeley in California. I moved out there to find her, but when I got there, it was too late. Marie had left me behind. But I stayed in California where things were - well - just easier for me." Aunt CeCe faltered, but Frankie took her fragile hand in her own, admiring the long fingers of an artist.

"Your grandmother never spoke to me again, Frankie. It's the biggest regret of my life, that we couldn't find our way back to each other." Aunt CeCe was crying softly now, and Frankie squeezed her hand.

"I'm so sorry, Aunt CeCe. I don't know what to say. My grandmother was always so kind and loving, a free spirit like you. I just can't imagine her any other way." Frankie was sad her aunt didn't have the same love from Felicity that Frankie enjoyed.

Aunt CeCe dried her tears, turned, and faced Frankie. "I don't blame my mother, Frankie. You see, her mother, my grandmother . . . well, she was raised in a strict Irish Catholic household. But, she fell in love with a Protestant. Her family forbid them to marry, so they ran away together, got married, and raised my mother and her siblings Catholic. But it didn't matter. My grandmother's family wouldn't see them, wouldn't be part of their lives. It crushed my grandmother, and my mother knew it. My mother wasn't about to let anyone come into our family and ruin it. She was protective of us, you see."

"But, Aunt CeCe, wasn't she being a hypocrite? She was doing exactly what her grandmother had done, sort of." Frankie felt Aunt CeCe was justified in feeling hurt.

Aunt CeCe just shrugged. "But I forgave her. I just wish she knew that. I just wish she would have forgiven me." She stared back at the creek, the sheen of the flowing dark currents and little puffs of foam on the surface heading toward Blackbird Bridge. "So much water moving underneath the bridge, Frankie." Aunt CeCe smiled softly and squeezed Frankie's hand this time.

*   *   *

Weeks later, at Bountiful Fruits, a lively gathering of Frankie's friends, family, and vineyard workers was taking place under a starry spring sky. Frankie made a toast to a newly christened vintage, Granite Red, made from a blend of red grapes and raspberries. "Let's raise our glasses to Emily Spurgeon, the Granite Quarry, and the end of the Quarry Curse!" Frankie toasted. Everyone cheered, but Tess and Tía Pepita both looked over their shoulders in case an evil spirit was lurking.

As glasses were refilled with a beautiful topaz-colored wine, Carmen raised her glass. "Frankie and I name this spirited apricot chardonnay after our aunts. Here's to the first Sweet Tía vintage and to Pepita and CeCe, our sweet tias." Carmen's husband, Ryan, and Frankie's brothers, James, Nick, and Will, made exaggerated bows toward the aunts, but Alonzo waggled a warning finger in their direction as he toasted.

Frankie invited Fitz Barnard and his wife Jaclyn Malone to the bottling party, figuring she owed them. The couple came into Bubble and Bake after the Roots Festival, Jaclyn formally introducing herself and smiling wryly at Frankie's suspicions about Fitz.

Frankie gave them two bottles of wine as a peace offering. When she learned Jaclyn was an introvert who didn't feel quite at home yet in Deep Lakes, and she hailed from Minneapolis, Frankie introduced the couple to James and Shauna.

Shauna and Jaclyn had much in common and bonded immediately over their Minneapolis roots. Frankie was grateful the doctor and Jaclyn didn't hold a grudge, and she was beginning to warm up to both of them.

The vineyard was aglow with strings of small mason jar party lights, and two picnic tables were laden with cookies, Carmen's black bean and queso fresco nachos with homemade salsa, Frankie's Guinness shredded beef sliders, and Garrett's twice-baked potato bar.

Manny Vega, along with his vineyard crew, played

guitar, violin, accordion, and tambourine while they sang songs - some in Spanish, some in English, some in both languages. The party-goers took turns singing along and even dancing to a couple of the slower numbers.

Carmen and Ryan drews oohs and aahs as they showed off some of the Latin steps they knew, and Peggy, with Dan Fitzpatrick at her side, took graceful turns around the lawn to claps of approval. Even Alonzo, after a few wine samples, led Jovie out to slow dance.

Garrett, however, had other plans, as he escorted Frankie to a darker part of the vineyard near the orchard, where they enjoyed a slow waltz, a couple of dips that left them laughing, then gazed upon a maze of twinkling stars.

Frankie pointed upward to the west at the constellation Boötes. After the new gazebo was unveiled, Frankie remembered to look up the unfamiliar constellation. Now, a bit tipsy from the wine toasts, she instructed Garrett.

"That constellation is the Ploughman or the Herdsman. Every culture has a different story about Boötes, but I like the Greek legend that says he was the man who taught the Greeks to plow the soil and grow grain and grapes. Pretty cool story for the vineyard, don't you think?"

Garrett tried not to laugh at Frankie, who was trying to tell a serious story amid a few slurred syllables, here and there. He took her hand, intertwining his fingers in hers.

"It's a good story, Frankie, but what I think, right now is: this is the perfect night. A spring vintage, time for new beginnings, beautiful sunny days ahead of us." Garrett kissed her under the canopy of stars. Frankie inhaled the heady scent of spring, welcoming its breath of promise. As Garrett held her tightly, Frankie saw two tiny glows ascend over his shoulder: the first fireflies of summer.

Epilogue:
The Newspaper Article in *Point Press*

A Treasured Legacy
By Francine Champagne

Many persons and organizations benefited from the life and death of Deep Lakes Granite Works heiress, Emily Spurgeon. Two of those persons are currently in jail, awaiting trial for their part in her murder. Emily Spurgeon died April 13 from renal failure due to poison and an overdose of a purgative in her system. Alana West, Emily's personal assistant, and Grant Foster, aka Rex Findlay, have been charged with intentional homicide and conspiracy to commit murder.

The Granite Works company and Emily Spurgeon have forever left their mark on Deep Lakes. The community has prospered from the granite quarry since operations began in the 1800s, bringing new families to town from various cultures and walks of life, making Deep Lakes a mini-melting pot in Wisconsin.

The granite mined in the quarry is considered some

of the highest quality in the world and is featured at the State Capitol and in Gettysburg Cemetery, among other famous locations.

But the storied history of the quarry is not without tragedies: workers' deaths from fires, explosions, falls, and lung disease throughout the years cannot be forgotten, nor can the founding families' own personal losses.

When a company is in business for one hundred years, stories become legends and sometimes are elaborated into curses. Such is the case with Granite Works. But, it wasn't a curse that killed Emily Spurgeon, but the greed of outsider Grant Foster, and more poignantly, the bitterness Alana West brought with her to Deep Lakes, bitterness that percolated into revenge.

Fortunately, sharp investigating skills of Sheriff Alonzo Goodman, Officer Shirley Lazaar, and others at Whitman County prevailed, and the culprits were apprehended quickly.

Unfortunately, Emily Spurgeon was unable to rededicate the beautiful city park with its granite outcroppings at the Deep Lakes Roots Festival.

Spurgeon Park with its new gazebo, concession area, and picnic grove will forever remind residents and visitors of the generosity of the Granite Works owner.

The Roots Festival, in fact, is celebrated annually to remind us of the importance of our roots, our family trees, and just how intertwined human beings are in a community. A community resembles a tree with all of the member branches offering their support, and one branch is not more important than another.

In my study of Emily Spurgeon's history and during the time I spent with her, I believe Emily lived the philosophy that every individual in the Granite Works company mattered. So much so that she constantly sought to right the wrongs of tragedies that had happened to those workers and within her own family.

Emily stepped into the shoes as hostess at the Granite Mansion after her mother died when Emily was just 12, opening their home to the workers and their families for celebrations, picnics, and holiday parties.

Emily established funds for workers who experienced losses of all kinds up until the quarry ceased operations. After that, she continued her charitable work in the community, especially supporting the local garden club and historical society and state-wide environmental and natural resources organizations.

However, Emily lived with an undercurrent of guilt, streaming from a dismissed lawsuit against the quarry company, brought by survivors of loved ones who had died from "quarry disease" or silicosis.

From Emily's own perspective, she tried to right the wrongs the victims suffered by supporting and providing for the survivors as best she could, but even the best of intentions cannot always ease bitterness felt by those who believe they have been wronged.

This bitterness took root in both Alana West, who lost

her father and brother to the quarry, and even in Emily's cousin, Cordelia McCoy, who blamed Emily for her own losses. Perhaps now Cordelia will be able to quell her bitterness and assume her own place in the Deep Lakes community. Cordelia certainly deserves that chance.

Trees and plants experience rot when too much water is collected at the roots and can no longer be absorbed by the rest of the tree. The tree begins to die inwardly and invisibly, unnoticed by the human eye until the leaves droop and fall. People experience the same kind of rot when bitterness takes root within, consuming the person covertly.

Bitterness is a toxic poison, and this is ironic, since the bearer of the bitterness in this case used poison to end Emily's life. But there is no end to bitter feelings once they take root. And Emily's death will give no relief to her murderer, who will certainly stew in the bitter broth she made for the remainder of her life.

For my part, I choose to replace the Quarry Curse with honored memories of those who founded the quarry and those who labored there. They gave Deep Lakes a renowned acclaim for the treasured granite monuments borne from the rocks, and for the jewel of Deep Lakes that is Spurgeon Park: rooted in earthly beauty, its granite cliffs and fresh waterfalls will outlast us all. Out of these cursed tragedies, blessings live.

Acknowledgments

I was inspired by my hometown's granite quarry and waterfalls as a backdrop for my second mystery. There is such a rich and storied history here in Montello and I can't help but wonder what those granite slabs and cliffs would say if they could speak. I am thankful to The Montello Historic Preservation Society and local authors, Bryan Troost, Thomas Freitag, and Kathleen McGwin for their compilation of Montello's quarry history. Through their book Etched in Stone: History of the Montello Granite Quarries, I learned enough about quarry operations, hopefully, for an authentic depiction in the novel. The story of the quarry heiress, granite mansion, and quarry events are fictional.

As far as learning about tending a vineyard in spring, I once again relied on the publication, Growing Grapes in Wisconsin, http://learningstore.uwex.edu/assets/pdfs/A1656.pdf, and conversations with vineyard owners throughout the state while on my Deep Dark Secrets book tour. After learning about the labor-intensive work in wine production, I hope that folks will head out to the more than 80 wineries in our state and sample their wares. And if you're visiting Wisconsin from I-don't-care-where, please give our wines a chance before passing judgment. I'm in awe of the wine varieties our state has to offer to please every palate. In fact, I christened Wisconsin the Golden Retriever of the 50 states, as our great residents just want to make everyone happy!

Authors can be difficult and fastidious about the most minuscule of details, so much gratitude goes out to friends and family who are with me for the long haul: John, you are indispensable as a husband, best friend and general manager. Mom, Jill, Kay, Daryl, Dale, Jack, Alan, Erica, Carly, Jen, Greg, Molly, Barbara: lots of love to you for your support. I am blessed that there are independent bookstores willing to take a chance on a relatively unknown author - please, people, go out and buy something from an indie bookstore - right now! Thank you to Shannon and Lauren at Orange Hat Publishing for their extra work in finalizing my book and my awesome illustrator, Tom Heffron.

Three cheers to my fellow Sisters in Crime members who reviewed my book and offered kind praise: Christine DeSmet, Kathleen Ernst and Patricia Skalka. You bothered to take time out from your busy writing careers to read my manuscript, and I only hope to pay your graciousness forward one day. Thank you Cozy Mystery Book Reviewer Missi Stockwell Martin for your heartfelt kindness. What can I say to my Beta Reader/Reviewer Janelle Bailey? John Steinbeck said, ``A writer who does not passionately believe in the perfectibility of man has no dedication nor any membership in literature." You proved you believed in perfecting an imperfect manuscript because you believe in me. I'm forever grateful. Please support all of these hardworking women who grace the world with their words.

- JAR

Recipes

Cha-Cha-Cha Quiche

A pie crust of your choice for a 9-inch plate (Pre-bake empty crust for 15 min at 400° and cool.

Break apart 6 oz. queso fresco onto the bottom of the crust

Brown ½ lb. chorizo, cool a bit then put on top of queso

Add ⅔ cup pico de gallo on top of that

Add a little salt

In a bowl: whisk 5 eggs with 1½ cups of whole milk.

Add any herbs you like: if your chorizo isn't well-seasoned, add some oregano and garlic powder, then pour egg mixture over the filling.

Final topping: 1 cup shredded cheddar cheese (I like sharp).

Bake at 350° until browned on top (actually burnt orange color!), about 30 minutes.

Cran-tastic Shortbread Cookies

2 sticks salted butter (at room temp)
1 cup powdered sugar
⅓ cup Craisins (soak them to soften first, then chop into pieces)
2 tsp vanilla extract
2 cups unbleached flour
⅓ cup shaved white chocolate (or chopped white chocolate chips)

Beat together butter, sugar and vanilla. Stir in Craisins. Beat in half of the flour. Stir in the white chocolate pieces. Beat in the other half of the flour. Dough will be stiff.

Chill dough for 30 minutes so it's easy to handle. Drop by teaspoonfuls onto parchment-lined cookie pan or non-stick pan. Flatten, then use a cookie stamp or something fun to make a design. Bake at 300° for 18-20 minutes - they will be firm but not brown. Cool on a rack.

Lavender Chai Sugar Cookies
(as voted on by Joy's readers)

2 cups flour

1½ tsp baking powder

½ tsp salt

⅔ cup of Brummel & Brown spread (or other buttery spread product)

1 cup sugar (plus extra for rolling cookies in)

1 egg

½ tsp vanilla extract

¼ cup ground lavender buds (I like to use a pestle and mortar, but a food processor is good too)

¾ tsp cinnamon

¼ tsp cardamom

⅛ tsp ground cloves

Whisk together flour, baking powder, and salt. Set aside. In mixing bowl, cream Brommel & Brown and sugar (Use the Brommel & Brown cold, not at room temp, as this mixture is thin and soupy - that's okay.) Add egg and vanilla. Again, the mix will look runny. Mix in the lavender and other spices.

Add in the dry ingredients in 2-3 increments.

Chill the dough for at least 30 minutes.

Preheat oven to 350°. Line cookie sheet with parchment.

Make about tablespoon-sized dough balls and roll in

sugar to coat. (If you can find lavender sugar, it's even more amazing.)

Flatten cookie balls slightly. Space about an inch apart. Bake 8-10 minutes. Let sit after baking for a couple minutes before removing from the sheet.

Rhubarb Custard Pie

Use your favorite 9 inch pie crust (you will need 2)
Line the pie plate with crust (no pre-bake)
Beat 3 eggs lightly
Add 3 TB milk
Mix and stir in: 2 cups sugar, ¼ cup flour, ¾ tsp nutmeg, 4 cups rhubarb (chopped)
Pour mixture into pie shell, dot with 1 TB butter
Cover with top crust and seal edges. You can cut diagonals into the top or another pretty design. You can add an egg wash or sprinkle cinnamon/sugar on top.
Bake at 400° for 50-60 minutes.

If this isn't the best rhubarb pie you've ever eaten, I want to hear from you! I grew up eating this pie, so it's a luscious seasonal memory for me. My 90-year-old mom still brings me this pie every spring!

Lemon Cheese Scones

(Thank you to Karen who made these and brought them to my book event at Pieper Porch Winery, Waukesha, WI)

2 ¼ cups flour

2 TB sugar

2½ tsp baking powder

½ tsp baking soda

¼ tsp red pepper (ground)

½ tsp salt

1 cup sharp cheddar cheese, shredded

1 cup buttermilk

1-2 TB lemon zest

1 egg

Stir together dry ingredients. Cut in butter with pastry blender or fork until it looks like coarse pea-sized crumbs.

Stir in cheese.

Add buttermilk and lemon zest and stir with a fork - dough will be sticky and soft.

Flour your hands and make the dough into a ball.

Knead gently on a floured surface - just 10 times

Pat into a ¾-inch thick round. Cut rounds (2.5 inches) or cut into wedges with a pizza cutter.

If making rounds, gather up the leftover scraps, re-shape into a round once more, and cut out more rounds.

Lay on cookie sheet. Brush the tops with egg. Bake at 425° for 12-14 minutes, until golden.

Dark Beer Beef Sliders

3 to 4 lb. rump or sirloin roast

2 onions chunked or sliced

1 lb mushrooms, quartered (I like baby bellas)

1 pkg. onion soup mix (or garlic herb) - I use one envelope plus ½ of second one

black pepper (sprinkle on top of beef)

12 oz Guinness or other dark beer with lots of body

On bottom of slow cooker, place onions and mushrooms. Set the roast on top of the veggies. Mix dried soup mix with enough water to pour it over the roast (maybe a ½ cup)

Last, pour a bottle of beer over the top.

Cooks about 4 hours on high in slow cooker. Adjust for Instant Pot or for slow cooking on low.

Cook until the roast can be shredded with a fork. Shred and mix all that good onion, mushroom, and beef together and pile it onto your favorite bun. Great dish to serve company!

Rum Raisin Cake
(makes two 9-inch round cakes)

1 cup raisins (soak in 1 cup of dark rum or coconut rum)
1½ cups cake flour
1½ cups all purpose flour
2½ tsp baking powder
¼ tsp salt
2 sticks butter (at room temp)
2 cups sugar
¾ to 1 cup coconut flakes (optional)
4 eggs (room temp)
2 tsp vanilla or rum extract
1 cup evaporated milk

Soak raisins in rum overnight. Strain, but keep the rum liquid.

Stir together dry ingredients and set aside.

Cream butter and sugar until fluffy. Add eggs, one at a time, beating well each time. (This makes the cake like chiffon!) Beat in extract and coconut.

FOLD in dry ingredients in 3 additions, alternating with evaporated milk each time. Fold in rum-soaked raisins with the final portion of milk. Begin with the dry ingredients and end with the dry.

Pour batter into greased and floured pans. Bake at 325° for 30-40 minutes. Do not overbake. Test with a toothpick. Rest cake 10 minutes and remove from pan to cool on racks. When cool, pierce the cake with skewer or large fork all over the surface. Spoon the reserved rum over the top. Seal the cake if you have time - either wrap in waxed paper and place in Ziploc bag or wrap and place in container with a lid and let sit overnight or even a couple of days. (Tip: If you don't want to use alcohol, soak the raisins in a cola beverage - not diet.)

Icing:
4 cups powdered sugar
2 sticks butter
1 tsp vanilla
3 TB pineapple rum or pineapple juice (play with the liquid for desired taste, consistency)
A little milk or half-and-half for creaminess (maybe a TB)

I've also added crushed pineapple instead of pineapple juice with rum or milk as the liquid. I like the pineapple bits in my frosting! If you love coconut, you can add some of that into your icing, too or instead of the pineapple.

Gluten-Free Cauliflower Quiche Crust
(fill with your favorite quiche recipe)

1 head cauliflower, cut into florets
½ cup grated parmesan cheese
½ teaspoon garlic powder
¼ teaspoon salt, divided
1 egg

Add the cauliflower to food processor and pulse until finely crumbled. Microwave the cauliflower for about 4-5 minutes (depending on your microwave). I like to use a steamer to cook mine. Cool. Ball up your cauliflower into a tea towel or cheesecloth and squeeze out the water. Throw away the liquid.

Add to the cauliflower: 1 egg, parmesan cheese, garlic powder, and salt.

Press crust into a pie plate (glass works the best) and be sure you cover the sides (it will take time to get this even. You don't want a really thick bottom - I made the mistake of making the bottom too thick the first time!). Bake the crust at 400° until golden for about 15-17 minutes. Let cool before filling.

Deep Bitter Roots
Book Club Discussion Questions

1. How did the setting of the book contribute to the mystery?

2. Discuss Tía Pepita and Aunt CeCe. What did they contribute to the story?

3. Discuss the relationship between Frankie and Carmen. How would you describe their partnership?

4. What do you like most and least about Frankie?

5. Discuss Cordelia McCoy, Mack Perry, Alana West, Garrett, and Donovan Pflug. Did you find them believable? Could you relate to any of them?

6. At what point did you think you knew the outcome of the mystery? Why? Were you right or wrong?

7. Read your favorite passage from the book? How do you think the author's style adds to the narrative in this passage?

8. Follow the clues given in the story. Which were helpful? Which led you astray?

9. Discuss the head of chapter quotes. Which ones did you like? How did they contribute to the theme of the novel?

10. What did you think of how the mystery was solved? Was it plausible? Would you have ended it differently?

11. The author believes in life lessons and invites readers to delve more deeply in a personal way during and after reading the novel. What would you like to share about the book's message? Did you make any personal connections in the lessons offered?

12. If you lived in Deep Lakes, where would you see yourself as a community member?

About the Author

Joy Ann Ribar lives in central Wisconsin where she writes the Deep Lakes Cozy Mystery Series, starring baker/vinter Frankie Champagne. Joy's writing is inspired by Wisconsin's four distinct seasons and other Wisconsin whimsical quirks, which she hopes to promote for all the world to enjoy. Joy is a member of Sisters in Crime and Wisconsin Writers Association. She teaches writing courses at Madison College and enjoys chatting with readers and writers from all over. Joy and her husband, John, someday plan to sell their house, buy an RV, and travel around the U.S. spreading good cheer and hygge! Joy is a little proud that her first mystery, *Deep Dark Secrets*, is the #1 best-selling fiction with Orange Hat Publishing for 2019.

*Sign up for email updates and see more about upcoming events at joyribar.com
Instagram: @authorjoyribar
Facebook: Joy Ann Ribar Wisconsin Author

If you enjoyed this book, please pass it along!

Leave a rating and review on:
Amazon.com
Goodreads.com
BookBub.com